THE RENEGADES

DEFENDERS OF THE PLANET

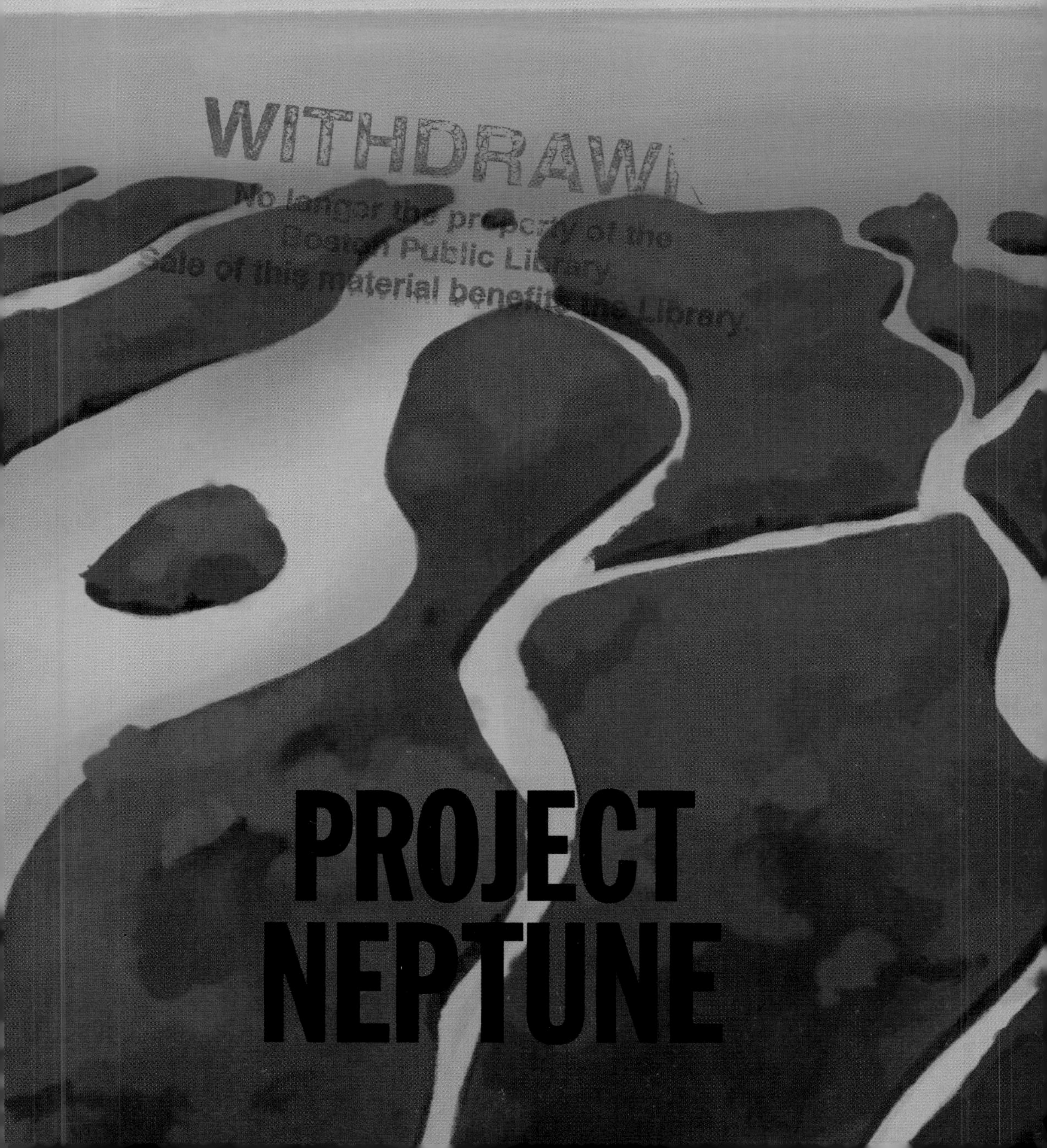

PROJECT NEPTUNE

DK Penguin Random House

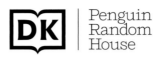

DK LONDON
Project Editor Vicky Richards
Project Art Editor Kit Lane
US Editor Kayla Dugger
Managing Editor Francesca Baines
Managing Art Editor Philip Letsu
Production Editor George Nimmo
Production Controller Sian Cheung
Jacket Designer Surabhi Wadhwa-Gandhi
Jacket Design Development Manager Sophia MTT
Publisher Andrew Mcintyre
Associate Publishing Director Liz Wheeler
Art Director Karen Self
Publishing Director Jonathan Metcalf

First American Edition, 2021
Published in the United States by DK Publishing
1450 Broadway, Suite 801, New York, NY 10018

21 22 23 24 25 10 9 8 7 6 5 4 3 2 1
001–326685–Oct/2021

A catalog record for this book
is available from the Library of Congress.
ISBN: 978-0-744-0-5132-2 (Paperback)
ISBN: 978-0-744-0-5133-9 (ALB)

Printed and bound in China

For the curious
www.dk.com

MIX
Paper from responsible sources
FSC™ C018179
FSC www.fsc.org

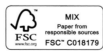

This book was made with
Forest Stewardship Council™ certified paper–
one small step in DK's commitment to a sustainable future.
For more information go to www.dk.com/our-green-pledge

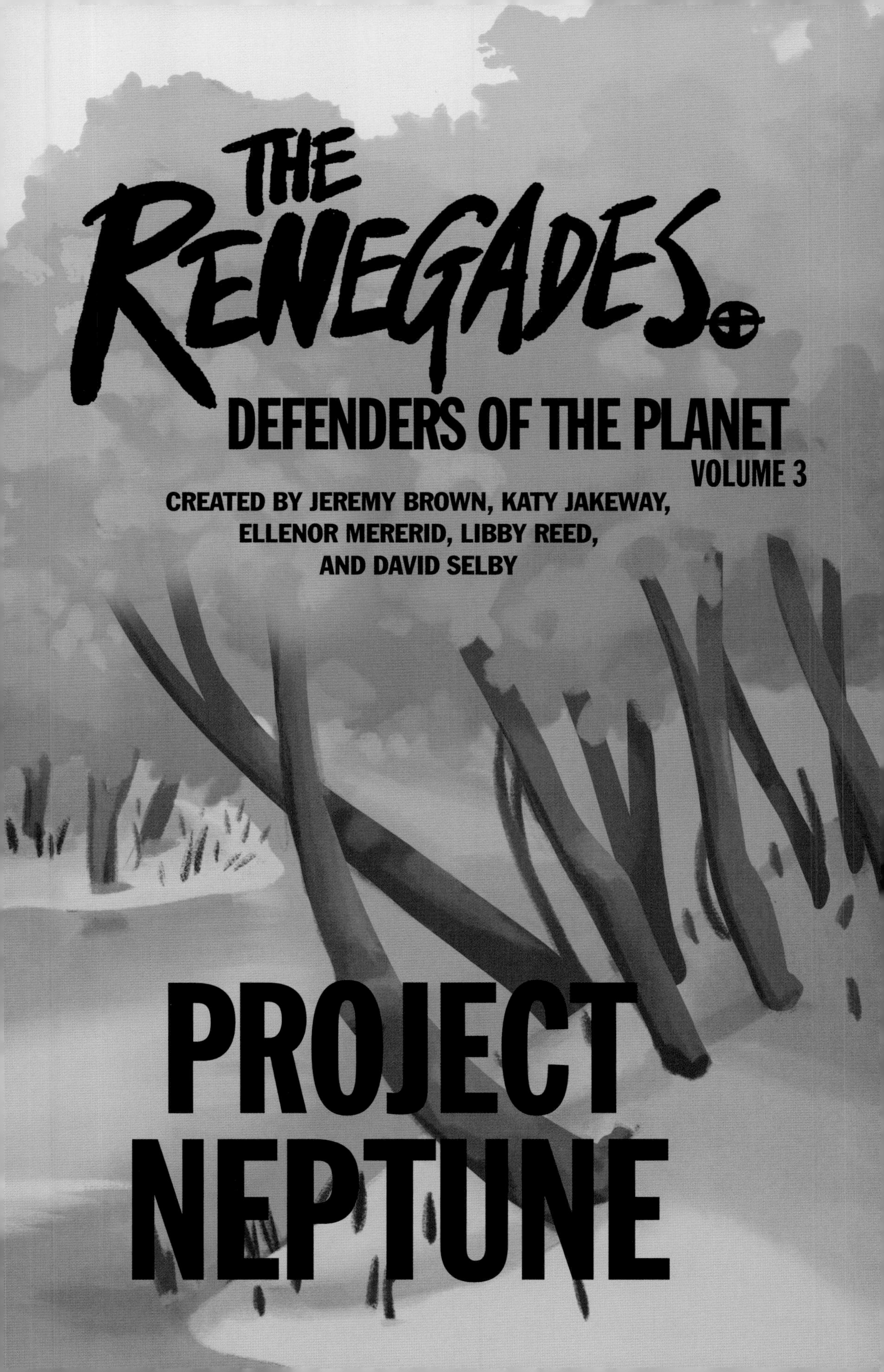

THE RENEGADES

DEFENDERS OF THE PLANET

VOLUME 3

CREATED BY JEREMY BROWN, KATY JAKEWAY,
ELLENOR MERERID, LIBBY REED,
AND DAVID SELBY

PROJECT NEPTUNE

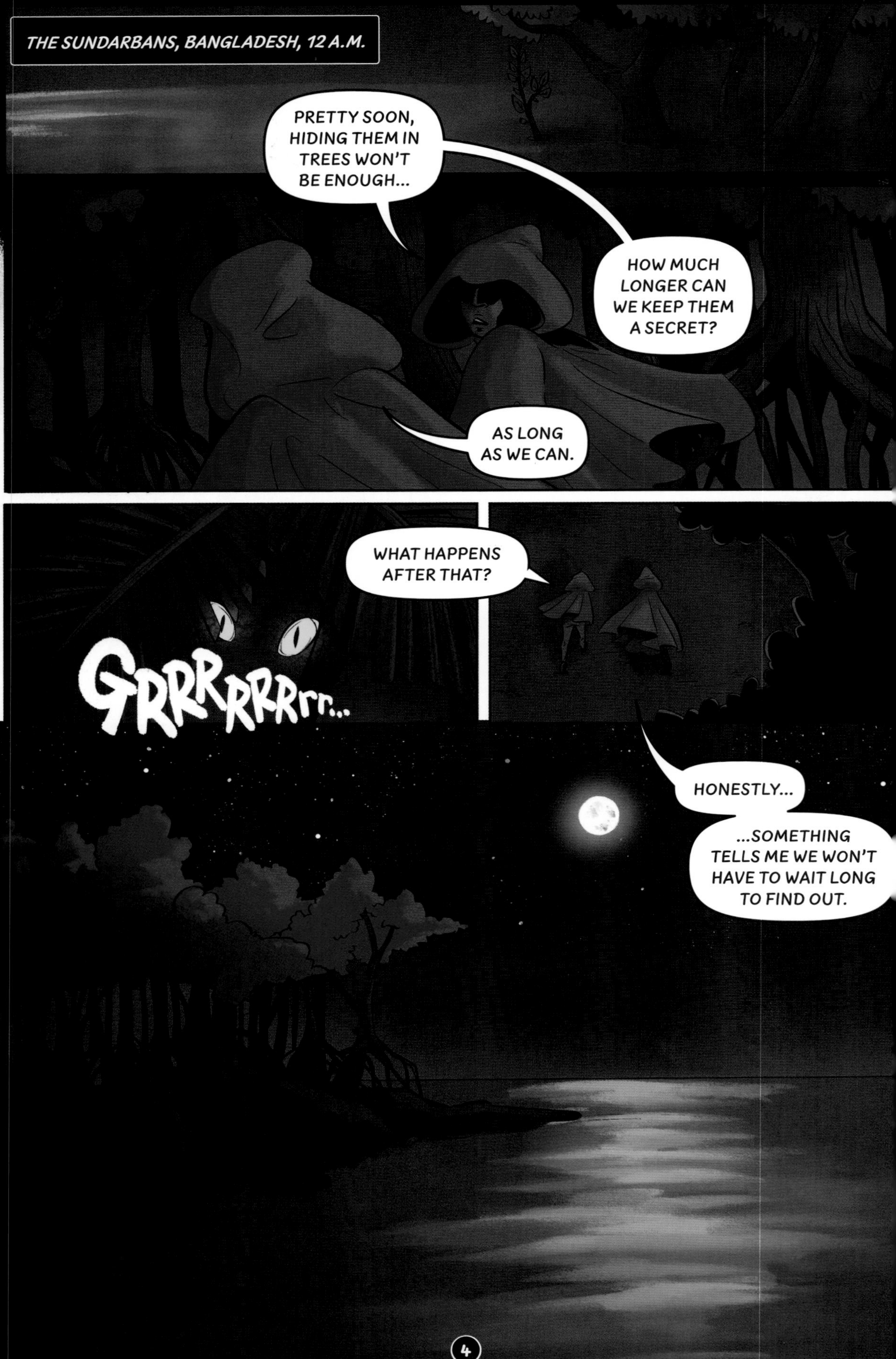
THE SUNDARBANS, BANGLADESH, 12 A.M.
PRETTY SOON, HIDING THEM IN TREES WON'T BE ENOUGH...
HOW MUCH LONGER CAN WE KEEP THEM A SECRET?
AS LONG AS WE CAN.
WHAT HAPPENS AFTER THAT?
GRRRRRRrr...
HONESTLY...
...SOMETHING TELLS ME WE WON'T HAVE TO WAIT LONG TO FIND OUT.

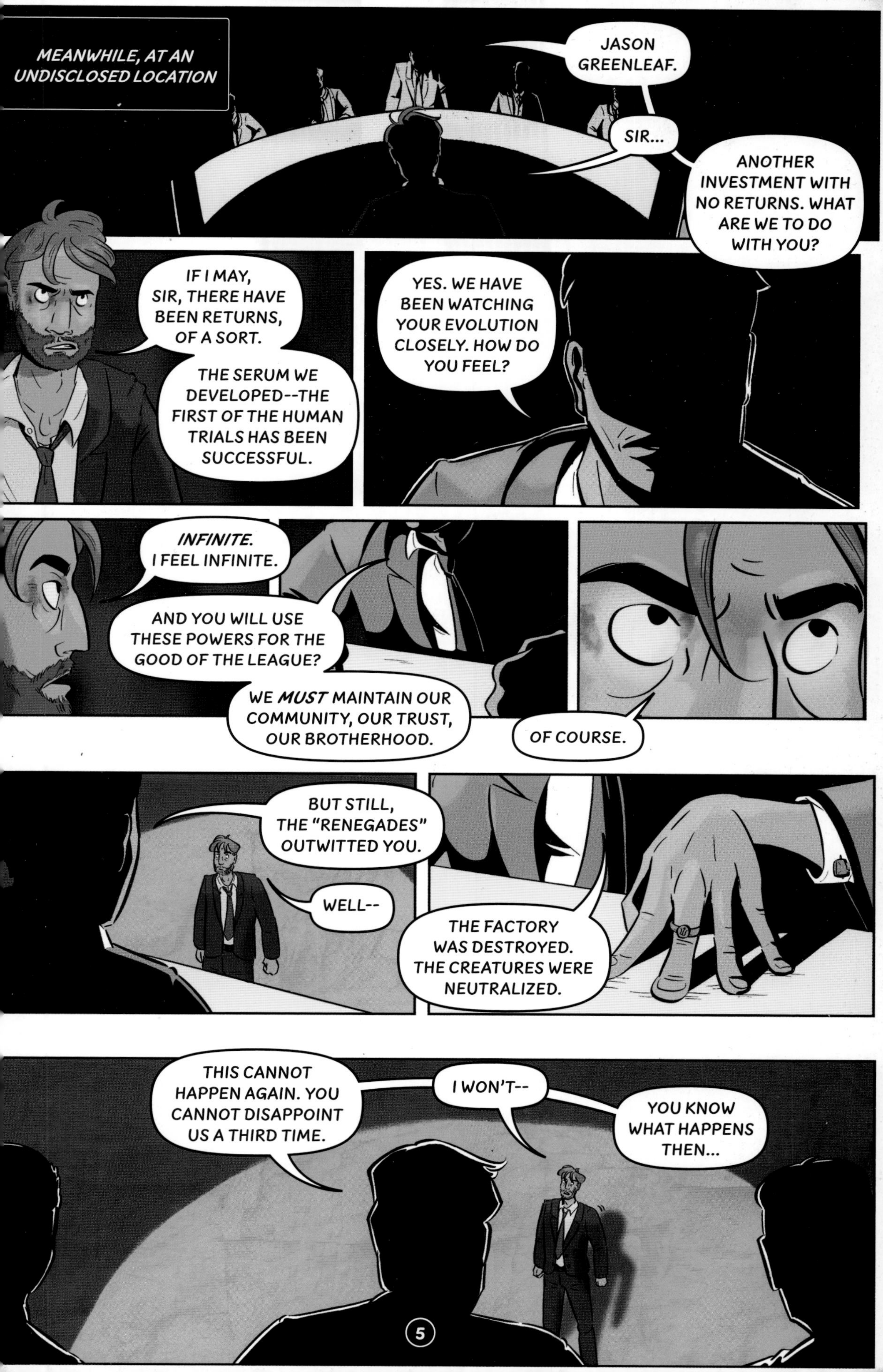
MEANWHILE, AT AN UNDISCLOSED LOCATION
JASON GREENLEAF.
SIR...
ANOTHER INVESTMENT WITH NO RETURNS. WHAT ARE WE TO DO WITH YOU?
IF I MAY, SIR, THERE HAVE BEEN RETURNS, OF A SORT.
THE SERUM WE DEVELOPED--THE FIRST OF THE HUMAN TRIALS HAS BEEN SUCCESSFUL.
YES. WE HAVE BEEN WATCHING YOUR EVOLUTION CLOSELY. HOW DO YOU FEEL?
INFINITE. I FEEL INFINITE.
AND YOU WILL USE THESE POWERS FOR THE GOOD OF THE LEAGUE?
WE *MUST* MAINTAIN OUR COMMUNITY, OUR TRUST, OUR BROTHERHOOD.
OF COURSE.
BUT STILL, THE "RENEGADES" OUTWITTED YOU.
WELL--
THE FACTORY WAS DESTROYED. THE CREATURES WERE NEUTRALIZED.
THIS CANNOT HAPPEN AGAIN. YOU CANNOT DISAPPOINT US A THIRD TIME.
I WON'T--
YOU KNOW WHAT HAPPENS THEN...

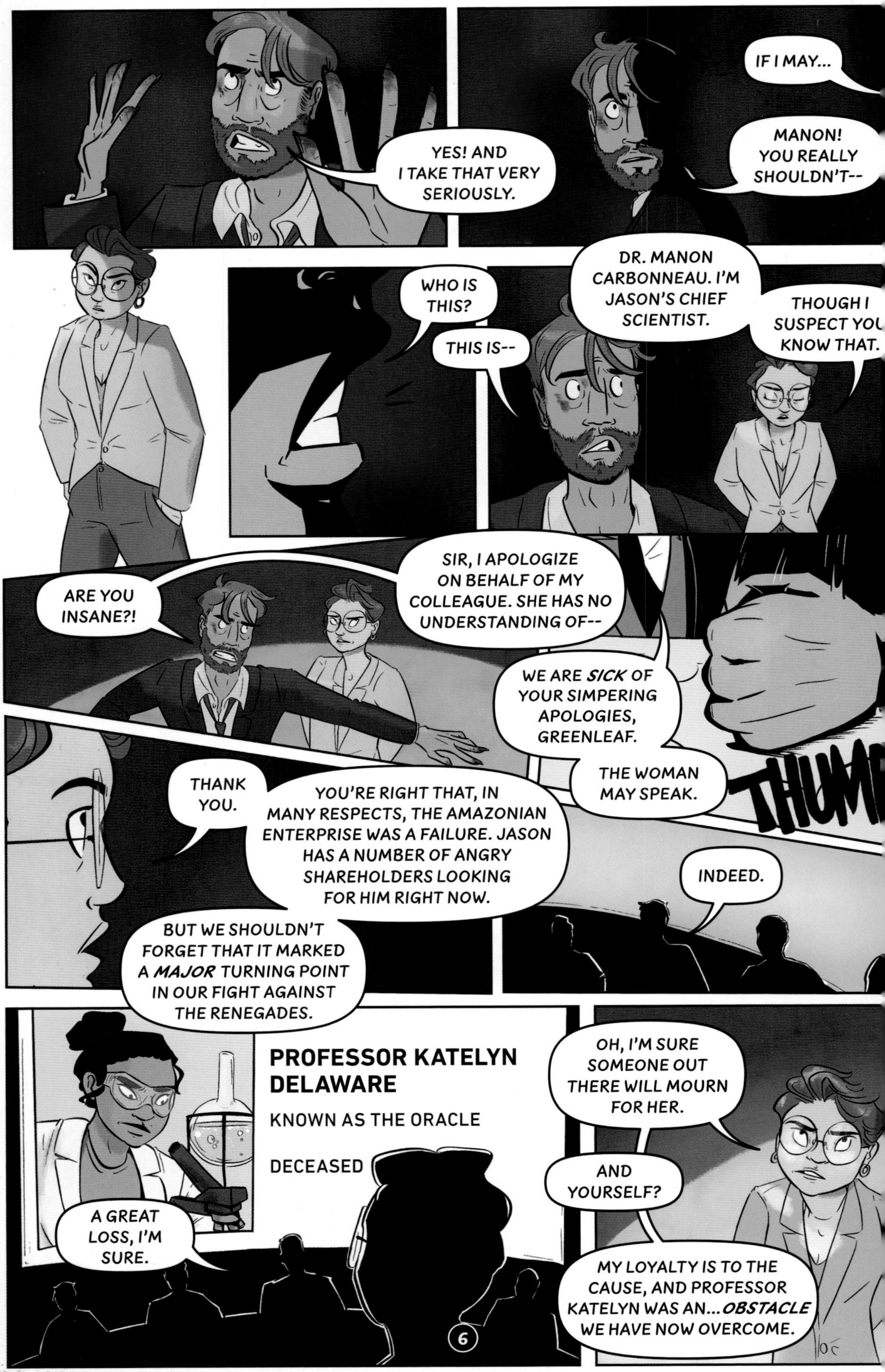
YES! AND I TAKE THAT VERY SERIOUSLY.
IF I MAY...
MANON! YOU REALLY SHOULDN'T--
WHO IS THIS?
THIS IS--
DR. MANON CARBONNEAU. I'M JASON'S CHIEF SCIENTIST.
THOUGH I SUSPECT YOU KNOW THAT.
ARE YOU INSANE?!
SIR, I APOLOGIZE ON BEHALF OF MY COLLEAGUE. SHE HAS NO UNDERSTANDING OF--
WE ARE *SICK* OF YOUR SIMPERING APOLOGIES, GREENLEAF.
THE WOMAN MAY SPEAK.
THUM
THANK YOU.
YOU'RE RIGHT THAT, IN MANY RESPECTS, THE AMAZONIAN ENTERPRISE WAS A FAILURE. JASON HAS A NUMBER OF ANGRY SHAREHOLDERS LOOKING FOR HIM RIGHT NOW.
BUT WE SHOULDN'T FORGET THAT IT MARKED A *MAJOR* TURNING POINT IN OUR FIGHT AGAINST THE RENEGADES.
INDEED.
PROFESSOR KATELYN DELAWARE
KNOWN AS THE ORACLE
DECEASED
A GREAT LOSS, I'M SURE.
OH, I'M SURE SOMEONE OUT THERE WILL MOURN FOR HER.
AND YOURSELF?
MY LOYALTY IS TO THE CAUSE, AND PROFESSOR KATELYN WAS AN...*OBSTACLE* WE HAVE NOW OVERCOME.

LEON MURPHY
KNOWN AS THE PHANTOM
ENVIRONMENTALIST
WHEREABOUTS UNKNOWN
AS FOR HER COLLEAGUES...
HUH, AN ENVIRONMENTALIST? HE'S HARDLY GRETA THUNBERG. AS FOR HIS LOCATION--
WE ARE LOOKING INTO HIS WHEREABOUTS.
IN FAIRNESS, HE CAN TURN INVISIBLE AND WALK THROUGH WALLS. MEN LIKE THAT ARE QUITE DIFFICULT TO PIN DOWN.
MO TEMBE
KNOWN AS SOL
ASPIRING CHEF
WHEREABOUTS UNKNOWN
ANOTHER OFF-GRID.
ALMA VARELA
AMAZON ACTIVIST
WHEREABOUTS UNKNOWN
AFTER AN UNFORTUNATE ENCOUNTER WITH A VAT FULL OF SERUM--WHICH I CAN ONLY APOLOGIZE FOR--MISS VARELA SEEMS TO HAVE DEVELOPED SOME POWERS OF HER OWN.
AS FOR THEIR RELATIVES...
NEITHER MO NOR KATELYN HAVE ANY IDENTIFIABLE BLOOD RELATIONS REMAINING.
AS FOR LEON, HE HAS SEVERAL, AND A SIGNIFICANT OTHER WHO HAS ALSO DISAPPEARED OFF-GRID.
SHE'S PROBABLY WHEREVER LEON IS. OR, IF NOT, SHE MIGHT HELP LEAD US TO HIM.
EITHER WAY, MY POINT IS THAT THE RENEGADES NO LONGER CONSTITUTE A SIGNIFICANT THREAT TO US.
OH, THEY'VE TRIED TO SALVAGE THEIR REPUTATION BY COMING UP WITH CUTESY SUPERHERO NAMES, BUT THEY'RE STILL WANTED CRIMINALS, AND THEIR RINGLEADER--THEIR PRECIOUS ORACLE--IS DEAD.
THEY'RE ABOUT AS DANGEROUS AS AN IRRITATED YORKSHIRE TERRIER. AND JUST AS ANNOYING.

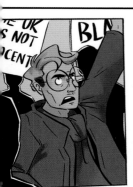

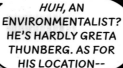

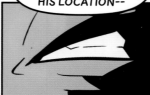

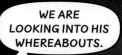

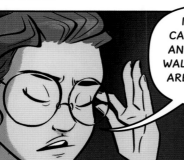

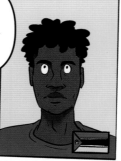

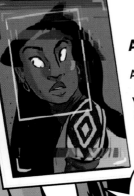

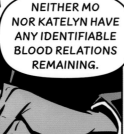

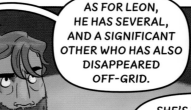

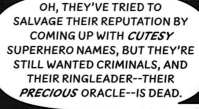

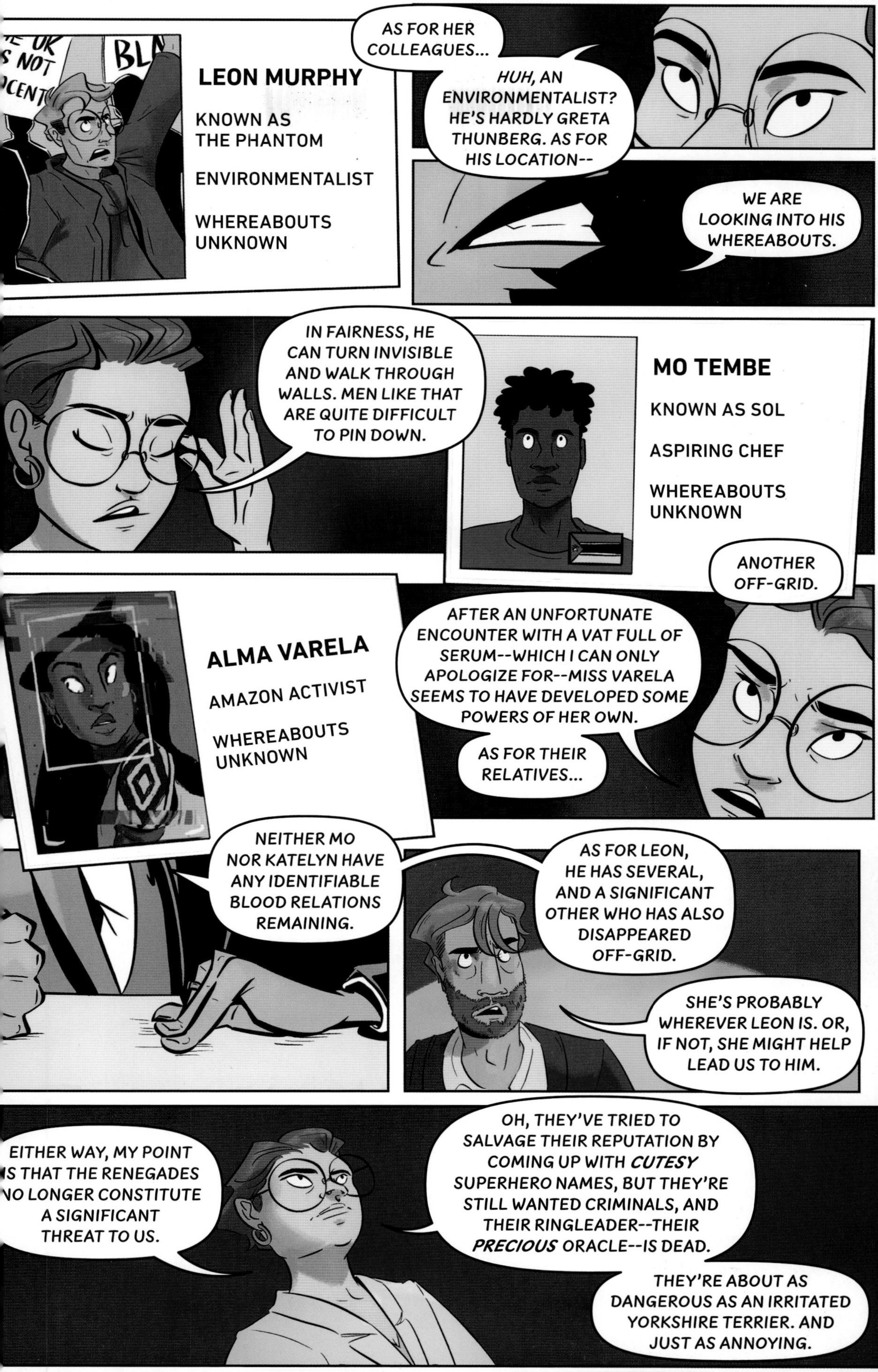

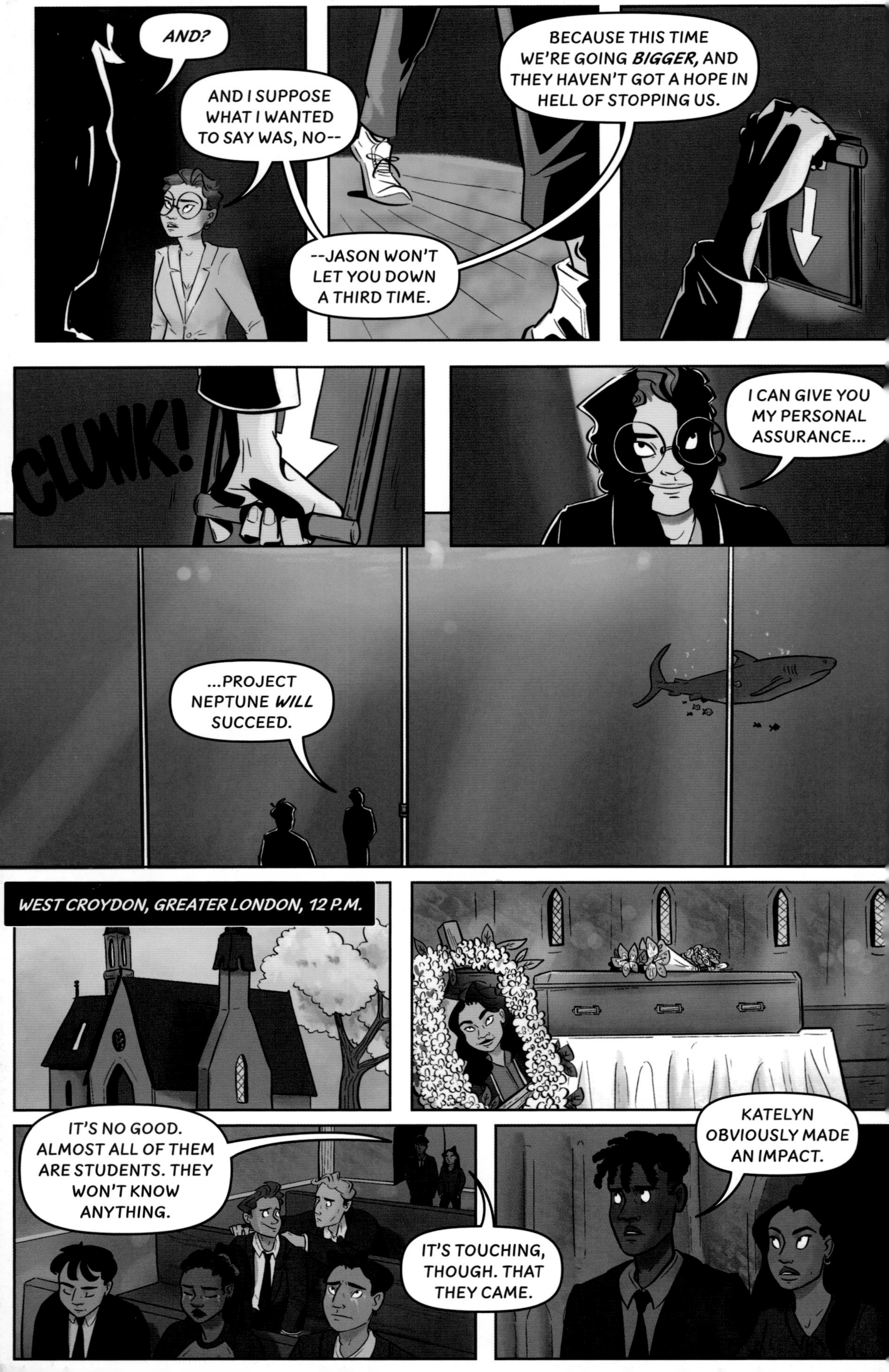
AND?
AND I SUPPOSE WHAT I WANTED TO SAY WAS, NO--
--JASON WON'T LET YOU DOWN A THIRD TIME.
BECAUSE THIS TIME WE'RE GOING BIGGER, AND THEY HAVEN'T GOT A HOPE IN HELL OF STOPPING US.
CLUNK!
I CAN GIVE YOU MY PERSONAL ASSURANCE...
...PROJECT NEPTUNE WILL SUCCEED.
WEST CROYDON, GREATER LONDON, 12 P.M.
IT'S NO GOOD. ALMOST ALL OF THEM ARE STUDENTS. THEY WON'T KNOW ANYTHING.
IT'S TOUCHING, THOUGH. THAT THEY CAME.
KATELYN OBVIOUSLY MADE AN IMPACT.

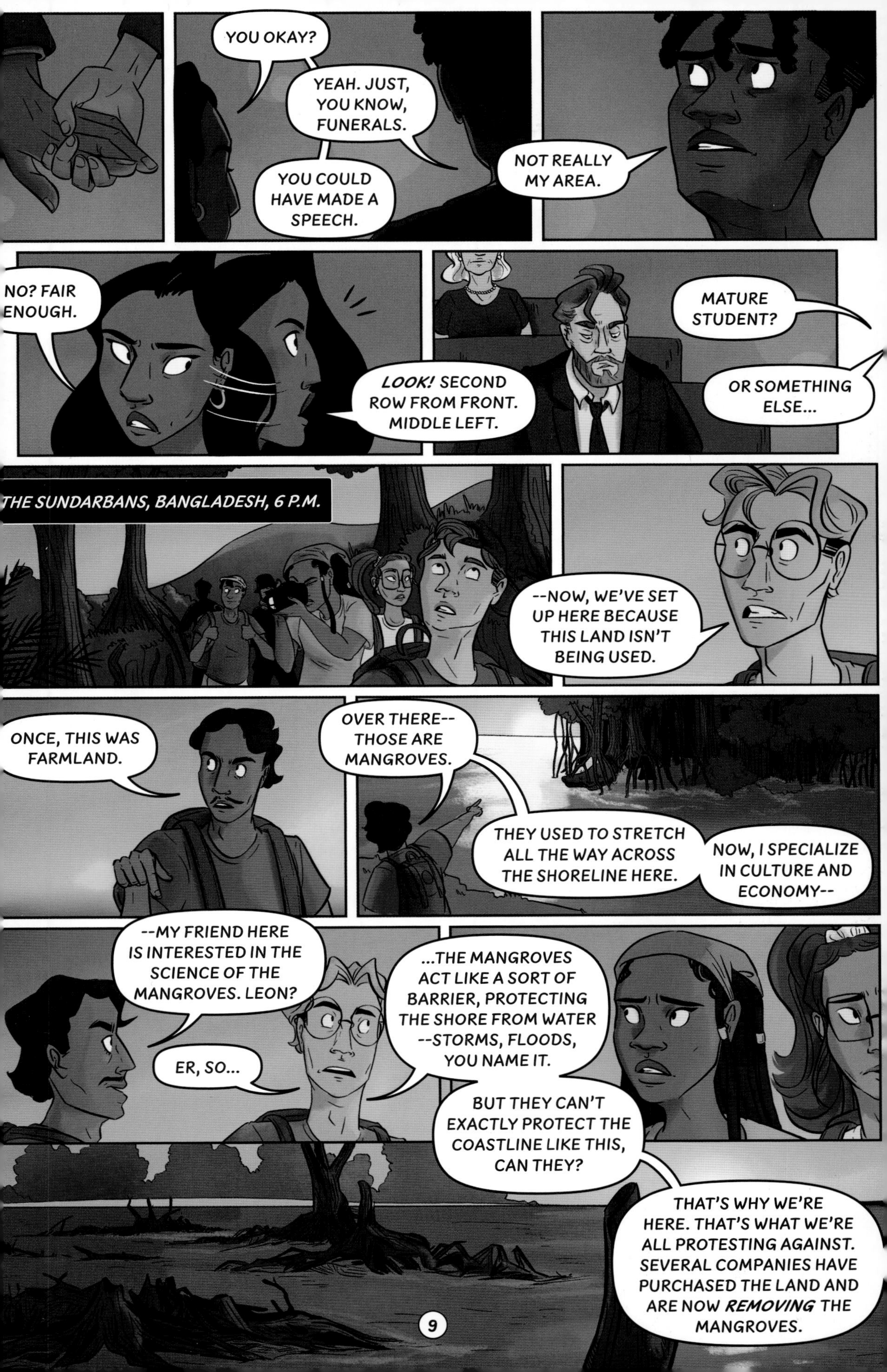
YOU OKAY?
YEAH. JUST, YOU KNOW, FUNERALS.
YOU COULD HAVE MADE A SPEECH.
NOT REALLY MY AREA.
NO? FAIR ENOUGH.
LOOK! SECOND ROW FROM FRONT. MIDDLE LEFT.
MATURE STUDENT?
OR SOMETHING ELSE...
THE SUNDARBANS, BANGLADESH, 6 P.M.
--NOW, WE'VE SET UP HERE BECAUSE THIS LAND ISN'T BEING USED.
ONCE, THIS WAS FARMLAND.
OVER THERE-- THOSE ARE MANGROVES.
THEY USED TO STRETCH ALL THE WAY ACROSS THE SHORELINE HERE.
NOW, I SPECIALIZE IN CULTURE AND ECONOMY--
--MY FRIEND HERE IS INTERESTED IN THE SCIENCE OF THE MANGROVES. LEON?
ER, SO...
...THE MANGROVES ACT LIKE A SORT OF BARRIER, PROTECTING THE SHORE FROM WATER --STORMS, FLOODS, YOU NAME IT.
BUT THEY CAN'T EXACTLY PROTECT THE COASTLINE LIKE THIS, CAN THEY?
THAT'S WHY WE'RE HERE. THAT'S WHAT WE'RE ALL PROTESTING AGAINST. SEVERAL COMPANIES HAVE PURCHASED THE LAND AND ARE NOW REMOVING THE MANGROVES.

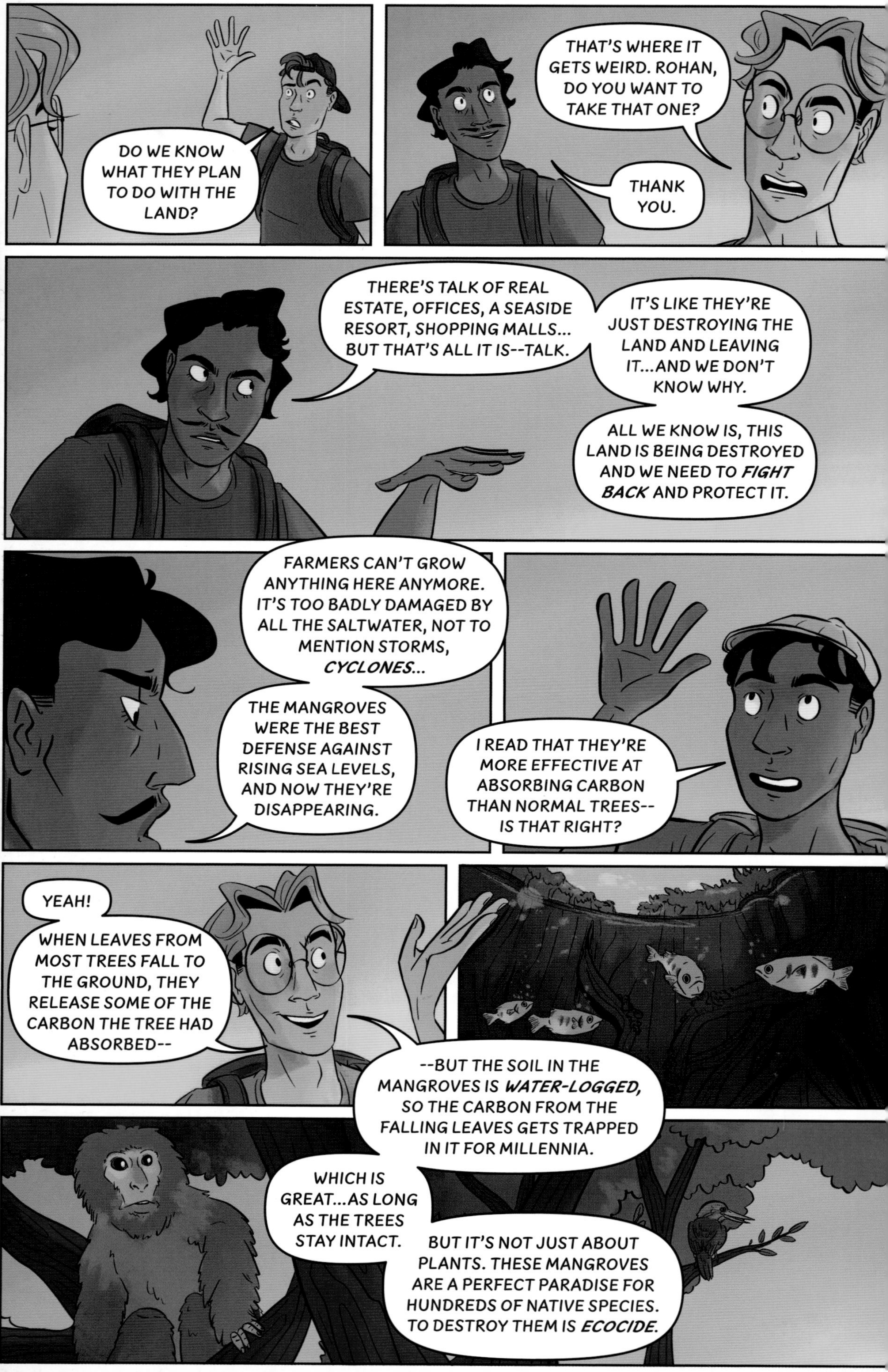
DO WE KNOW WHAT THEY PLAN TO DO WITH THE LAND?
THAT'S WHERE IT GETS WEIRD. ROHAN, DO YOU WANT TO TAKE THAT ONE?
THANK YOU.
THERE'S TALK OF REAL ESTATE, OFFICES, A SEASIDE RESORT, SHOPPING MALLS... BUT THAT'S ALL IT IS--TALK.
IT'S LIKE THEY'RE JUST DESTROYING THE LAND AND LEAVING IT...AND WE DON'T KNOW WHY.
ALL WE KNOW IS, THIS LAND IS BEING DESTROYED AND WE NEED TO *FIGHT BACK* AND PROTECT IT.
FARMERS CAN'T GROW ANYTHING HERE ANYMORE. IT'S TOO BADLY DAMAGED BY ALL THE SALTWATER, NOT TO MENTION STORMS, *CYCLONES*...
THE MANGROVES WERE THE BEST DEFENSE AGAINST RISING SEA LEVELS, AND NOW THEY'RE DISAPPEARING.
I READ THAT THEY'RE MORE EFFECTIVE AT ABSORBING CARBON THAN NORMAL TREES-- IS THAT RIGHT?
YEAH!
WHEN LEAVES FROM MOST TREES FALL TO THE GROUND, THEY RELEASE SOME OF THE CARBON THE TREE HAD ABSORBED--
--BUT THE SOIL IN THE MANGROVES IS *WATER-LOGGED,* SO THE CARBON FROM THE FALLING LEAVES GETS TRAPPED IN IT FOR MILLENNIA.
WHICH IS GREAT...AS LONG AS THE TREES STAY INTACT.
BUT IT'S NOT JUST ABOUT PLANTS. THESE MANGROVES ARE A PERFECT PARADISE FOR HUNDREDS OF NATIVE SPECIES. TO DESTROY THEM IS *ECOCIDE.*

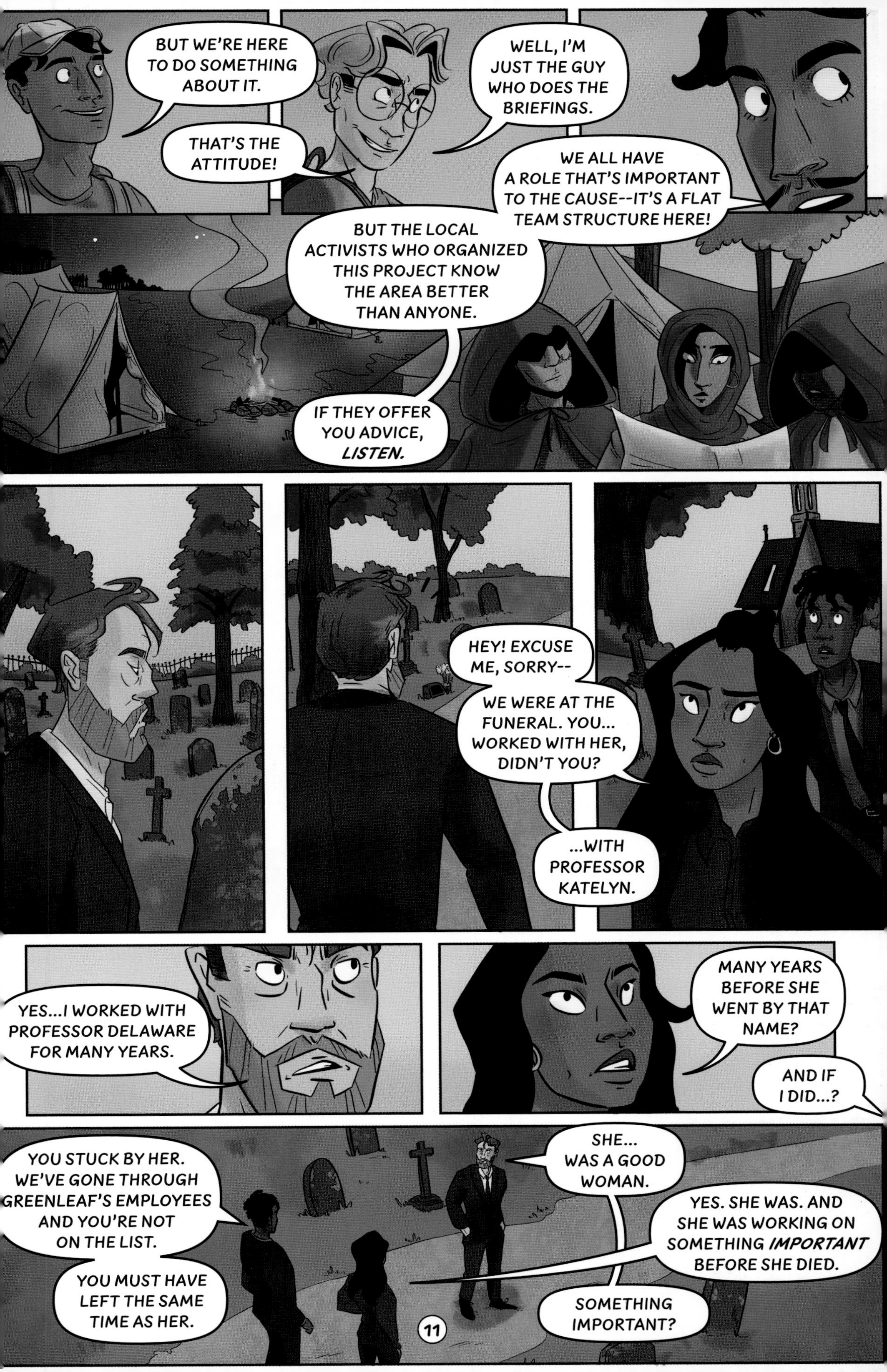

BUT WE'RE HERE TO DO SOMETHING ABOUT IT.
THAT'S THE ATTITUDE!
WELL, I'M JUST THE GUY WHO DOES THE BRIEFINGS.
WE ALL HAVE A ROLE THAT'S IMPORTANT TO THE CAUSE--IT'S A FLAT TEAM STRUCTURE HERE!
BUT THE LOCAL ACTIVISTS WHO ORGANIZED THIS PROJECT KNOW THE AREA BETTER THAN ANYONE.
IF THEY OFFER YOU ADVICE, *LISTEN.*
HEY! EXCUSE ME, SORRY--
WE WERE AT THE FUNERAL. YOU... WORKED WITH HER, DIDN'T YOU?
...WITH PROFESSOR KATELYN.
YES...I WORKED WITH PROFESSOR DELAWARE FOR MANY YEARS.
MANY YEARS BEFORE SHE WENT BY THAT NAME?
AND IF I DID...?
YOU STUCK BY HER. WE'VE GONE THROUGH GREENLEAF'S EMPLOYEES AND YOU'RE NOT ON THE LIST.
YOU MUST HAVE LEFT THE SAME TIME AS HER.
SHE... WAS A GOOD WOMAN.
YES. SHE WAS. AND SHE WAS WORKING ON SOMETHING *IMPORTANT* BEFORE SHE DIED.
SOMETHING IMPORTANT?

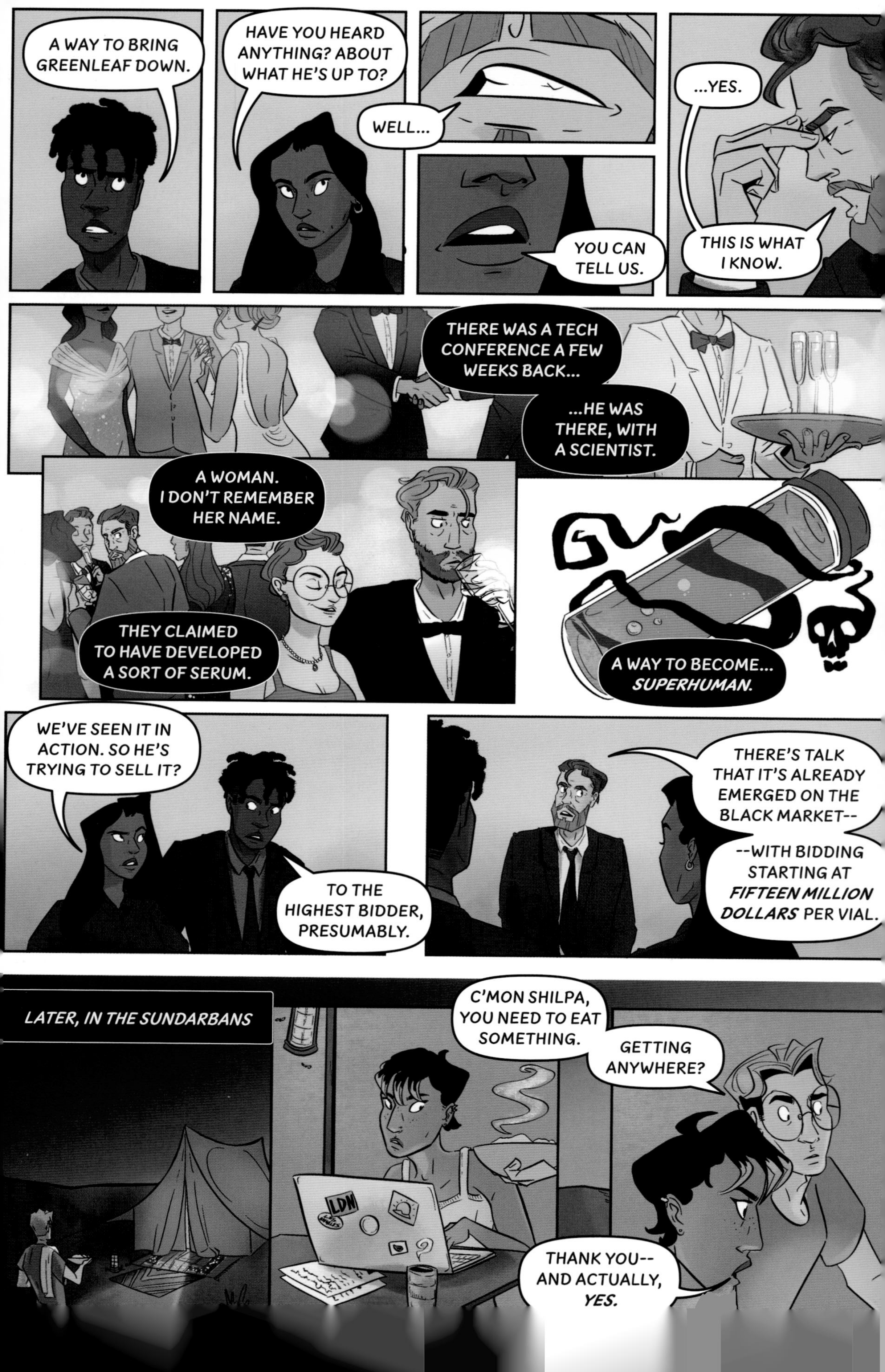
A WAY TO BRING GREENLEAF DOWN.
HAVE YOU HEARD ANYTHING? ABOUT WHAT HE'S UP TO?
WELL...
YOU CAN TELL US.
...YES.
THIS IS WHAT I KNOW.
THERE WAS A TECH CONFERENCE A FEW WEEKS BACK...
...HE WAS THERE, WITH A SCIENTIST.
A WOMAN. I DON'T REMEMBER HER NAME.
THEY CLAIMED TO HAVE DEVELOPED A SORT OF SERUM.
A WAY TO BECOME... *SUPERHUMAN.*
WE'VE SEEN IT IN ACTION. SO HE'S TRYING TO SELL IT?
TO THE HIGHEST BIDDER, PRESUMABLY.
THERE'S TALK THAT IT'S ALREADY EMERGED ON THE BLACK MARKET--
--WITH BIDDING STARTING AT *FIFTEEN MILLION DOLLARS* PER VIAL.
LATER, IN THE SUNDARBANS
C'MON SHILPA, YOU NEED TO EAT SOMETHING.
GETTING ANYWHERE?
THANK YOU-- AND ACTUALLY, *YES.*
LDN

THAT ENCRYPTED TRANSACTION, FROM MONTHS AGO--

YEAH, WE FOLLOWED IT. AND WE CHECKED ALL THE ORDERS, ALL THOSE TRUCKING COMPANIES...

WELL, AFTER YOU GAVE UP, I CARRIED ON CHECKING. AND WE WERE *RIGHT*.

THAT EQUIPMENT WAS MOVED. IF I'VE GOT THIS RIGHT, THEN IT'S ALL BEEN MOVED TO A PRIVATE STORAGE FACILITY--

--JUST TEN MINUTES AWAY FROM US.

AND LOOK *WHO* PLACED THE ORDER.

DR. MANON CARBONNEAU.

HEY! SHE WAS THERE IN THE AMAZON. SO IF SHE'S HERE, THEN...

...SO IS *GREENLEAF*.

YOU'RE BRILLIANT!

UHH... AHEM--

I, UH, GUESS YOU NEED SOMEONE TO CHECK OUT THAT STORAGE FACILITY!

I GUESS I DO...

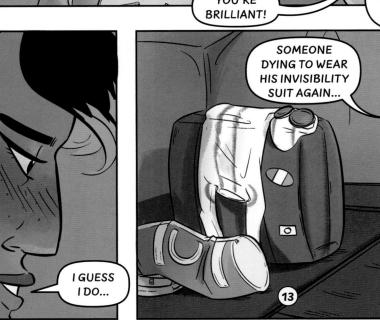

SOMEONE DYING TO WEAR HIS INVISIBILITY SUIT AGAIN...

THEN *SOMEONE* HAD BETTER BE CAREFUL. THERE ARE DANGEROUS PEOPLE OUT THERE...

13

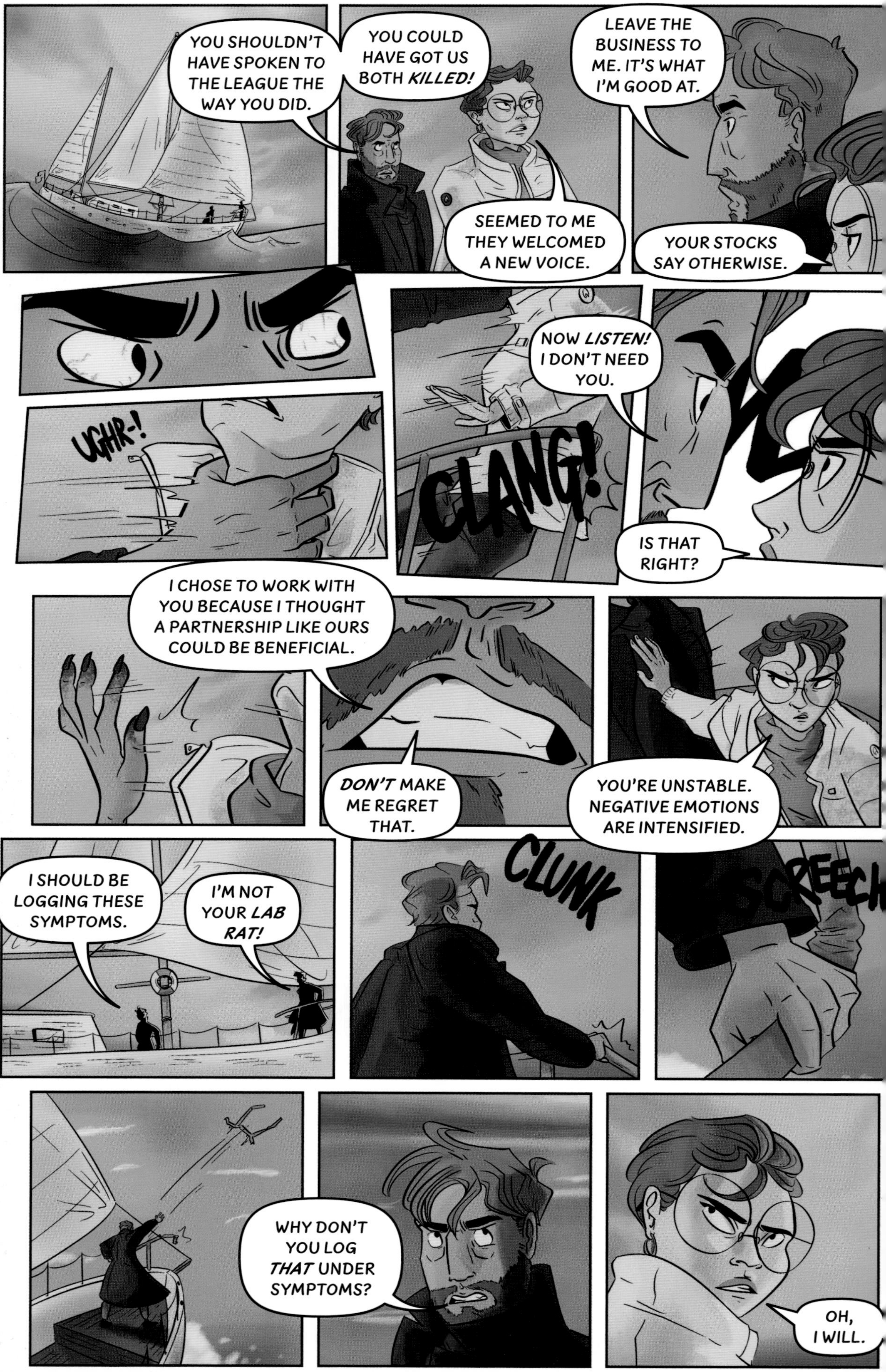
YOU SHOULDN'T HAVE SPOKEN TO THE LEAGUE THE WAY YOU DID.
YOU COULD HAVE GOT US BOTH *KILLED!*
SEEMED TO ME THEY WELCOMED A NEW VOICE.
LEAVE THE BUSINESS TO ME. IT'S WHAT I'M GOOD AT.
YOUR STOCKS SAY OTHERWISE.
UGHR-!
NOW *LISTEN!* I DON'T NEED YOU.
CLANG!
IS THAT RIGHT?
I CHOSE TO WORK WITH YOU BECAUSE I THOUGHT A PARTNERSHIP LIKE OURS COULD BE BENEFICIAL.
DON'T MAKE ME REGRET THAT.
YOU'RE UNSTABLE. NEGATIVE EMOTIONS ARE INTENSIFIED.
I SHOULD BE LOGGING THESE SYMPTOMS.
I'M NOT YOUR *LAB RAT!*
CLUNK
SCREECH
WHY DON'T YOU LOG *THAT* UNDER SYMPTOMS?
OH, I WILL.

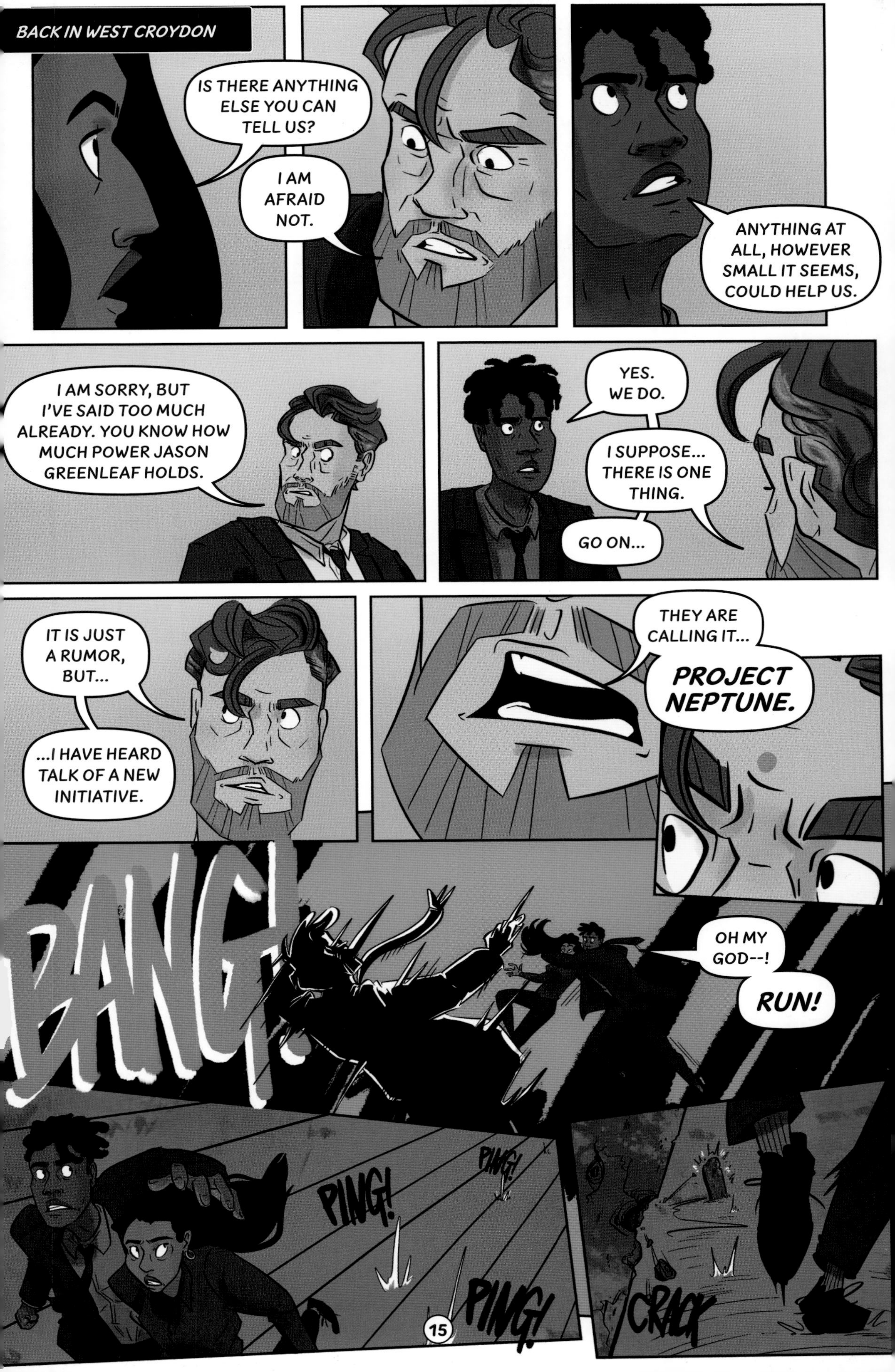
BACK IN WEST CROYDON
IS THERE ANYTHING ELSE YOU CAN TELL US?
I AM AFRAID NOT.
ANYTHING AT ALL, HOWEVER SMALL IT SEEMS, COULD HELP US.
I AM SORRY, BUT I'VE SAID TOO MUCH ALREADY. YOU KNOW HOW MUCH POWER JASON GREENLEAF HOLDS.
YES. WE DO.
I SUPPOSE... THERE IS ONE THING.
GO ON...
IT IS JUST A RUMOR, BUT...
...I HAVE HEARD TALK OF A NEW INITIATIVE.
THEY ARE CALLING IT...
PROJECT NEPTUNE.
BANG!
OH MY GOD--!
RUN!
PING!
PING!
PING!
CRACK

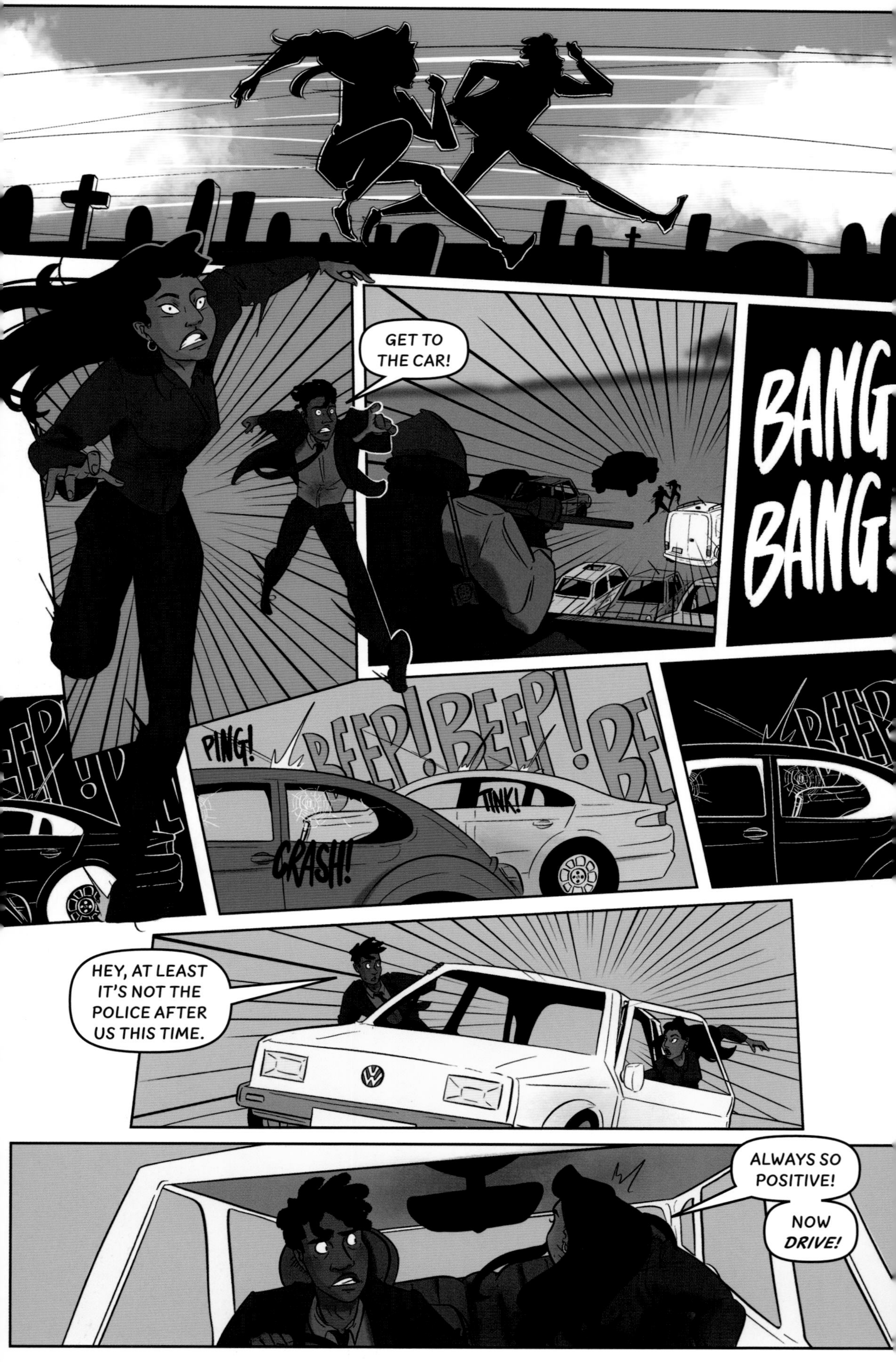
GET TO THE CAR!
BANG BANG!
PING!
BEEP! BEEP!
TINK!
CRASH!
HEY, AT LEAST IT'S NOT THE POLICE AFTER US THIS TIME.
ALWAYS SO POSITIVE!
NOW *DRIVE!*

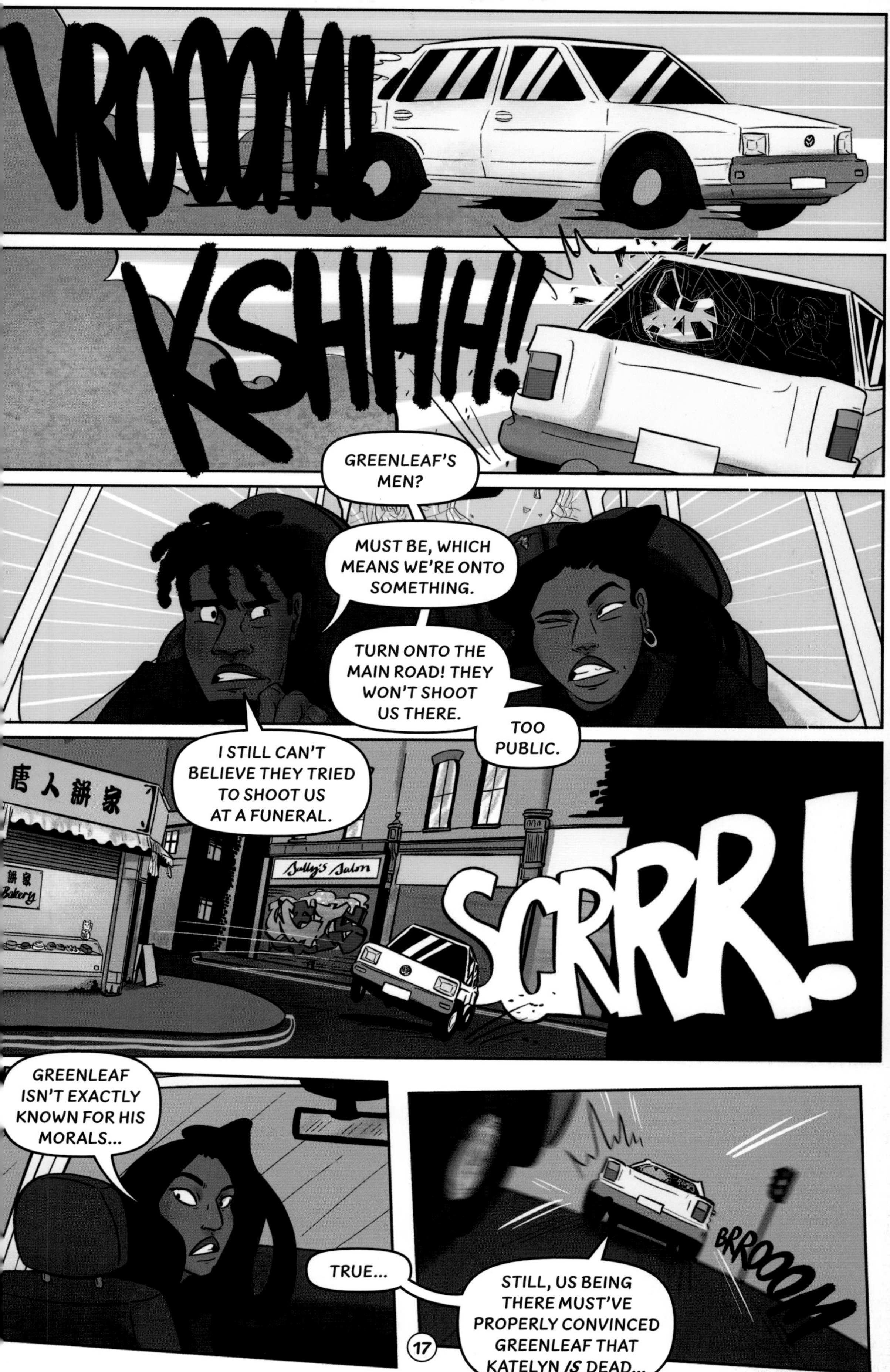
VROOOM!
KSHHH!
GREENLEAF'S MEN?
MUST BE, WHICH MEANS WE'RE ONTO SOMETHING.
TURN ONTO THE MAIN ROAD! THEY WON'T SHOOT US THERE.
TOO PUBLIC.
I STILL CAN'T BELIEVE THEY TRIED TO SHOOT US AT A FUNERAL.
唐人餅家
餅家
Bakery
Sally's Salon
SCRRR!
GREENLEAF ISN'T EXACTLY KNOWN FOR HIS MORALS...
TRUE...
BRROOOOM
STILL, US BEING THERE MUST'VE PROPERLY CONVINCED GREENLEAF THAT KATELYN *IS* DEAD...

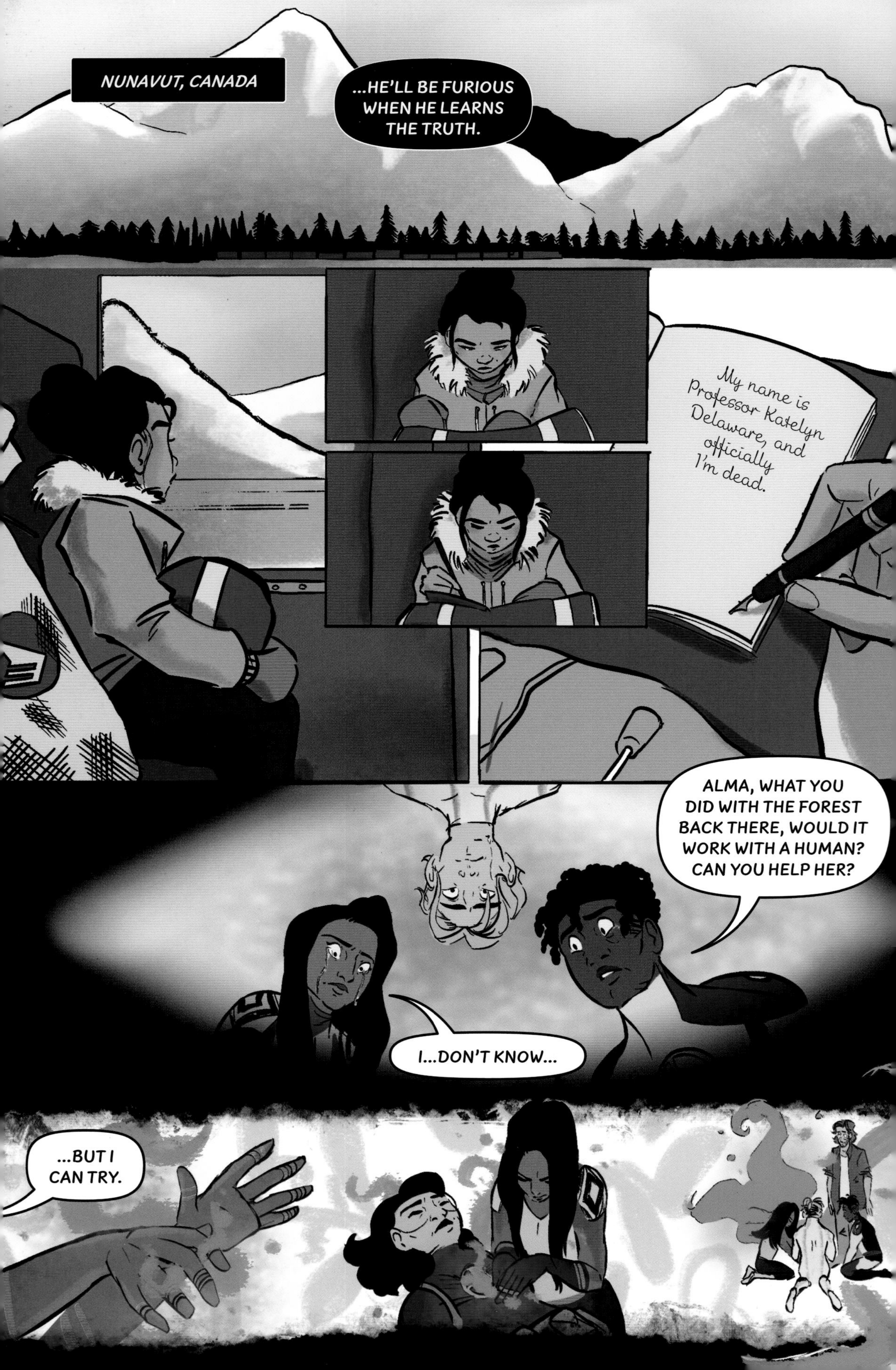
NUNAVUT, CANADA
...HE'LL BE FURIOUS WHEN HE LEARNS THE TRUTH.
My name is Professor Katelyn Delaware, and officially I'm dead.
ALMA, WHAT YOU DID WITH THE FOREST BACK THERE, WOULD IT WORK WITH A HUMAN? CAN YOU HELP HER?
I...DON'T KNOW...
...BUT I CAN TRY.

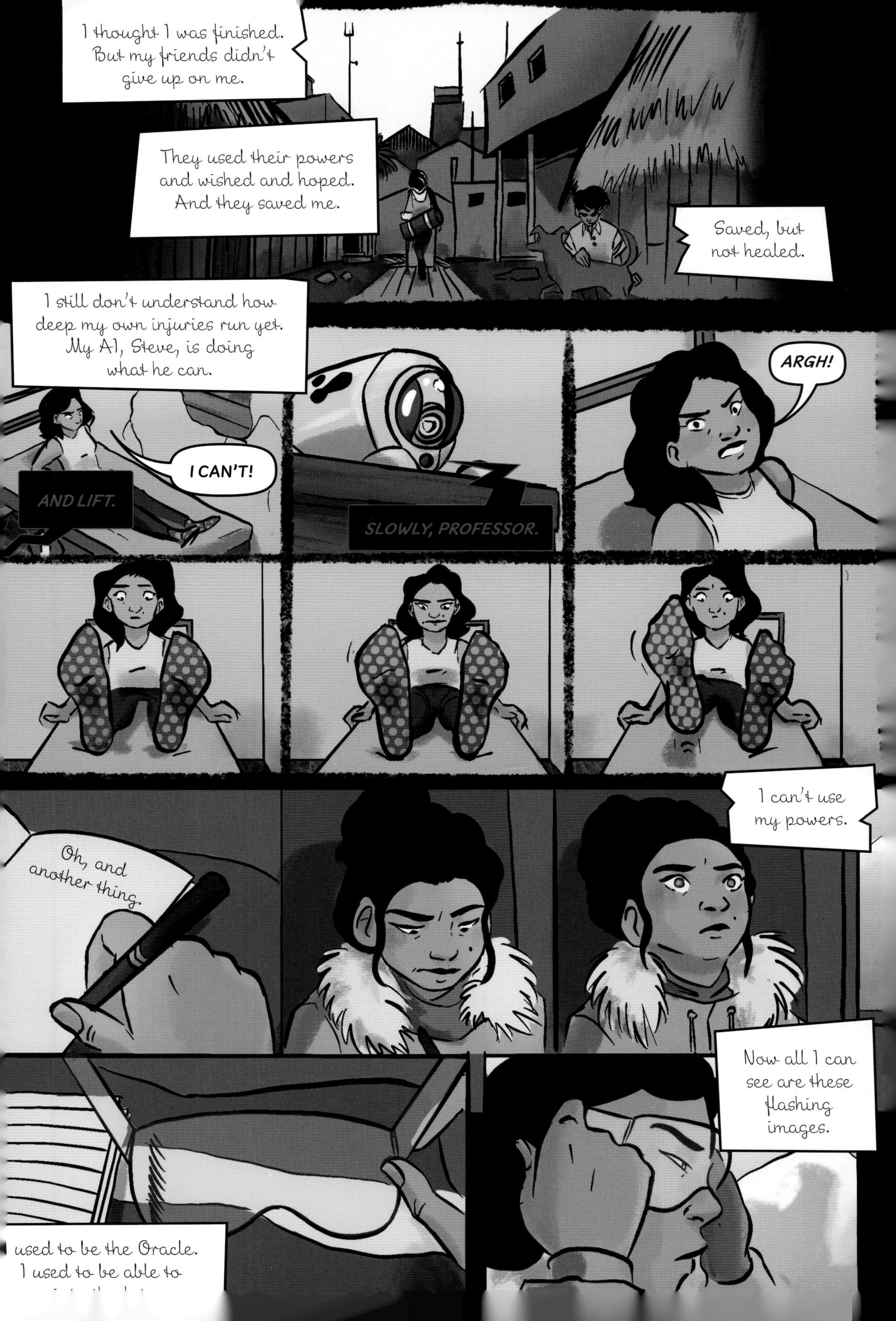

I thought I was finished. But my friends didn't give up on me.
They used their powers and wished and hoped. And they saved me.
Saved, but not healed.
I still don't understand how deep my own injuries run yet. My AI, Steve, is doing what he can.
AND LIFT.
I CAN'T!
SLOWLY, PROFESSOR.
ARGH!
Oh, and another thing.
I can't use my powers.
Now all I can see are these flashing images.
used to be the Oracle. I used to be able to

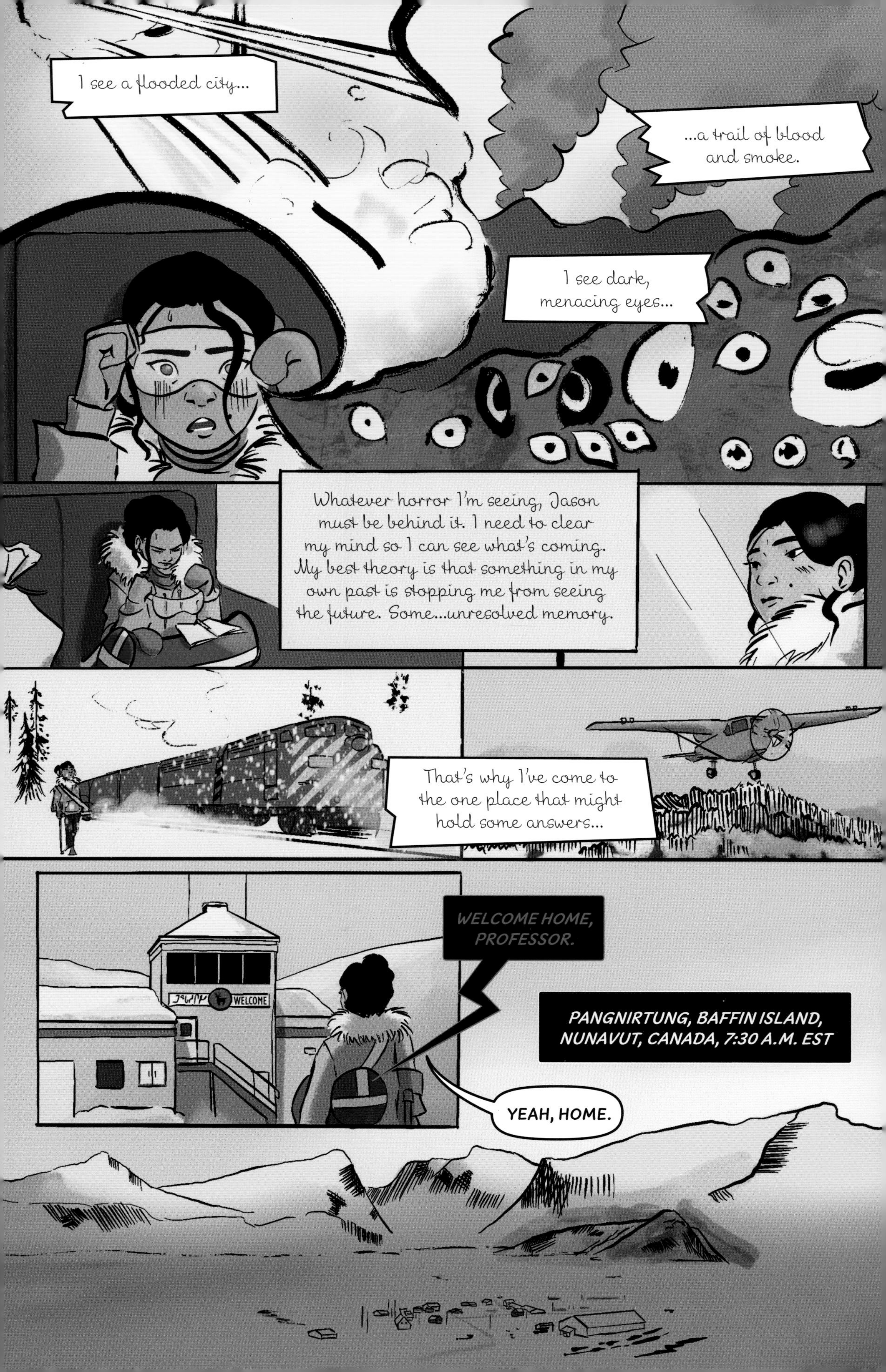
I see a flooded city...
...a trail of blood and smoke.
I see dark, menacing eyes...
Whatever horror I'm seeing, Jason must be behind it. I need to clear my mind so I can see what's coming. My best theory is that something in my own past is stopping me from seeing the future. Some...unresolved memory.
That's why I've come to the one place that might hold some answers...
WELCOME
WELCOME HOME, PROFESSOR.
PANGNIRTUNG, BAFFIN ISLAND, NUNAVUT, CANADA, 7:30 A.M. EST
YEAH, HOME.

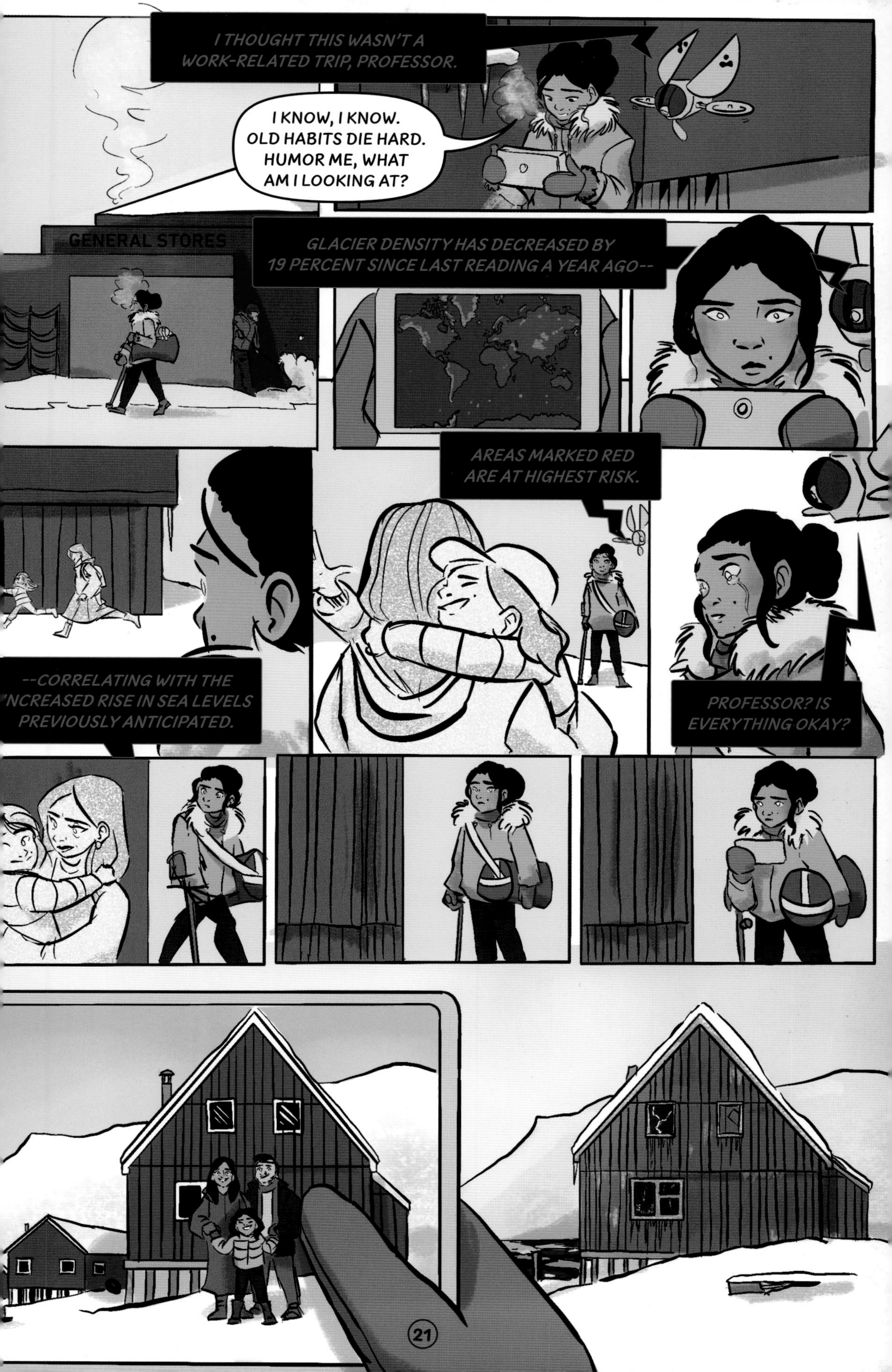
I THOUGHT THIS WASN'T A WORK-RELATED TRIP, PROFESSOR.
I KNOW, I KNOW. OLD HABITS DIE HARD. HUMOR ME, WHAT AM I LOOKING AT?
GENERAL STORES
GLACIER DENSITY HAS DECREASED BY 19 PERCENT SINCE LAST READING A YEAR AGO--
AREAS MARKED RED ARE AT HIGHEST RISK.
--CORRELATING WITH THE 'NCREASED RISE IN SEA LEVELS PREVIOUSLY ANTICIPATED.
PROFESSOR? IS EVERYTHING OKAY?

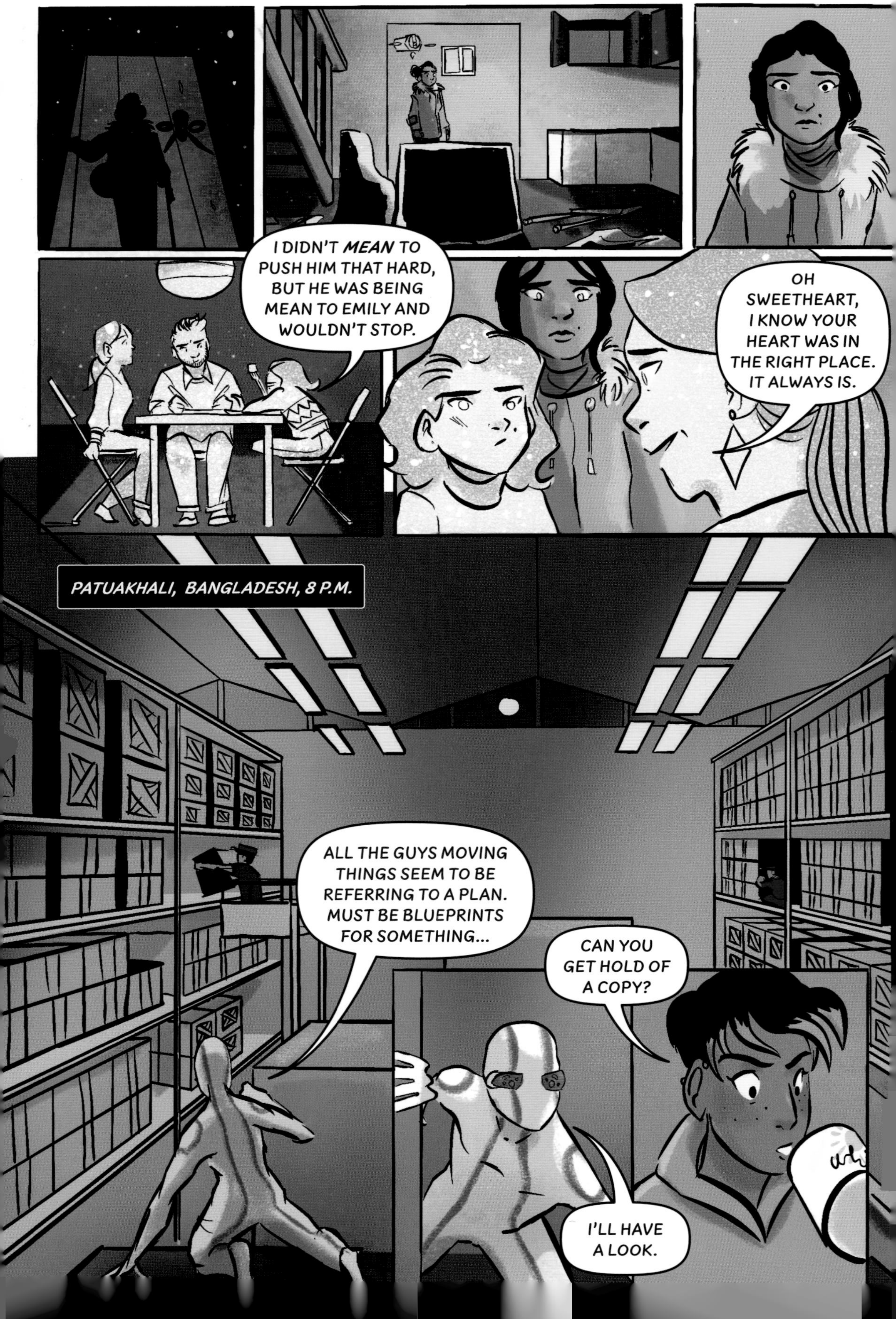
I DIDN'T *MEAN* TO PUSH HIM THAT HARD, BUT HE WAS BEING MEAN TO EMILY AND WOULDN'T STOP.
OH SWEETHEART, I KNOW YOUR HEART WAS IN THE RIGHT PLACE. IT ALWAYS IS.
PATUAKHALI, BANGLADESH, 8 P.M.
ALL THE GUYS MOVING THINGS SEEM TO BE REFERRING TO A PLAN. MUST BE BLUEPRINTS FOR SOMETHING...
CAN YOU GET HOLD OF A COPY?
I'LL HAVE A LOOK.

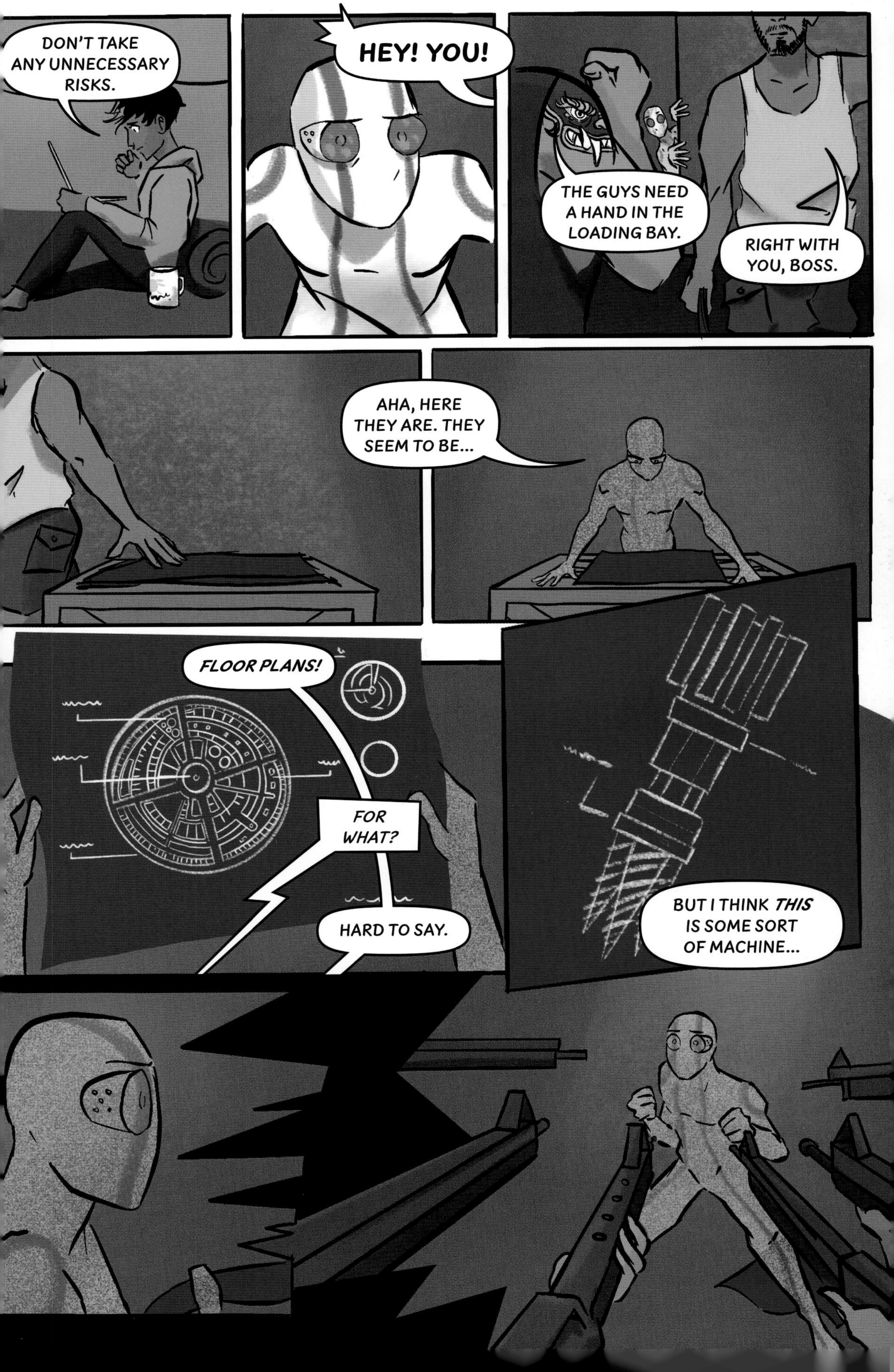
DON'T TAKE ANY UNNECESSARY RISKS.
HEY! YOU!
THE GUYS NEED A HAND IN THE LOADING BAY.
RIGHT WITH YOU, BOSS.
AHA, HERE THEY ARE. THEY SEEM TO BE...
FLOOR PLANS!
FOR WHAT?
HARD TO SAY.
BUT I THINK *THIS* IS SOME SORT OF MACHINE...

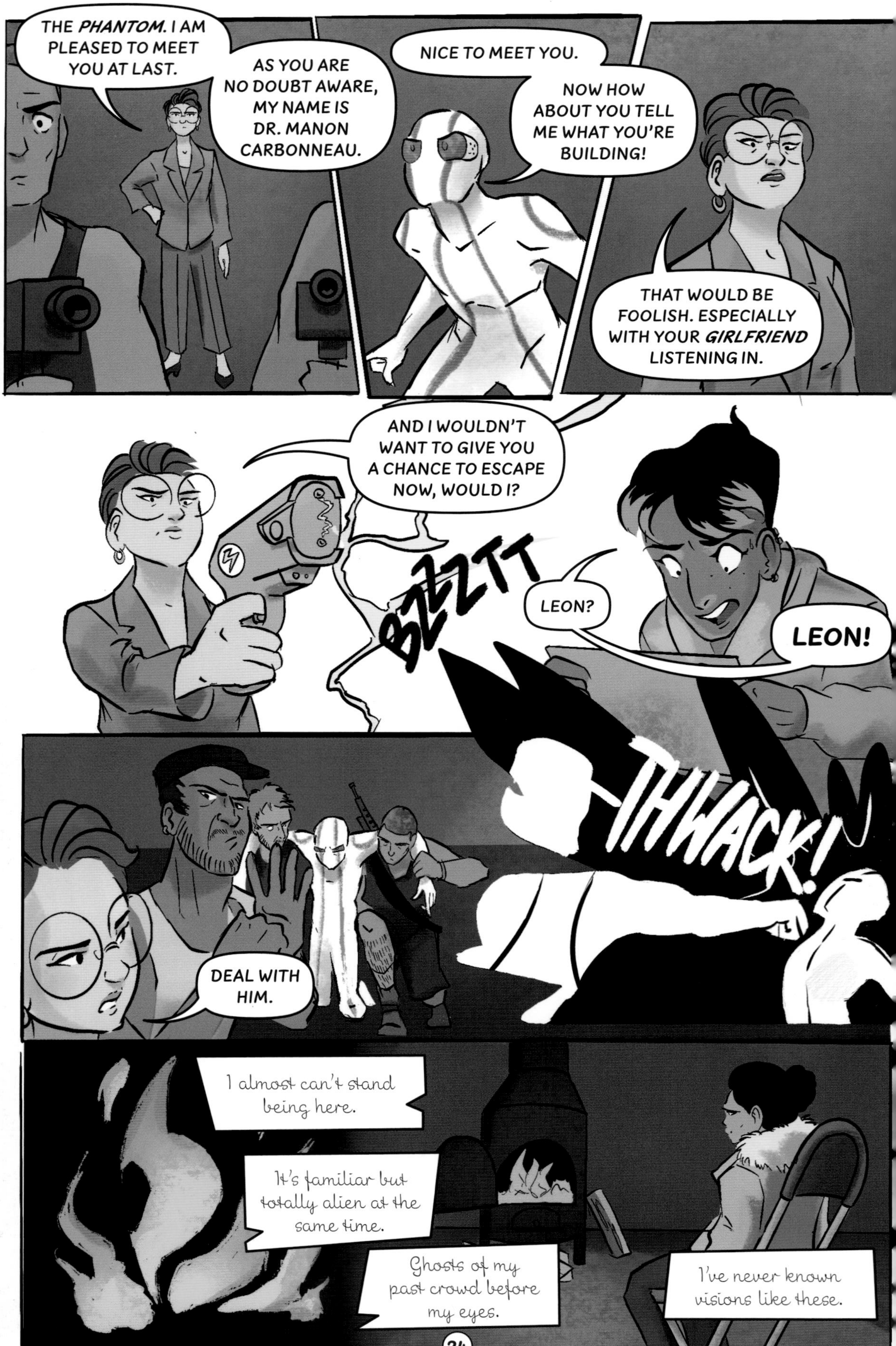
THE *PHANTOM*. I AM PLEASED TO MEET YOU AT LAST.
AS YOU ARE NO DOUBT AWARE, MY NAME IS DR. MANON CARBONNEAU.
NICE TO MEET YOU.
NOW HOW ABOUT YOU TELL ME WHAT YOU'RE BUILDING!
THAT WOULD BE FOOLISH. ESPECIALLY WITH YOUR *GIRLFRIEND* LISTENING IN.
AND I WOULDN'T WANT TO GIVE YOU A CHANCE TO ESCAPE NOW, WOULD I?
BZZZTT
LEON?
LEON!
THWACK!
DEAL WITH HIM.
I almost can't stand being here.
It's familiar but totally alien at the same time.
Ghosts of my past crowd before my eyes.
I've never known visions like these.

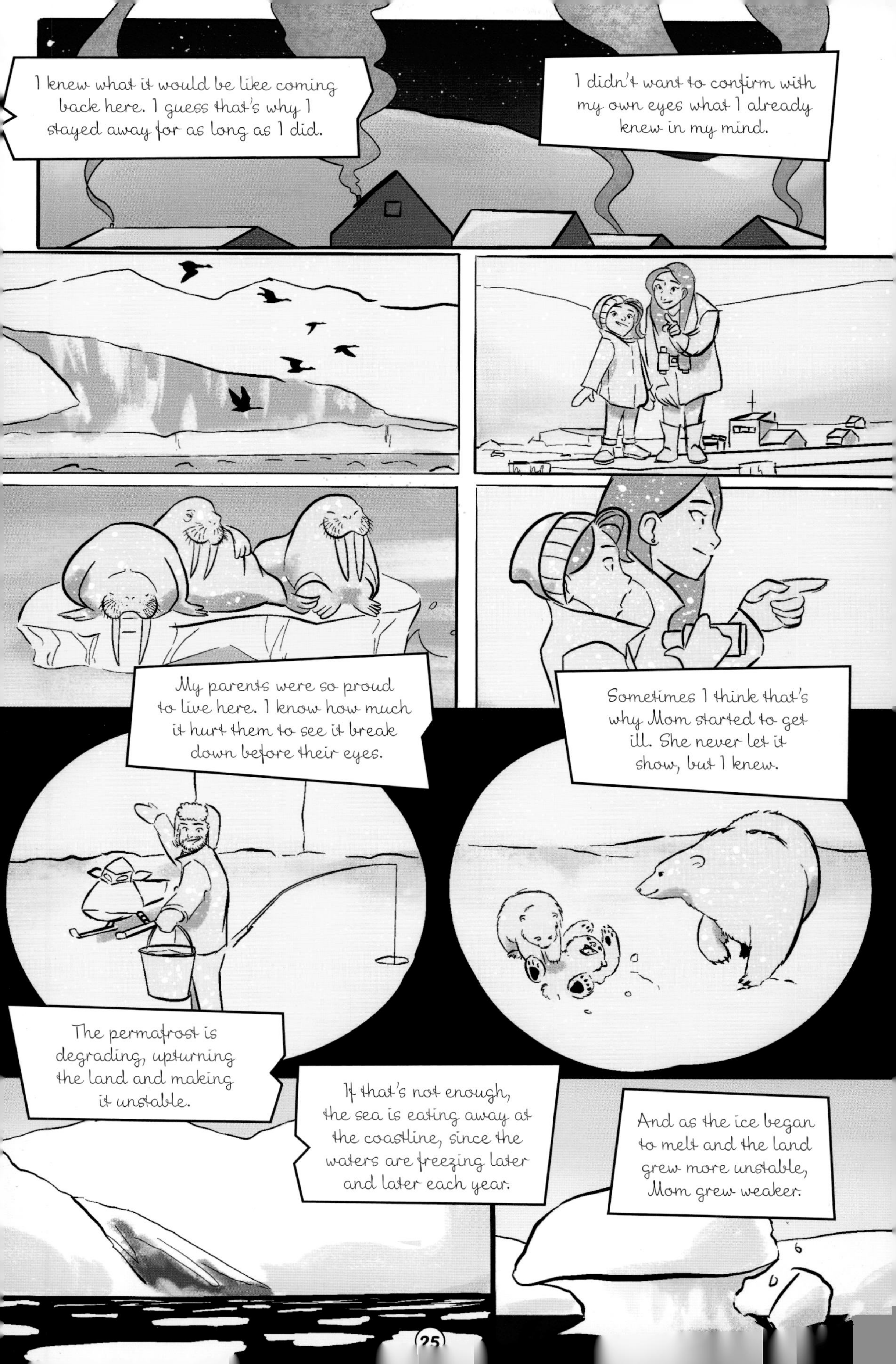
I knew what it would be like coming back here. I guess that's why I stayed away for as long as I did.
I didn't want to confirm with my own eyes what I already knew in my mind.
My parents were so proud to live here. I know how much it hurt them to see it break down before their eyes.
Sometimes I think that's why Mom started to get ill. She never let it show, but I knew.
The permafrost is degrading, upturning the land and making it unstable.
If that's not enough, the sea is eating away at the coastline, since the waters are freezing later and later each year.
And as the ice began to melt and the land grew more unstable, Mom grew weaker.

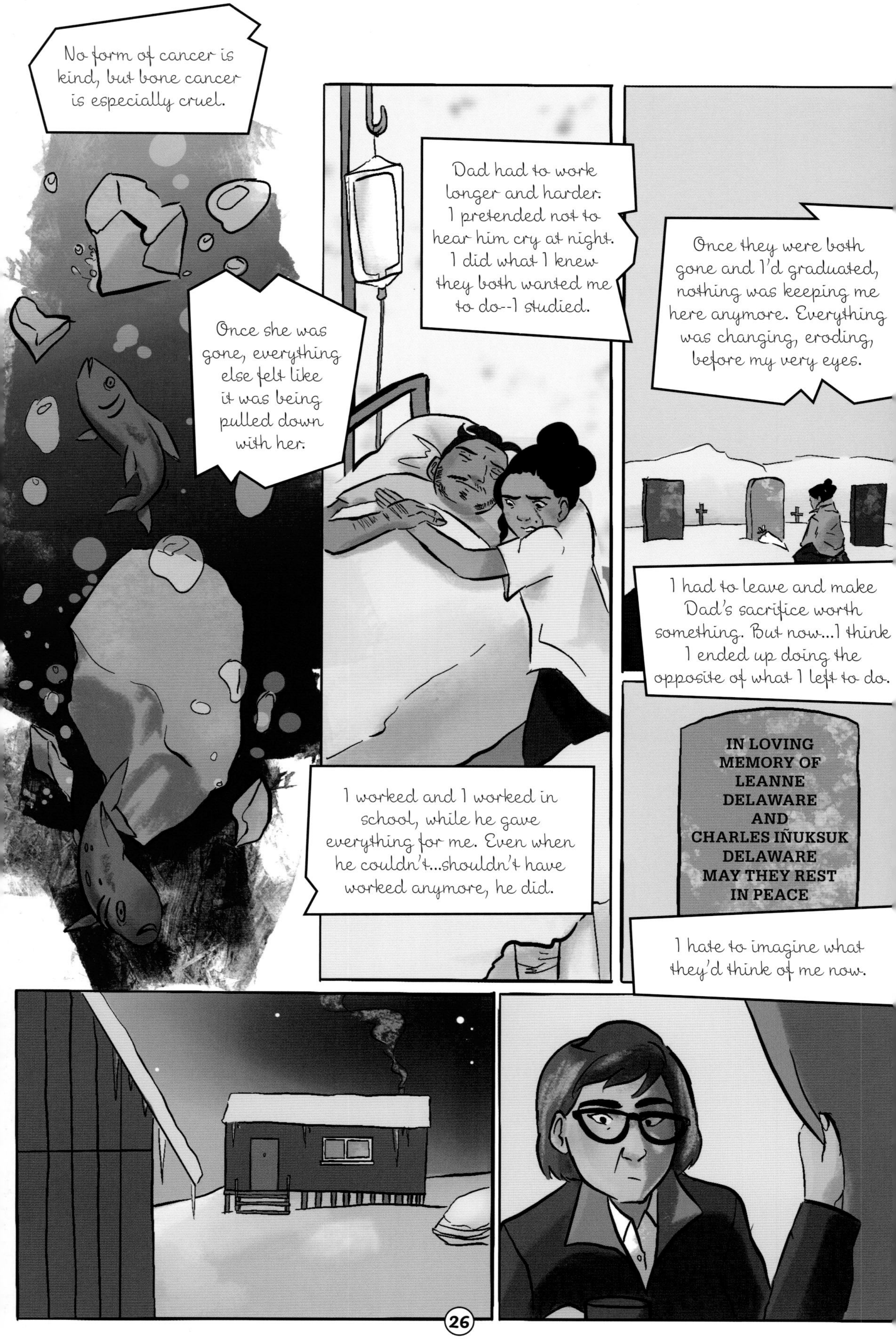
No form of cancer is kind, but bone cancer is especially cruel.
Once she was gone, everything else felt like it was being pulled down with her.
Dad had to work longer and harder. I pretended not to hear him cry at night. I did what I knew they both wanted me to do--I studied.
I worked and I worked in school, while he gave everything for me. Even when he couldn't...shouldn't have worked anymore, he did.
Once they were both gone and I'd graduated, nothing was keeping me here anymore. Everything was changing, eroding, before my very eyes.
I had to leave and make Dad's sacrifice worth something. But now...I think I ended up doing the opposite of what I left to do.
IN LOVING MEMORY OF LEANNE DELAWARE AND CHARLES IÑUKSUK DELAWARE MAY THEY REST IN PEACE
I hate to imagine what they'd think of me now.

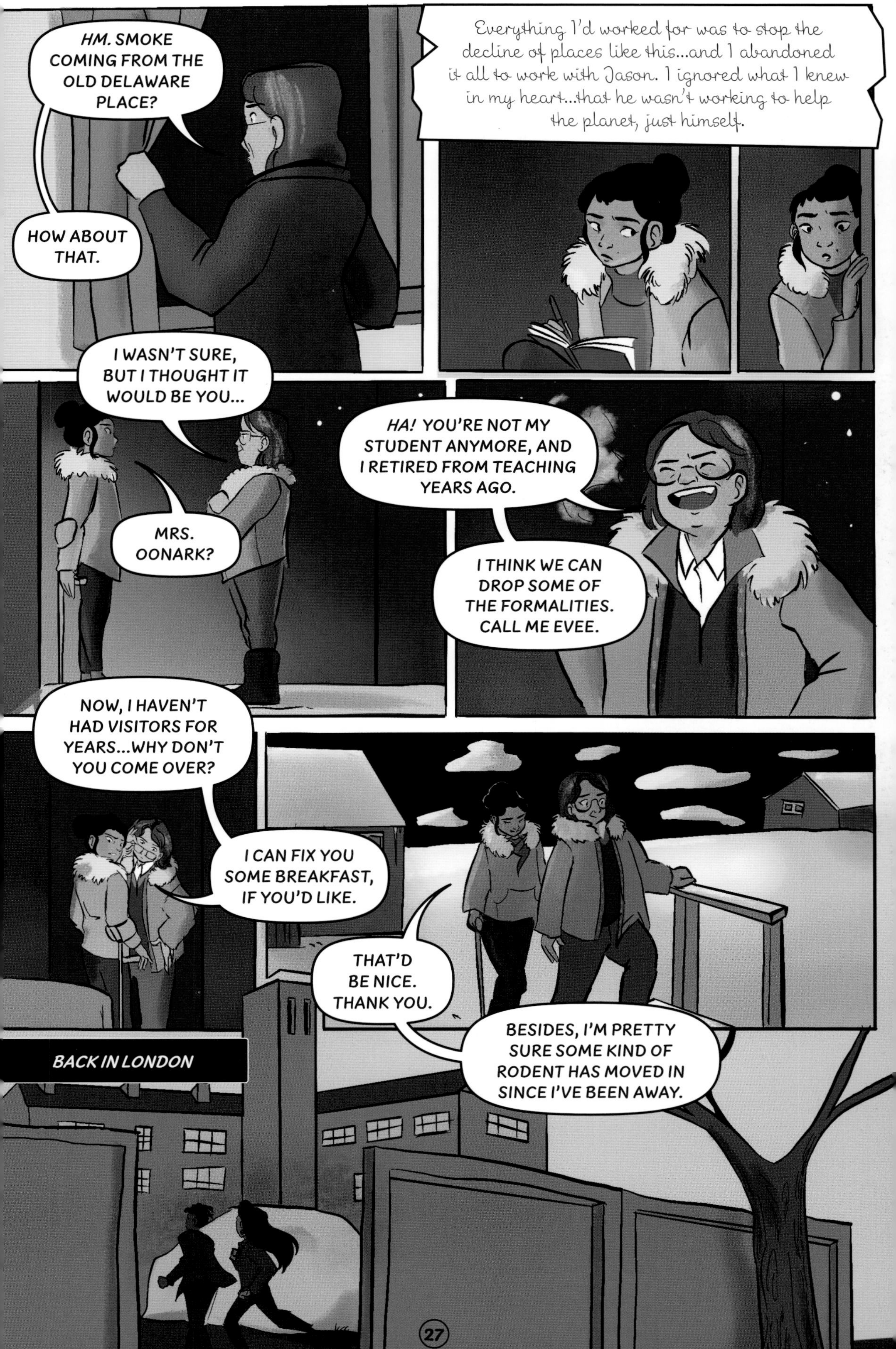

HM. SMOKE COMING FROM THE OLD DELAWARE PLACE?
HOW ABOUT THAT.
Everything I'd worked for was to stop the decline of places like this...and I abandoned it all to work with Jason. I ignored what I knew in my heart...that he wasn't working to help the planet, just himself.
I WASN'T SURE, BUT I THOUGHT IT WOULD BE YOU...
MRS. OONARK?
HA! YOU'RE NOT MY STUDENT ANYMORE, AND I RETIRED FROM TEACHING YEARS AGO.
I THINK WE CAN DROP SOME OF THE FORMALITIES. CALL ME EVEE.
NOW, I HAVEN'T HAD VISITORS FOR YEARS...WHY DON'T YOU COME OVER?
I CAN FIX YOU SOME BREAKFAST, IF YOU'D LIKE.
THAT'D BE NICE. THANK YOU.
BESIDES, I'M PRETTY SURE SOME KIND OF RODENT HAS MOVED IN SINCE I'VE BEEN AWAY.
BACK IN LONDON

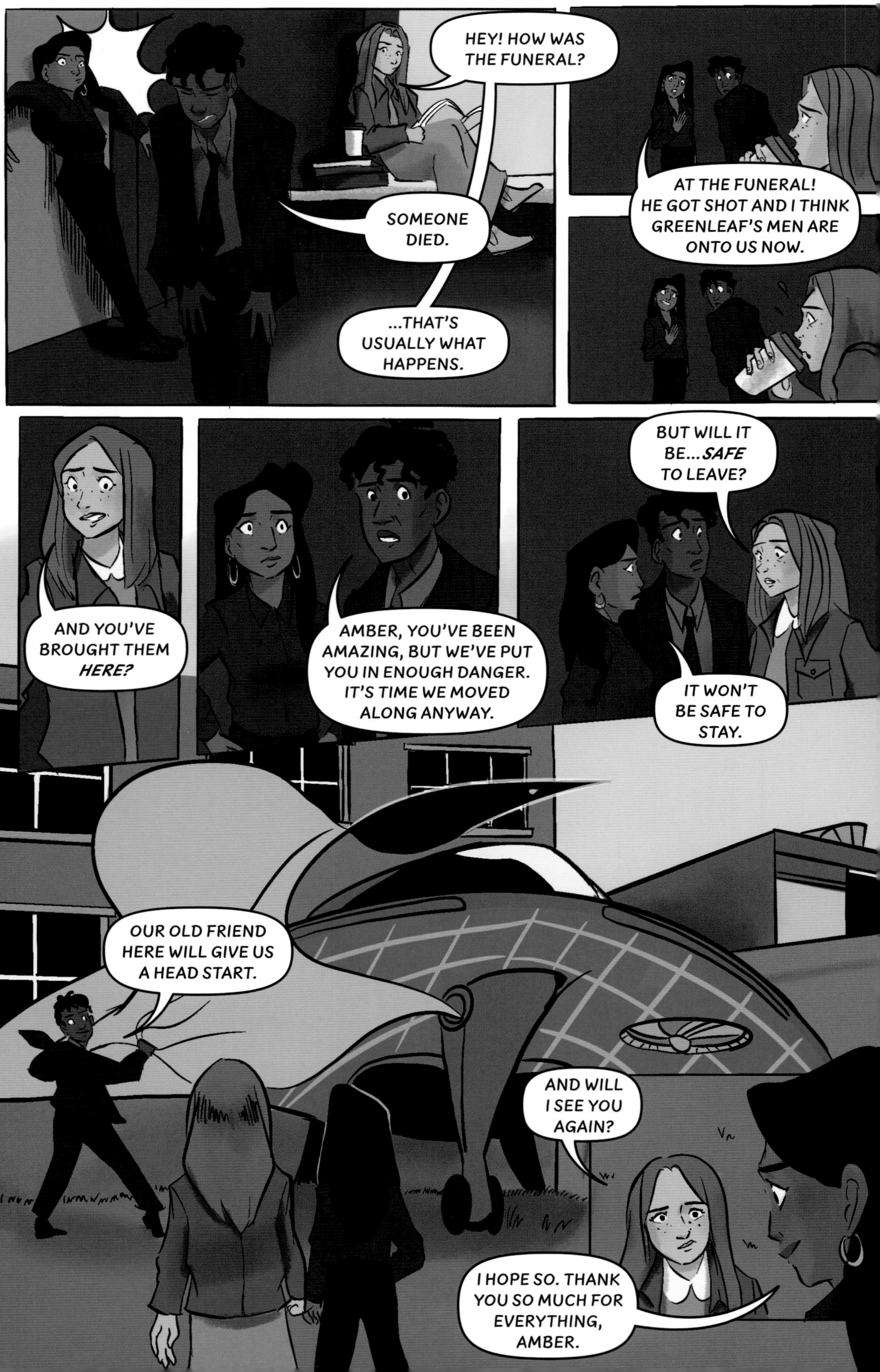
HEY! HOW WAS THE FUNERAL?
SOMEONE DIED.
...THAT'S USUALLY WHAT HAPPENS.
AT THE FUNERAL! HE GOT SHOT AND I THINK GREENLEAF'S MEN ARE ONTO US NOW.
AND YOU'VE BROUGHT THEM *HERE?*
AMBER, YOU'VE BEEN AMAZING, BUT WE'VE PUT YOU IN ENOUGH DANGER. IT'S TIME WE MOVED ALONG ANYWAY.
BUT WILL IT BE... ***SAFE*** TO LEAVE?
IT WON'T BE SAFE TO STAY.
OUR OLD FRIEND HERE WILL GIVE US A HEAD START.
AND WILL I SEE YOU AGAIN?
I HOPE SO. THANK YOU SO MUCH FOR EVERYTHING, AMBER.

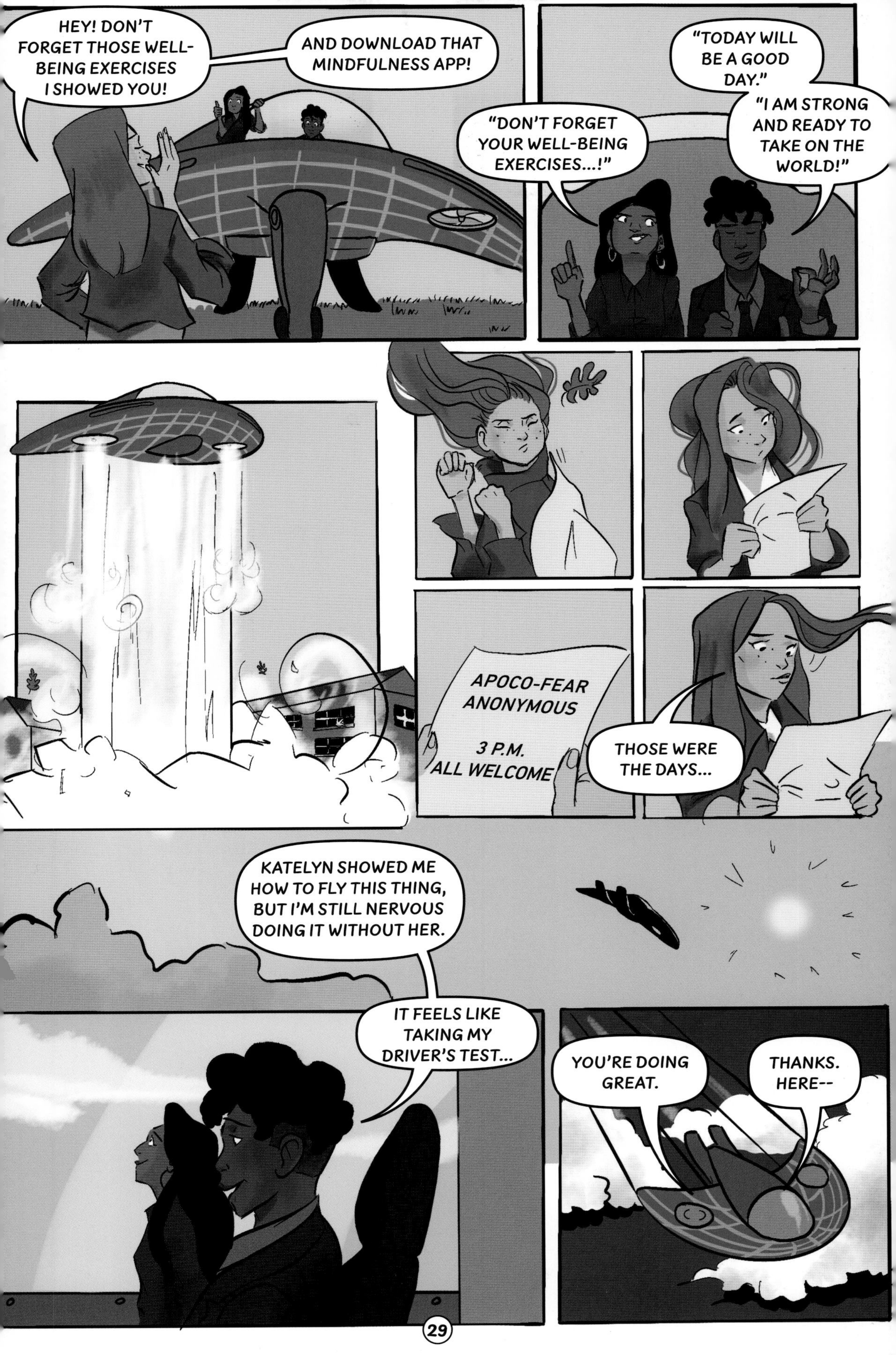
HEY! DON'T FORGET THOSE WELL-BEING EXERCISES I SHOWED YOU!
AND DOWNLOAD THAT MINDFULNESS APP!
"DON'T FORGET YOUR WELL-BEING EXERCISES...!"
"TODAY WILL BE A GOOD DAY."
"I AM STRONG AND READY TO TAKE ON THE WORLD!"
APOCO-FEAR ANONYMOUS
3 P.M.
ALL WELCOME
THOSE WERE THE DAYS...
KATELYN SHOWED ME HOW TO FLY THIS THING, BUT I'M STILL NERVOUS DOING IT WITHOUT HER.
IT FEELS LIKE TAKING MY DRIVER'S TEST...
YOU'RE DOING GREAT.
THANKS. HERE--

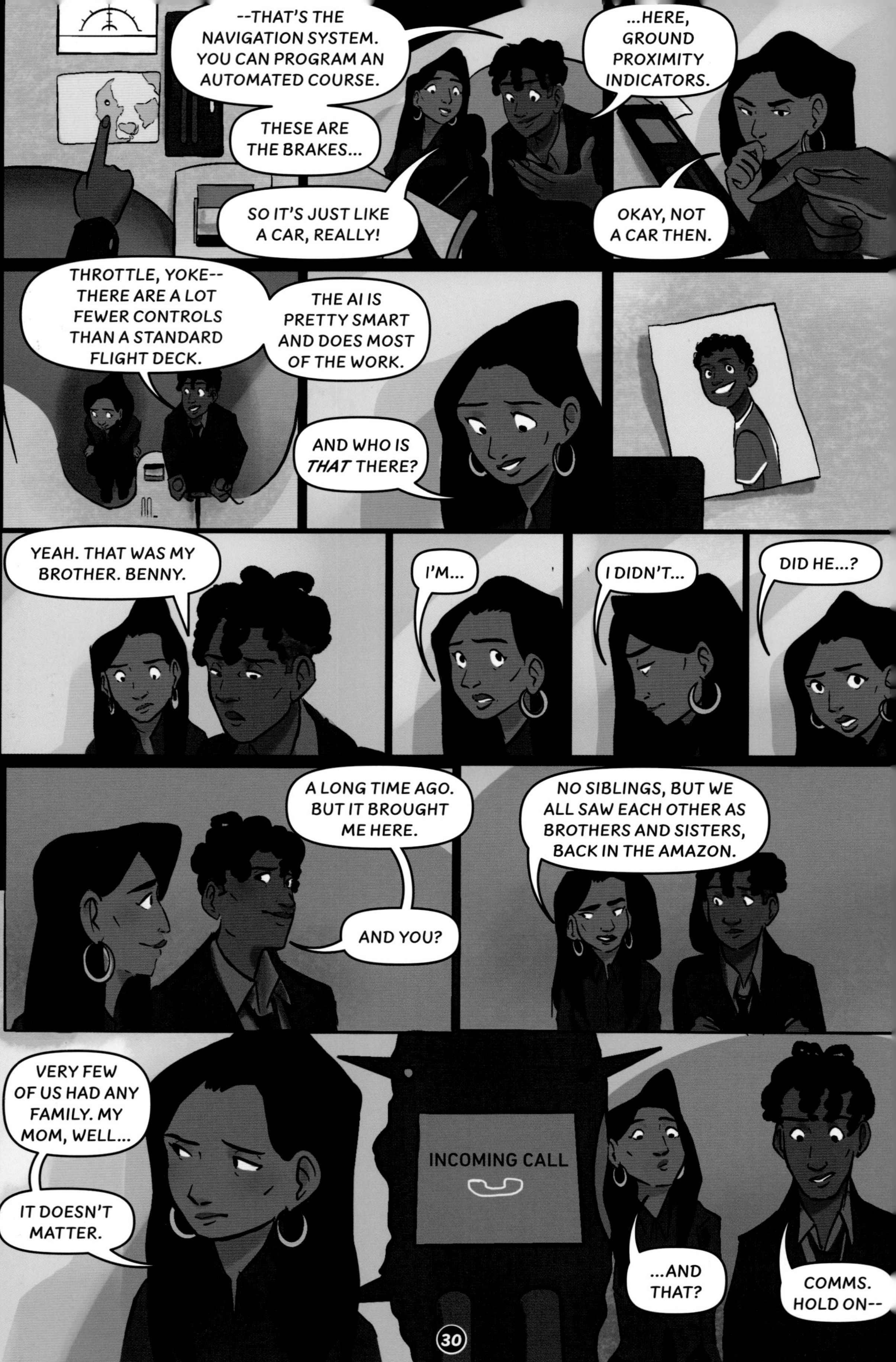
--THAT'S THE NAVIGATION SYSTEM. YOU CAN PROGRAM AN AUTOMATED COURSE.
THESE ARE THE BRAKES...
SO IT'S JUST LIKE A CAR, REALLY!
...HERE, GROUND PROXIMITY INDICATORS.
OKAY, NOT A CAR THEN.
THROTTLE, YOKE-- THERE ARE A LOT FEWER CONTROLS THAN A STANDARD FLIGHT DECK.
THE AI IS PRETTY SMART AND DOES MOST OF THE WORK.
AND WHO IS *THAT* THERE?
YEAH. THAT WAS MY BROTHER. BENNY.
I'M...
I DIDN'T...
DID HE...?
A LONG TIME AGO. BUT IT BROUGHT ME HERE.
AND YOU?
NO SIBLINGS, BUT WE ALL SAW EACH OTHER AS BROTHERS AND SISTERS, BACK IN THE AMAZON.
VERY FEW OF US HAD ANY FAMILY. MY MOM, WELL...
IT DOESN'T MATTER.
INCOMING CALL
...AND THAT?
COMMS. HOLD ON--

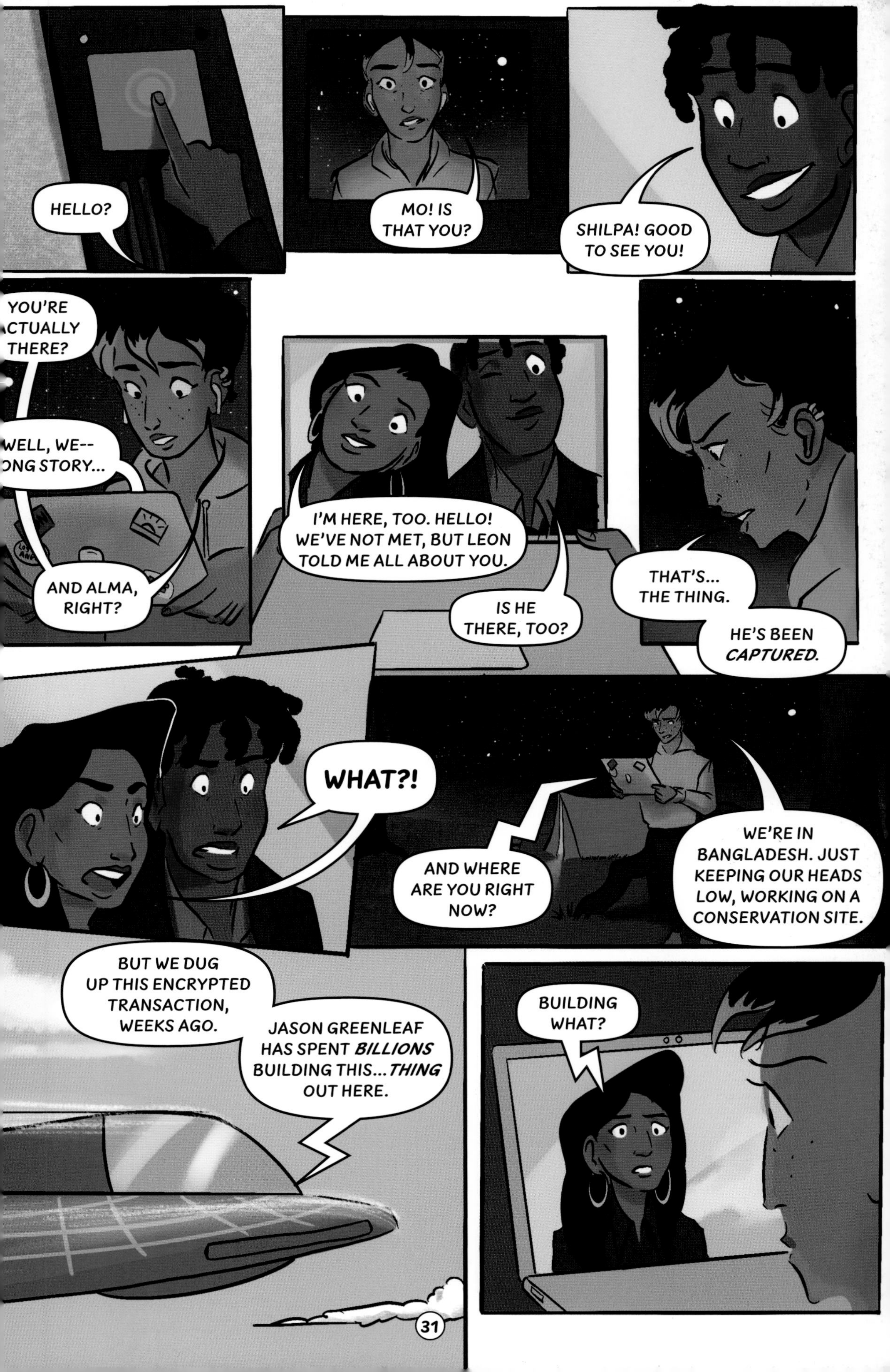
HELLO?
MO! IS THAT YOU?
SHILPA! GOOD TO SEE YOU!
YOU'RE ACTUALLY THERE?
WELL, WE-- LONG STORY...
AND ALMA, RIGHT?
I'M HERE, TOO. HELLO! WE'VE NOT MET, BUT LEON TOLD ME ALL ABOUT YOU.
IS HE THERE, TOO?
THAT'S... THE THING.
HE'S BEEN *CAPTURED.*
WHAT?!
AND WHERE ARE YOU RIGHT NOW?
WE'RE IN BANGLADESH. JUST KEEPING OUR HEADS LOW, WORKING ON A CONSERVATION SITE.
BUT WE DUG UP THIS ENCRYPTED TRANSACTION, WEEKS AGO.
JASON GREENLEAF HAS SPENT *BILLIONS* BUILDING THIS...*THING* OUT HERE.
BUILDING WHAT?

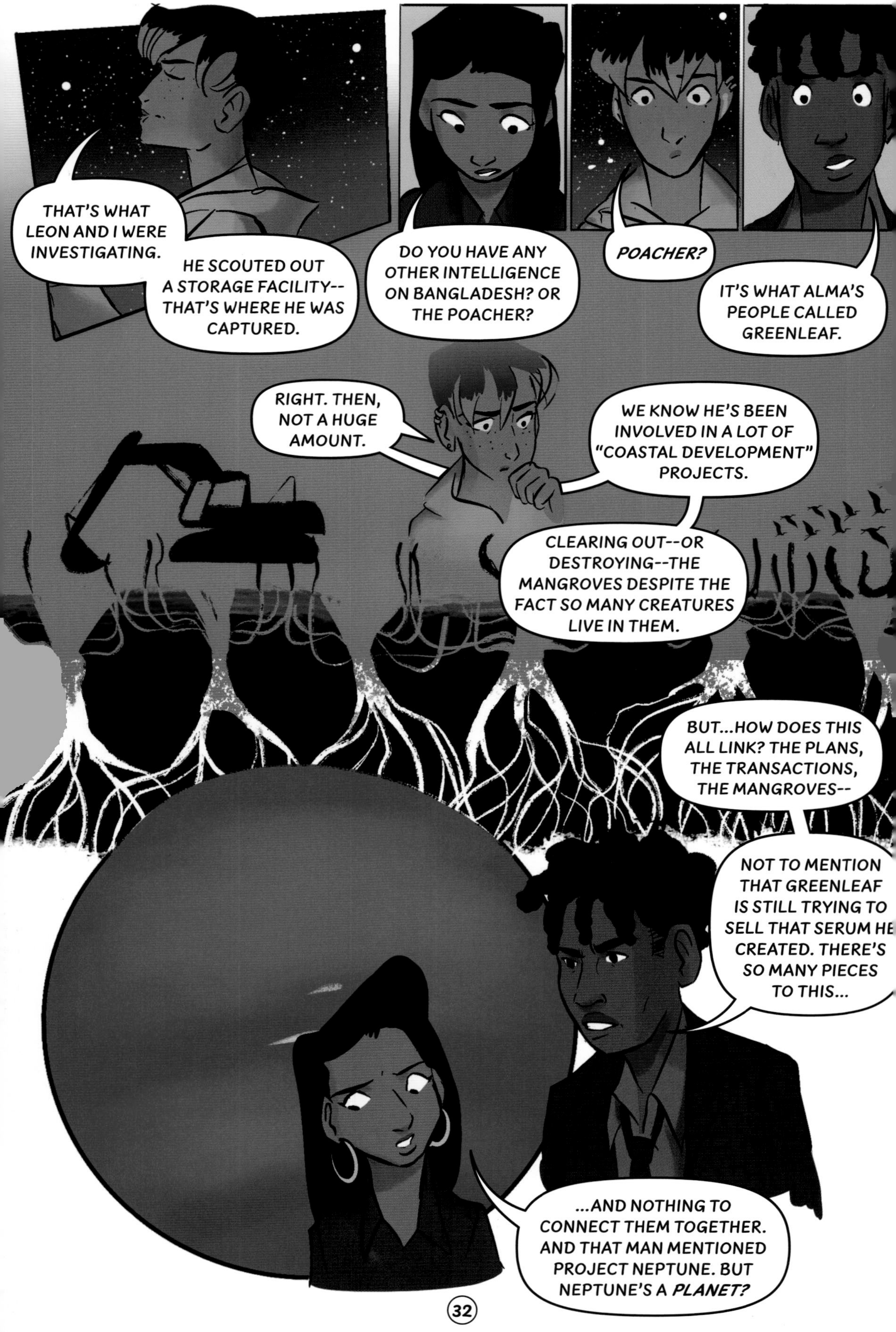
THAT'S WHAT LEON AND I WERE INVESTIGATING.
HE SCOUTED OUT A STORAGE FACILITY--THAT'S WHERE HE WAS CAPTURED.
DO YOU HAVE ANY OTHER INTELLIGENCE ON BANGLADESH? OR THE POACHER?
POACHER?
IT'S WHAT ALMA'S PEOPLE CALLED GREENLEAF.
RIGHT. THEN, NOT A HUGE AMOUNT.
WE KNOW HE'S BEEN INVOLVED IN A LOT OF "COASTAL DEVELOPMENT" PROJECTS.
CLEARING OUT--OR DESTROYING--THE MANGROVES DESPITE THE FACT SO MANY CREATURES LIVE IN THEM.
BUT...HOW DOES THIS ALL LINK? THE PLANS, THE TRANSACTIONS, THE MANGROVES--
NOT TO MENTION THAT GREENLEAF IS STILL TRYING TO SELL THAT SERUM HE CREATED. THERE'S SO MANY PIECES TO THIS...
...AND NOTHING TO CONNECT THEM TOGETHER. AND THAT MAN MENTIONED PROJECT NEPTUNE. BUT NEPTUNE'S A *PLANET?*

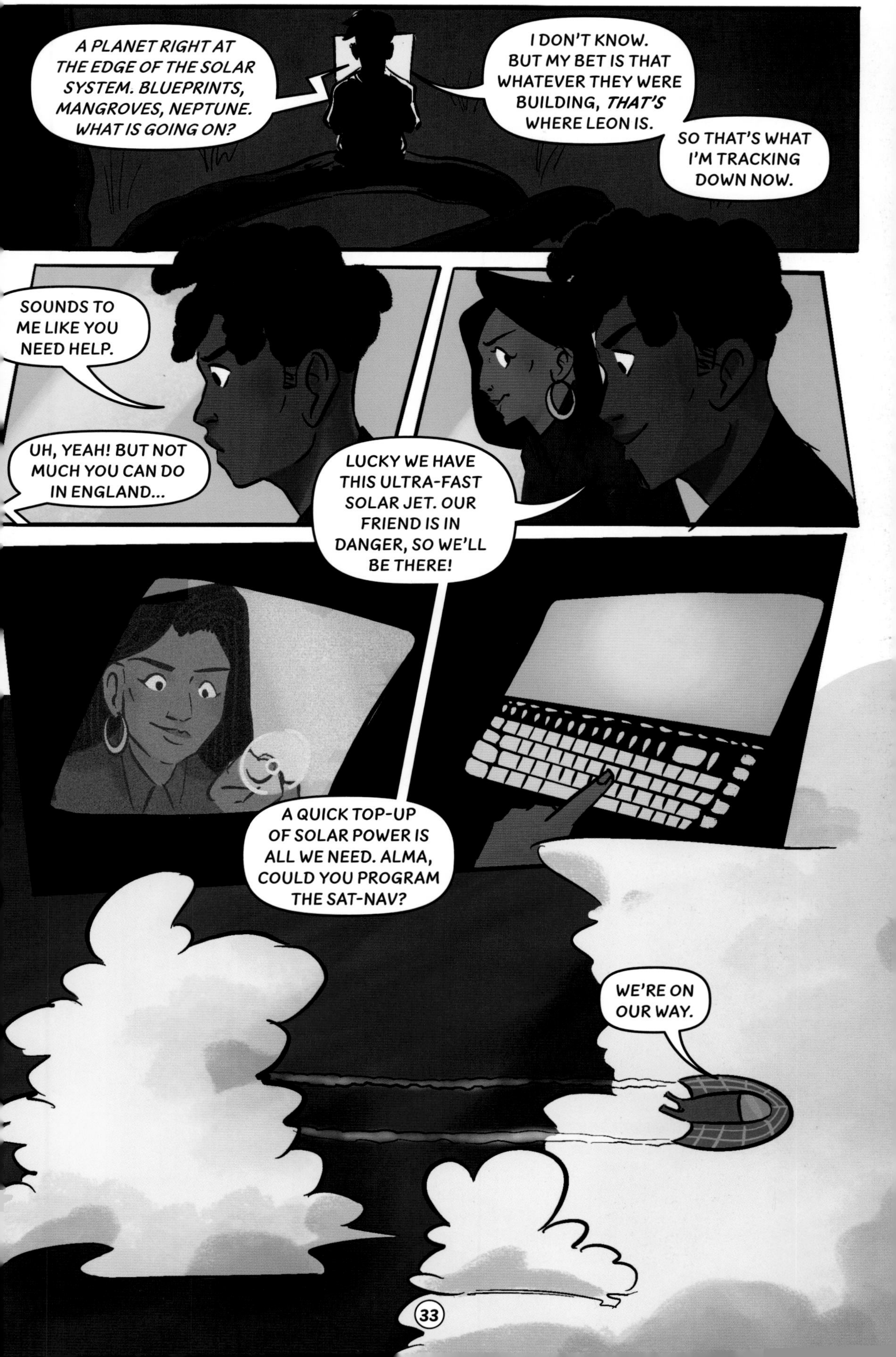
A PLANET RIGHT AT THE EDGE OF THE SOLAR SYSTEM. BLUEPRINTS, MANGROVES, NEPTUNE. WHAT IS GOING ON?
I DON'T KNOW. BUT MY BET IS THAT WHATEVER THEY WERE BUILDING, THAT'S WHERE LEON IS.
SO THAT'S WHAT I'M TRACKING DOWN NOW.
SOUNDS TO ME LIKE YOU NEED HELP.
UH, YEAH! BUT NOT MUCH YOU CAN DO IN ENGLAND...
LUCKY WE HAVE THIS ULTRA-FAST SOLAR JET. OUR FRIEND IS IN DANGER, SO WE'LL BE THERE!
A QUICK TOP-UP OF SOLAR POWER IS ALL WE NEED. ALMA, COULD YOU PROGRAM THE SAT-NAV?
WE'RE ON OUR WAY.

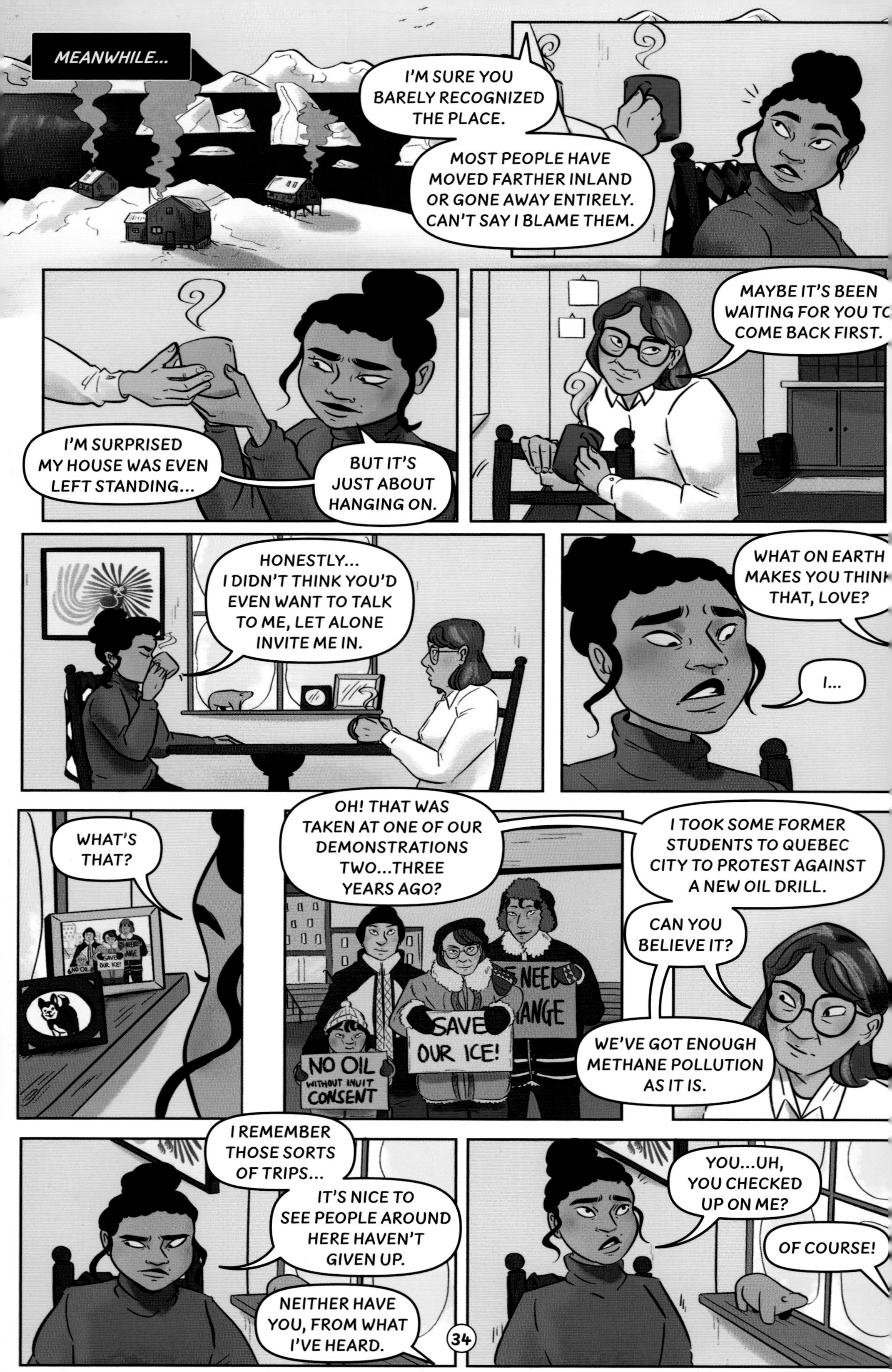
MEANWHILE...
I'M SURE YOU BARELY RECOGNIZED THE PLACE.
MOST PEOPLE HAVE MOVED FARTHER INLAND OR GONE AWAY ENTIRELY. CAN'T SAY I BLAME THEM.
I'M SURPRISED MY HOUSE WAS EVEN LEFT STANDING...
BUT IT'S JUST ABOUT HANGING ON.
MAYBE IT'S BEEN WAITING FOR YOU TO COME BACK FIRST.
HONESTLY... I DIDN'T THINK YOU'D EVEN WANT TO TALK TO ME, LET ALONE INVITE ME IN.
WHAT ON EARTH MAKES YOU THINK THAT, LOVE?
I...
WHAT'S THAT?
OH! THAT WAS TAKEN AT ONE OF OUR DEMONSTRATIONS TWO...THREE YEARS AGO?
I TOOK SOME FORMER STUDENTS TO QUEBEC CITY TO PROTEST AGAINST A NEW OIL DRILL.
CAN YOU BELIEVE IT?
WE'VE GOT ENOUGH METHANE POLLUTION AS IT IS.
NO OIL WITHOUT INUIT CONSENT
SAVE OUR ICE!
I REMEMBER THOSE SORTS OF TRIPS...
IT'S NICE TO SEE PEOPLE AROUND HERE HAVEN'T GIVEN UP.
NEITHER HAVE YOU, FROM WHAT I'VE HEARD.
YOU...UH, YOU CHECKED UP ON ME?
OF COURSE!

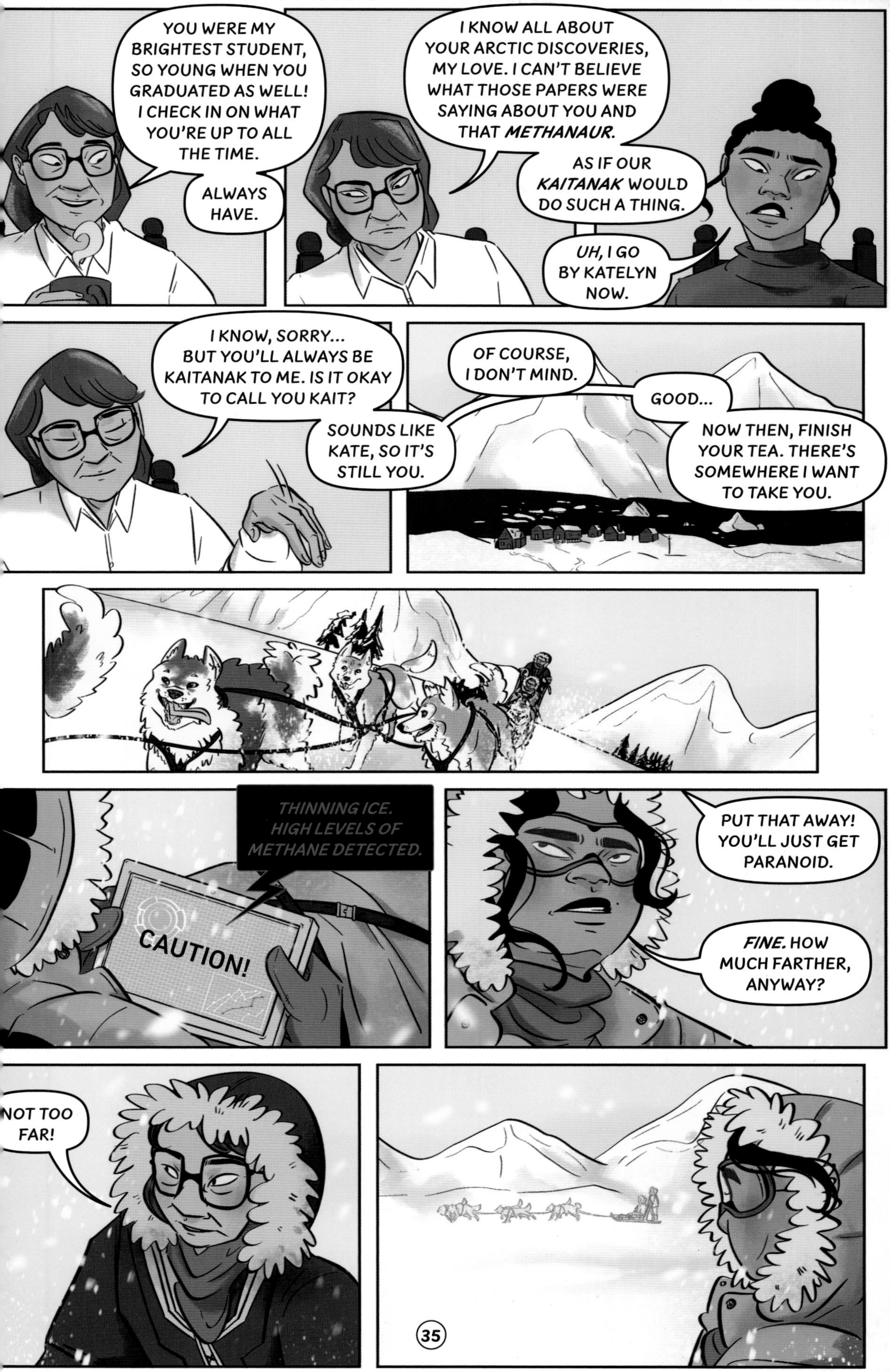
YOU WERE MY BRIGHTEST STUDENT, SO YOUNG WHEN YOU GRADUATED AS WELL! I CHECK IN ON WHAT YOU'RE UP TO ALL THE TIME.
ALWAYS HAVE.
I KNOW ALL ABOUT YOUR ARCTIC DISCOVERIES, MY LOVE. I CAN'T BELIEVE WHAT THOSE PAPERS WERE SAYING ABOUT YOU AND THAT *METHANAUR.*
AS IF OUR *KAITANAK* WOULD DO SUCH A THING.
UH, I GO BY KATELYN NOW.
I KNOW, SORRY... BUT YOU'LL ALWAYS BE KAITANAK TO ME. IS IT OKAY TO CALL YOU KAIT?
SOUNDS LIKE KATE, SO IT'S STILL YOU.
OF COURSE, I DON'T MIND.
GOOD...
NOW THEN, FINISH YOUR TEA. THERE'S SOMEWHERE I WANT TO TAKE YOU.
THINNING ICE. HIGH LEVELS OF METHANE DETECTED.
CAUTION!
PUT THAT AWAY! YOU'LL JUST GET PARANOID.
FINE. HOW MUCH FARTHER, ANYWAY?
NOT TOO FAR!

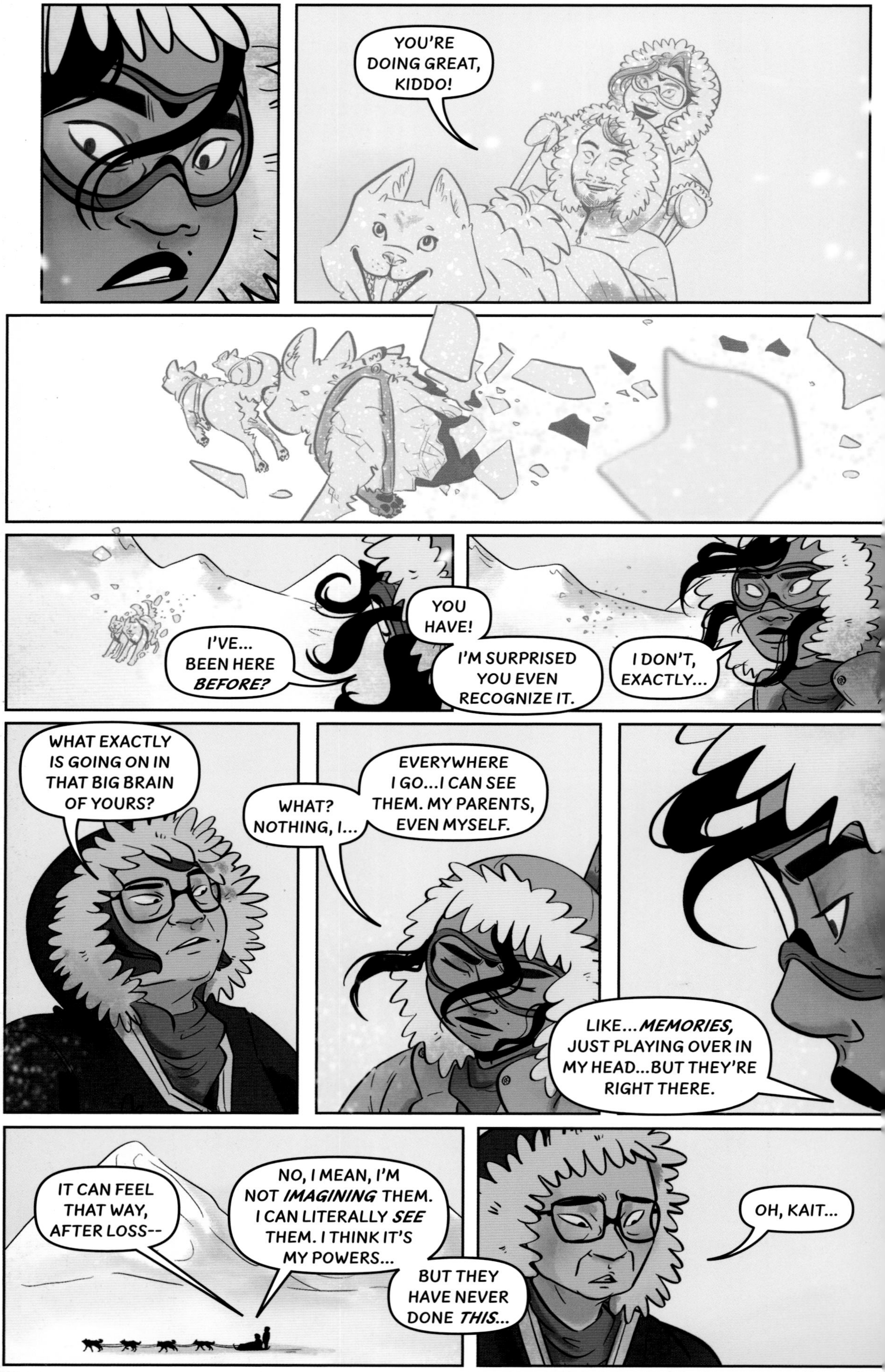
YOU'RE DOING GREAT, KIDDO!
I'VE... BEEN HERE *BEFORE?*
YOU HAVE!
I'M SURPRISED YOU EVEN RECOGNIZE IT.
I DON'T, EXACTLY...
WHAT EXACTLY IS GOING ON IN THAT BIG BRAIN OF YOURS?
WHAT? NOTHING, I...
EVERYWHERE I GO...I CAN SEE THEM. MY PARENTS, EVEN MYSELF.
LIKE...*MEMORIES,* JUST PLAYING OVER IN MY HEAD...BUT THEY'RE RIGHT THERE.
IT CAN FEEL THAT WAY, AFTER LOSS--
NO, I MEAN, I'M NOT *IMAGINING* THEM. I CAN LITERALLY *SEE* THEM. I THINK IT'S MY POWERS...
BUT THEY HAVE NEVER DONE *THIS*...
OH, KAIT...

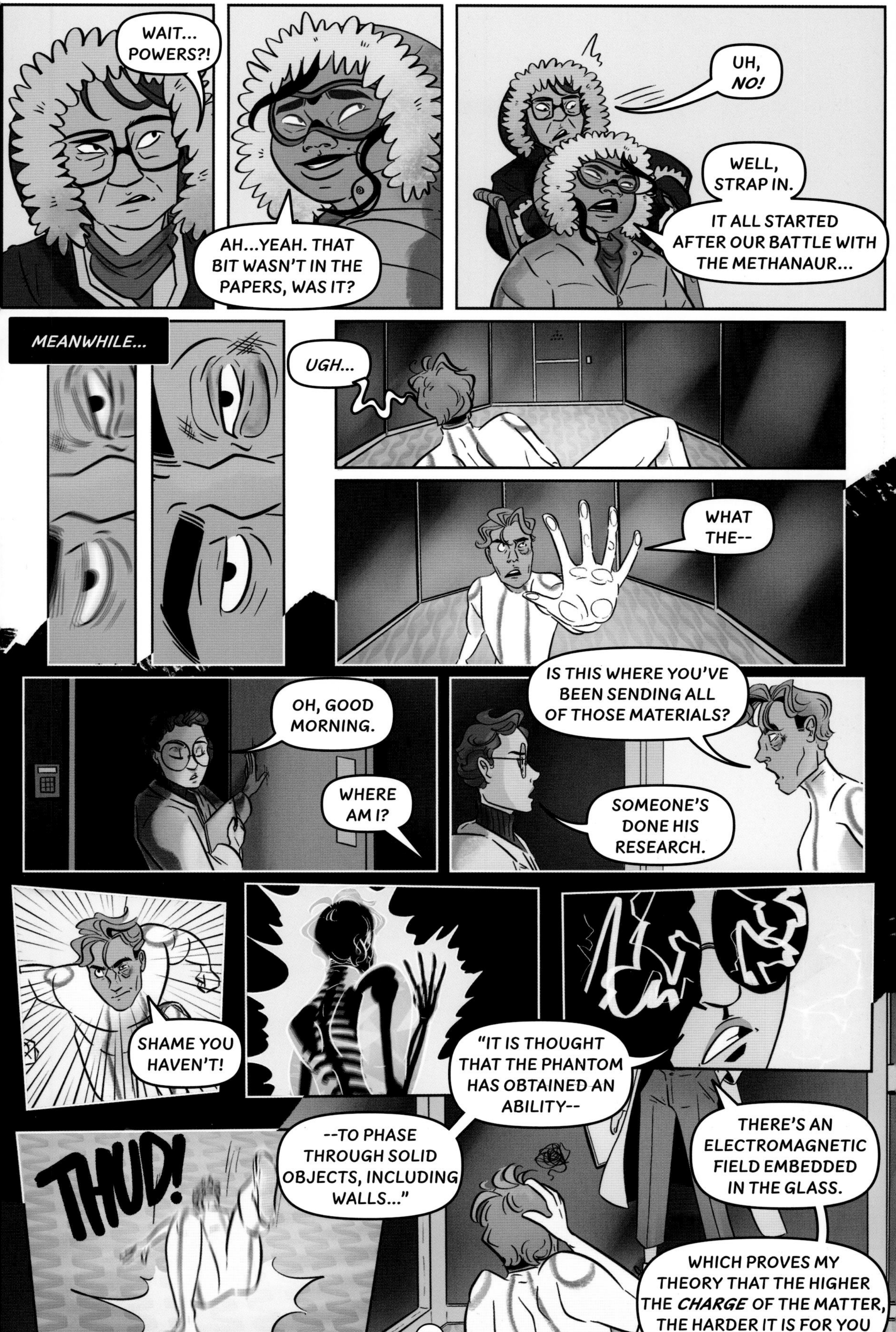

WAIT... POWERS?!
AH...YEAH. THAT BIT WASN'T IN THE PAPERS, WAS IT?
UH, *NO!*
WELL, STRAP IN.
IT ALL STARTED AFTER OUR BATTLE WITH THE METHANAUR...
MEANWHILE...
UGH...
WHAT THE--
OH, GOOD MORNING.
WHERE AM I?
IS THIS WHERE YOU'VE BEEN SENDING ALL OF THOSE MATERIALS?
SOMEONE'S DONE HIS RESEARCH.
SHAME YOU HAVEN'T!
THUD!
"IT IS THOUGHT THAT THE PHANTOM HAS OBTAINED AN ABILITY--
--TO PHASE THROUGH SOLID OBJECTS, INCLUDING WALLS..."
THERE'S AN ELECTROMAGNETIC FIELD EMBEDDED IN THE GLASS.
WHICH PROVES MY THEORY THAT THE HIGHER THE *CHARGE* OF THE MATTER, THE HARDER IT IS FOR YOU TO PASS THROUGH.

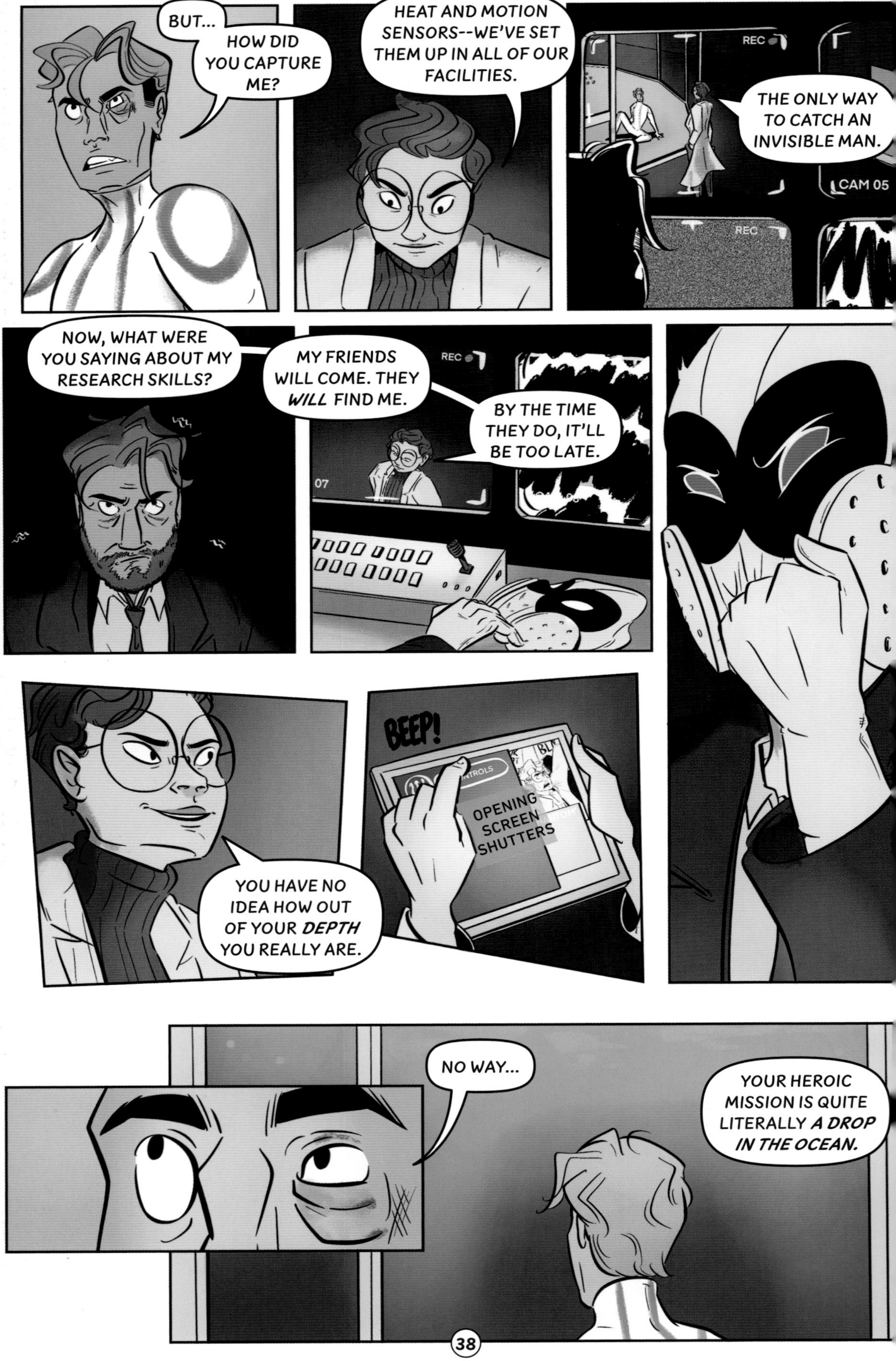
BUT...
HOW DID YOU CAPTURE ME?
HEAT AND MOTION SENSORS--WE'VE SET THEM UP IN ALL OF OUR FACILITIES.
REC
THE ONLY WAY TO CATCH AN INVISIBLE MAN.
CAM 05
REC
NOW, WHAT WERE YOU SAYING ABOUT MY RESEARCH SKILLS?
MY FRIENDS WILL COME. THEY *WILL* FIND ME.
REC
BY THE TIME THEY DO, IT'LL BE TOO LATE.
07
YOU HAVE NO IDEA HOW OUT OF YOUR *DEPTH* YOU REALLY ARE.
BEEP!
OPENING SCREEN SHUTTERS
NO WAY...
YOUR HEROIC MISSION IS QUITE LITERALLY *A DROP IN THE OCEAN.*

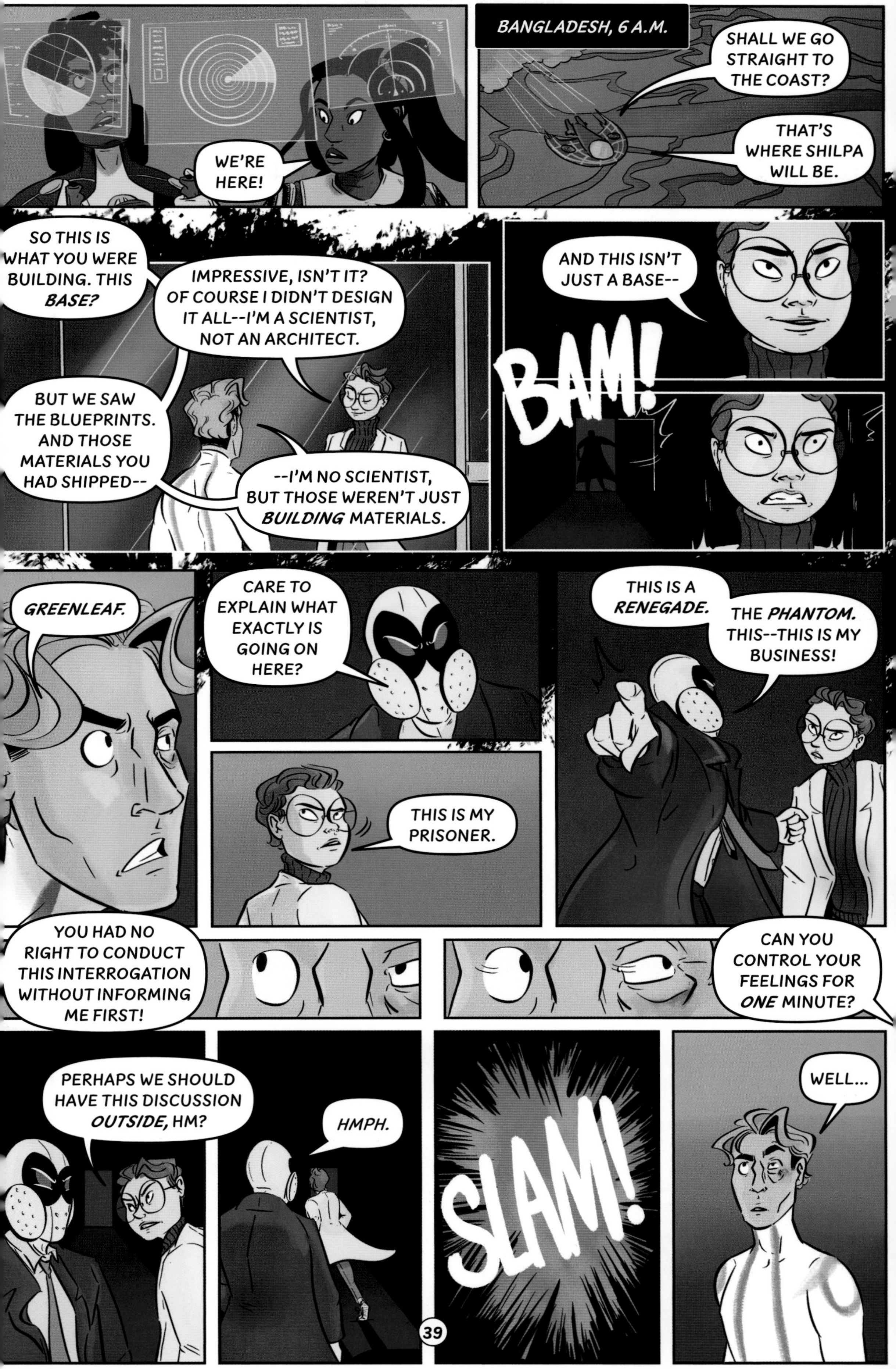
WE'RE HERE!
BANGLADESH, 6 A.M.
SHALL WE GO STRAIGHT TO THE COAST?
THAT'S WHERE SHILPA WILL BE.
SO THIS IS WHAT YOU WERE BUILDING. THIS BASE?
IMPRESSIVE, ISN'T IT? OF COURSE I DIDN'T DESIGN IT ALL--I'M A SCIENTIST, NOT AN ARCHITECT.
BUT WE SAW THE BLUEPRINTS. AND THOSE MATERIALS YOU HAD SHIPPED--
--I'M NO SCIENTIST, BUT THOSE WEREN'T JUST BUILDING MATERIALS.
AND THIS ISN'T JUST A BASE--
BAM!
GREENLEAF.
CARE TO EXPLAIN WHAT EXACTLY IS GOING ON HERE?
THIS IS MY PRISONER.
THIS IS A RENEGADE.
THE PHANTOM. THIS--THIS IS MY BUSINESS!
YOU HAD NO RIGHT TO CONDUCT THIS INTERROGATION WITHOUT INFORMING ME FIRST!
CAN YOU CONTROL YOUR FEELINGS FOR ONE MINUTE?
PERHAPS WE SHOULD HAVE THIS DISCUSSION OUTSIDE, HM?
HMPH.
SLAM!
WELL...

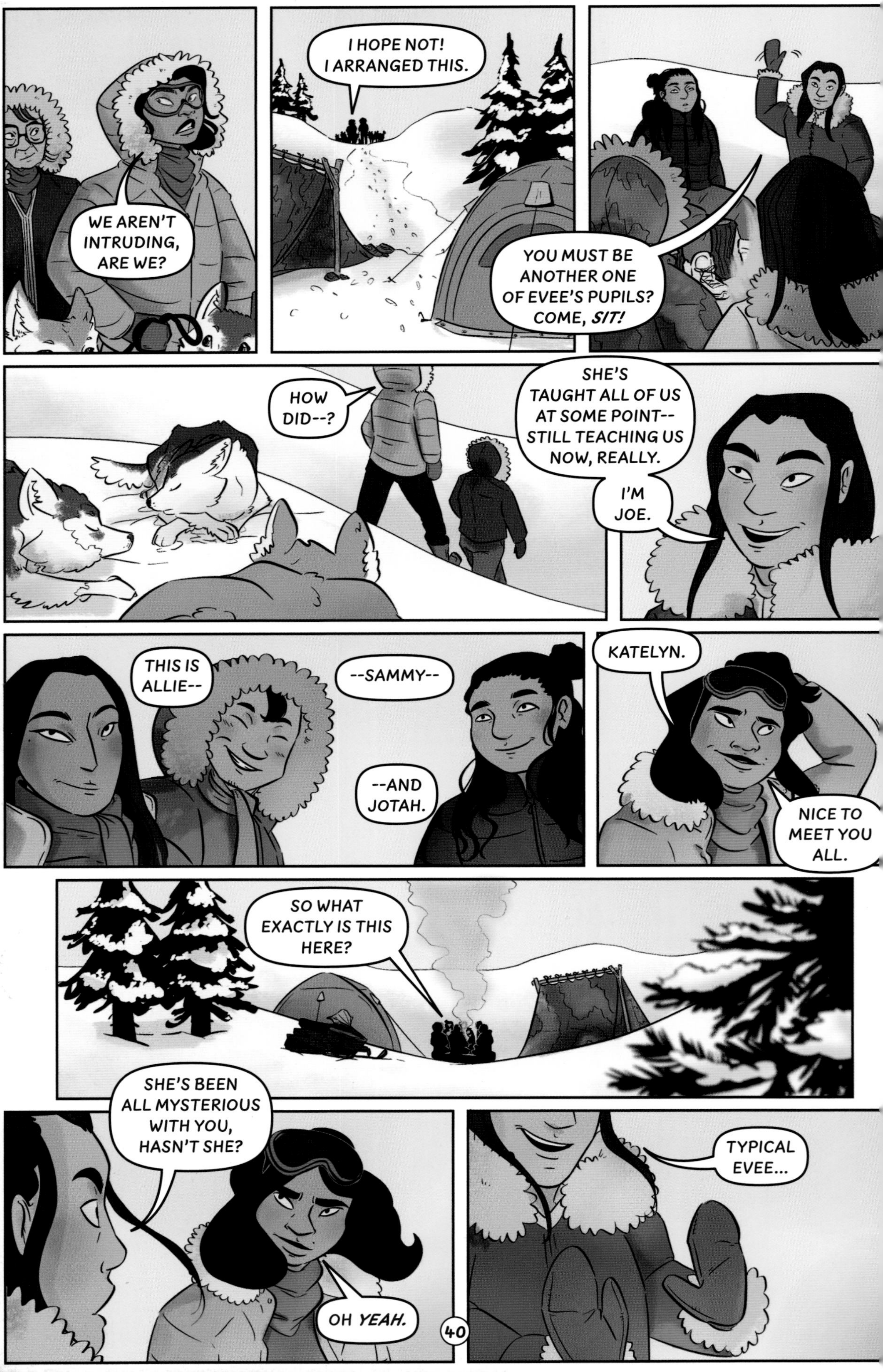
WE AREN'T INTRUDING, ARE WE?
I HOPE NOT! I ARRANGED THIS.
YOU MUST BE ANOTHER ONE OF EVEE'S PUPILS? COME, *SIT!*
HOW DID--?
SHE'S TAUGHT ALL OF US AT SOME POINT-- STILL TEACHING US NOW, REALLY.
I'M JOE.
THIS IS ALLIE--
--SAMMY--
--AND JOTAH.
KATELYN.
NICE TO MEET YOU ALL.
SO WHAT EXACTLY IS THIS HERE?
SHE'S BEEN ALL MYSTERIOUS WITH YOU, HASN'T SHE?
OH *YEAH.*
TYPICAL EVEE...

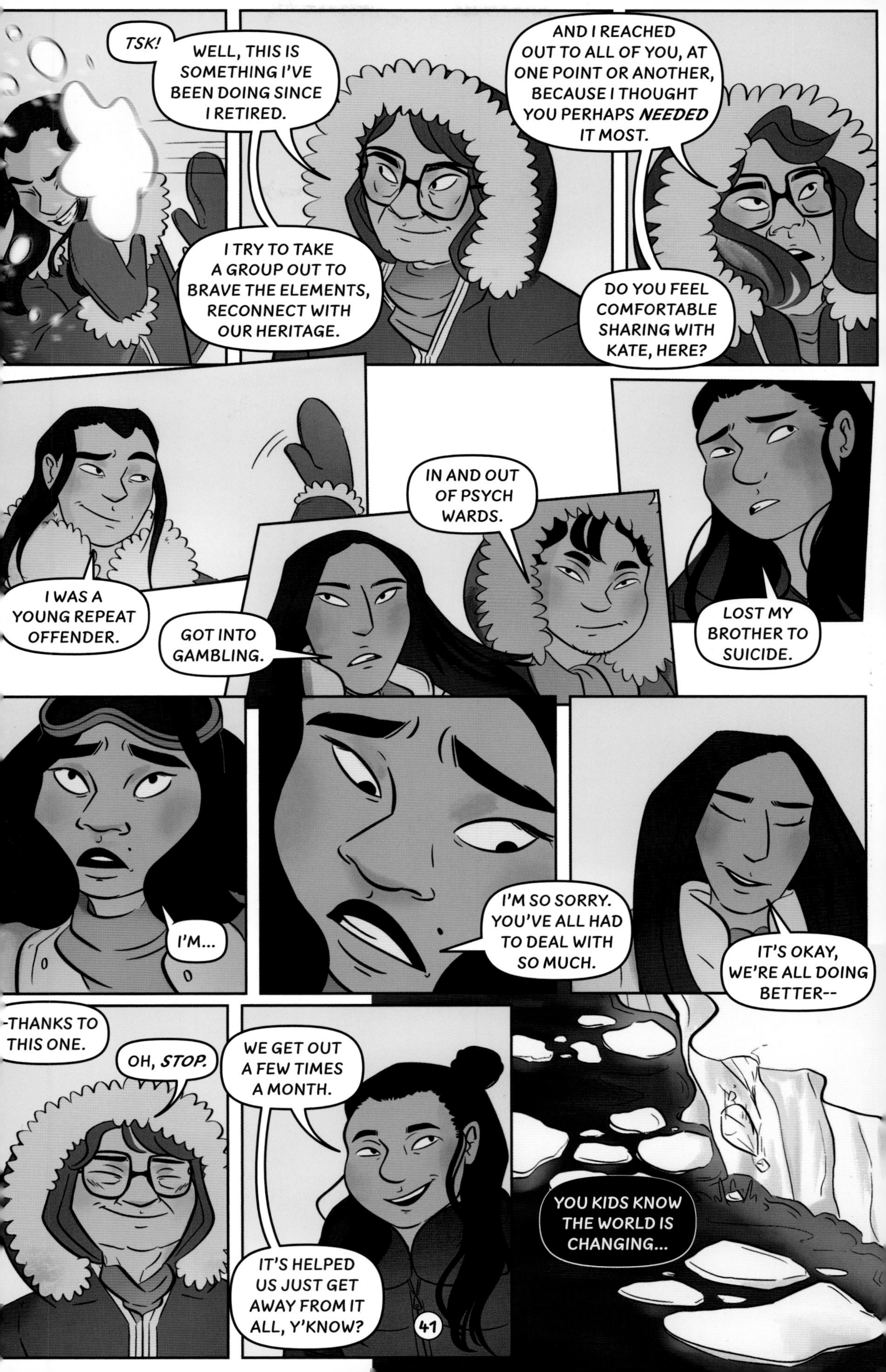
TSK!
WELL, THIS IS SOMETHING I'VE BEEN DOING SINCE I RETIRED.
I TRY TO TAKE A GROUP OUT TO BRAVE THE ELEMENTS, RECONNECT WITH OUR HERITAGE.
AND I REACHED OUT TO ALL OF YOU, AT ONE POINT OR ANOTHER, BECAUSE I THOUGHT YOU PERHAPS *NEEDED* IT MOST.
DO YOU FEEL COMFORTABLE SHARING WITH KATE, HERE?
I WAS A YOUNG REPEAT OFFENDER.
GOT INTO GAMBLING.
IN AND OUT OF PSYCH WARDS.
LOST MY BROTHER TO SUICIDE.
I'M...
I'M SO SORRY. YOU'VE ALL HAD TO DEAL WITH SO MUCH.
IT'S OKAY, WE'RE ALL DOING BETTER--
-THANKS TO THIS ONE.
OH, *STOP.*
WE GET OUT A FEW TIMES A MONTH.
IT'S HELPED US JUST GET AWAY FROM IT ALL, Y'KNOW?
YOU KIDS KNOW THE WORLD IS CHANGING...

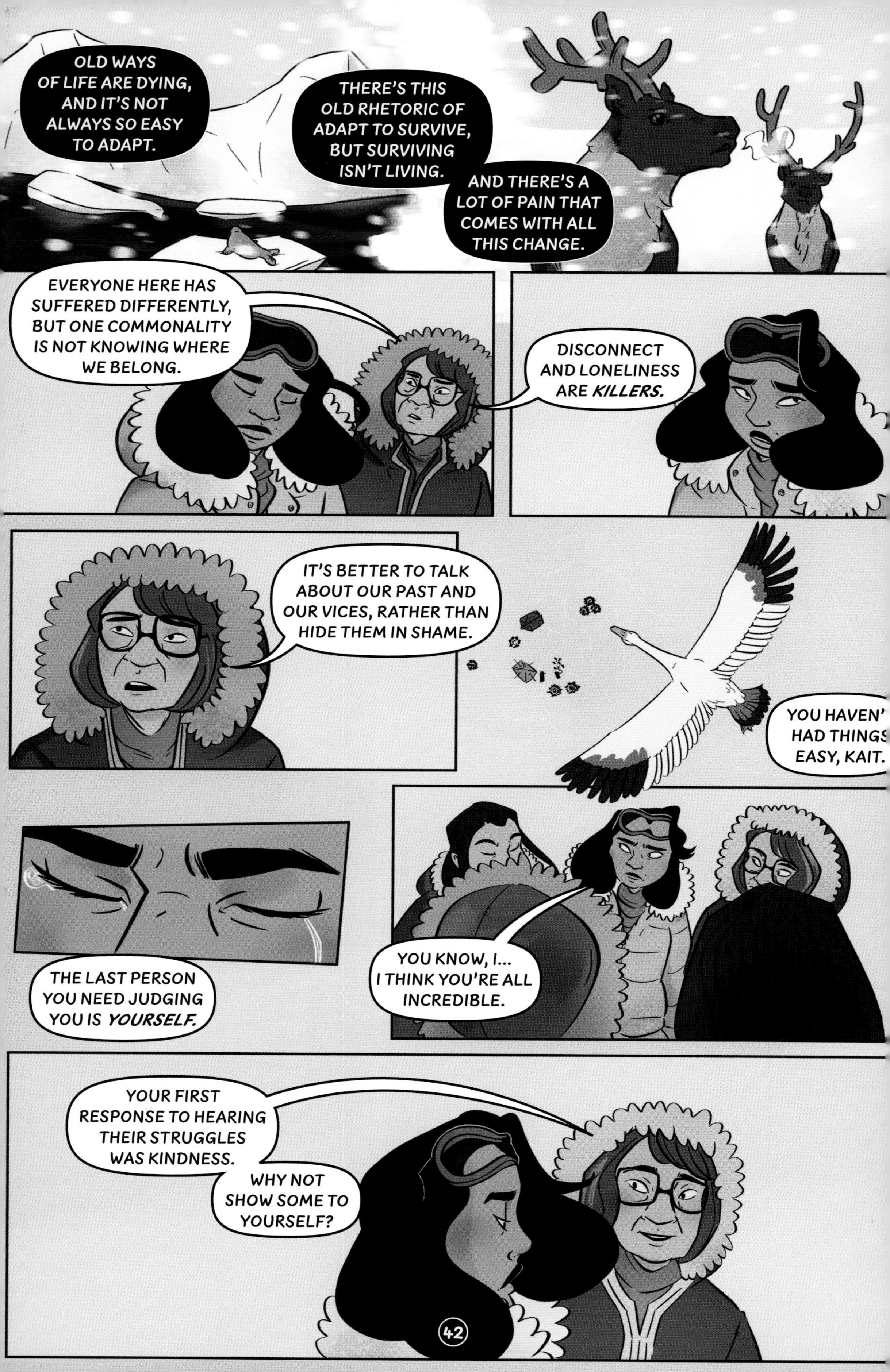
OLD WAYS OF LIFE ARE DYING, AND IT'S NOT ALWAYS SO EASY TO ADAPT.
THERE'S THIS OLD RHETORIC OF ADAPT TO SURVIVE, BUT SURVIVING ISN'T LIVING.
AND THERE'S A LOT OF PAIN THAT COMES WITH ALL THIS CHANGE.
EVERYONE HERE HAS SUFFERED DIFFERENTLY, BUT ONE COMMONALITY IS NOT KNOWING WHERE WE BELONG.
DISCONNECT AND LONELINESS ARE *KILLERS.*
IT'S BETTER TO TALK ABOUT OUR PAST AND OUR VICES, RATHER THAN HIDE THEM IN SHAME.
YOU HAVEN' HAD THINGS EASY, KAIT.
THE LAST PERSON YOU NEED JUDGING YOU IS *YOURSELF.*
YOU KNOW, I... I THINK YOU'RE ALL INCREDIBLE.
YOUR FIRST RESPONSE TO HEARING THEIR STRUGGLES WAS KINDNESS.
WHY NOT SHOW SOME TO YOURSELF?

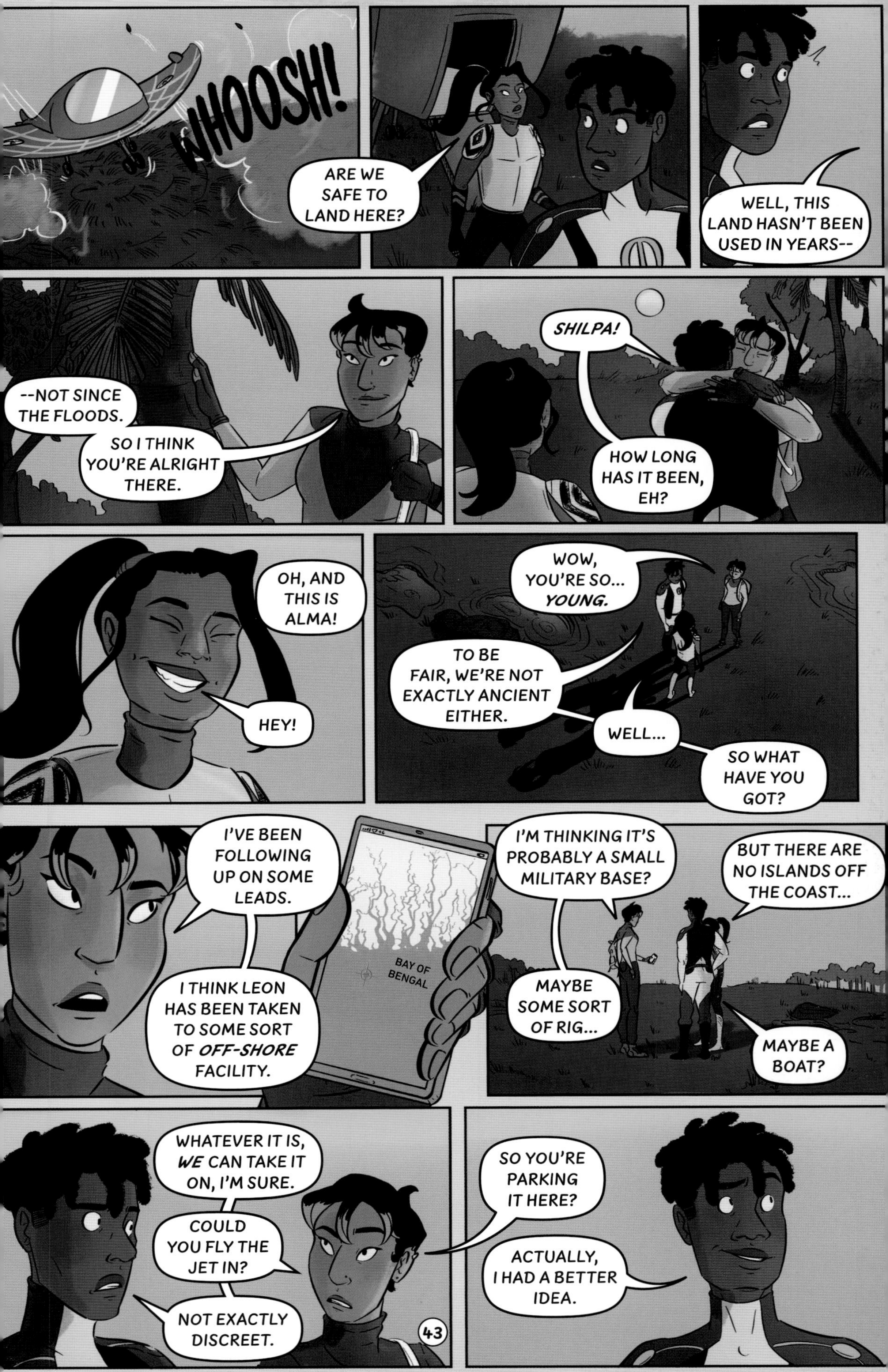
WHOOSH!
ARE WE SAFE TO LAND HERE?
WELL, THIS LAND HASN'T BEEN USED IN YEARS--
--NOT SINCE THE FLOODS.
SO I THINK YOU'RE ALRIGHT THERE.
SHILPA!
HOW LONG HAS IT BEEN, EH?
OH, AND THIS IS ALMA!
HEY!
WOW, YOU'RE SO... YOUNG.
TO BE FAIR, WE'RE NOT EXACTLY ANCIENT EITHER.
WELL...
SO WHAT HAVE YOU GOT?
I'VE BEEN FOLLOWING UP ON SOME LEADS.
BAY OF BENGAL
I THINK LEON HAS BEEN TAKEN TO SOME SORT OF OFF-SHORE FACILITY.
I'M THINKING IT'S PROBABLY A SMALL MILITARY BASE?
BUT THERE ARE NO ISLANDS OFF THE COAST...
MAYBE SOME SORT OF RIG...
MAYBE A BOAT?
WHATEVER IT IS, WE CAN TAKE IT ON, I'M SURE.
COULD YOU FLY THE JET IN?
NOT EXACTLY DISCREET.
SO YOU'RE PARKING IT HERE?
ACTUALLY, I HAD A BETTER IDEA.

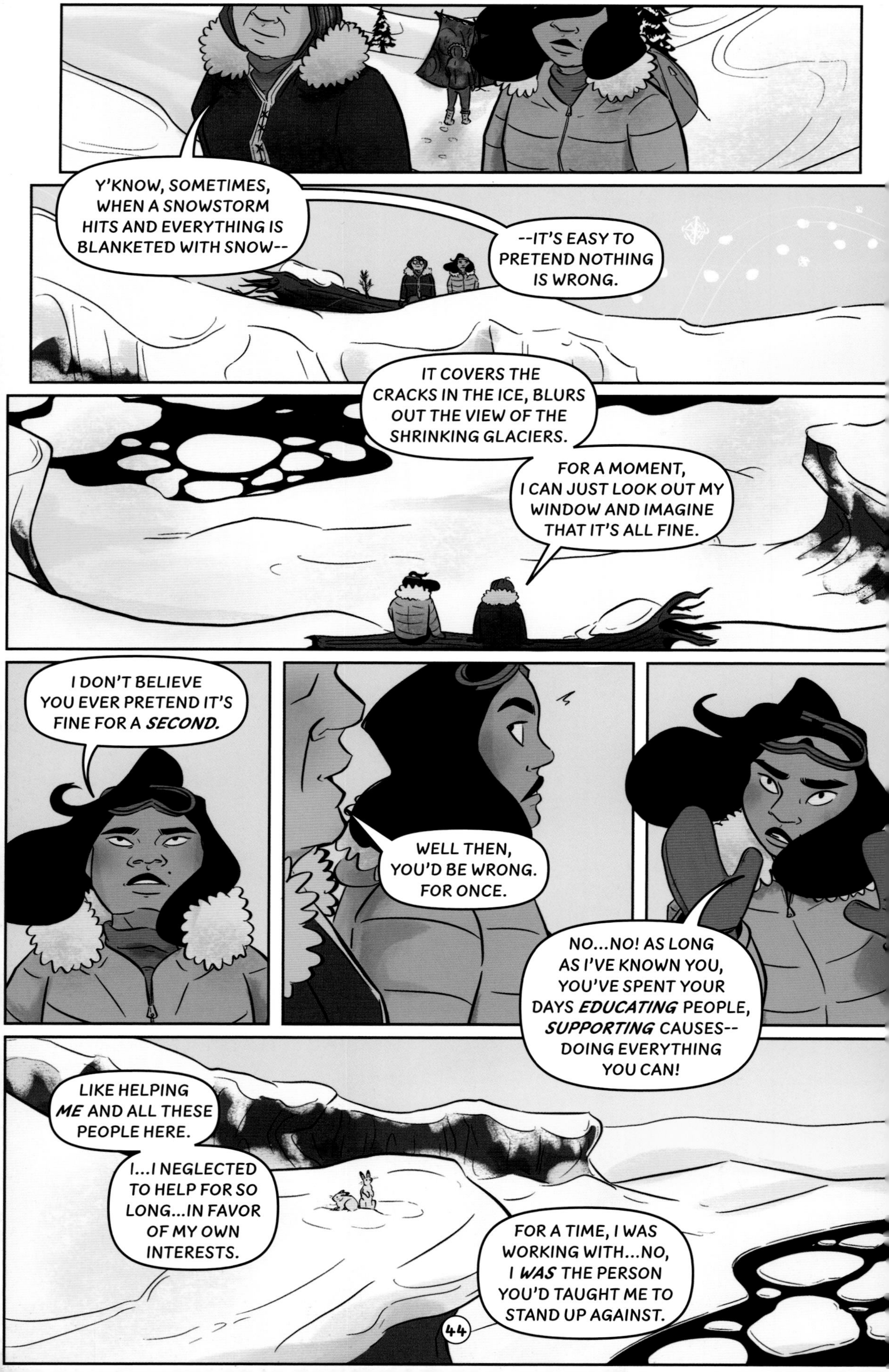
Y'KNOW, SOMETIMES, WHEN A SNOWSTORM HITS AND EVERYTHING IS BLANKETED WITH SNOW--
--IT'S EASY TO PRETEND NOTHING IS WRONG.
IT COVERS THE CRACKS IN THE ICE, BLURS OUT THE VIEW OF THE SHRINKING GLACIERS.
FOR A MOMENT, I CAN JUST LOOK OUT MY WINDOW AND IMAGINE THAT IT'S ALL FINE.
I DON'T BELIEVE YOU EVER PRETEND IT'S FINE FOR A *SECOND.*
WELL THEN, YOU'D BE WRONG. FOR ONCE.
NO...NO! AS LONG AS I'VE KNOWN YOU, YOU'VE SPENT YOUR DAYS *EDUCATING* PEOPLE, *SUPPORTING* CAUSES-- DOING EVERYTHING YOU CAN!
LIKE HELPING *ME* AND ALL THESE PEOPLE HERE.
I...I NEGLECTED TO HELP FOR SO LONG...IN FAVOR OF MY OWN INTERESTS.
FOR A TIME, I WAS WORKING WITH...NO, I *WAS* THE PERSON YOU'D TAUGHT ME TO STAND UP AGAINST.

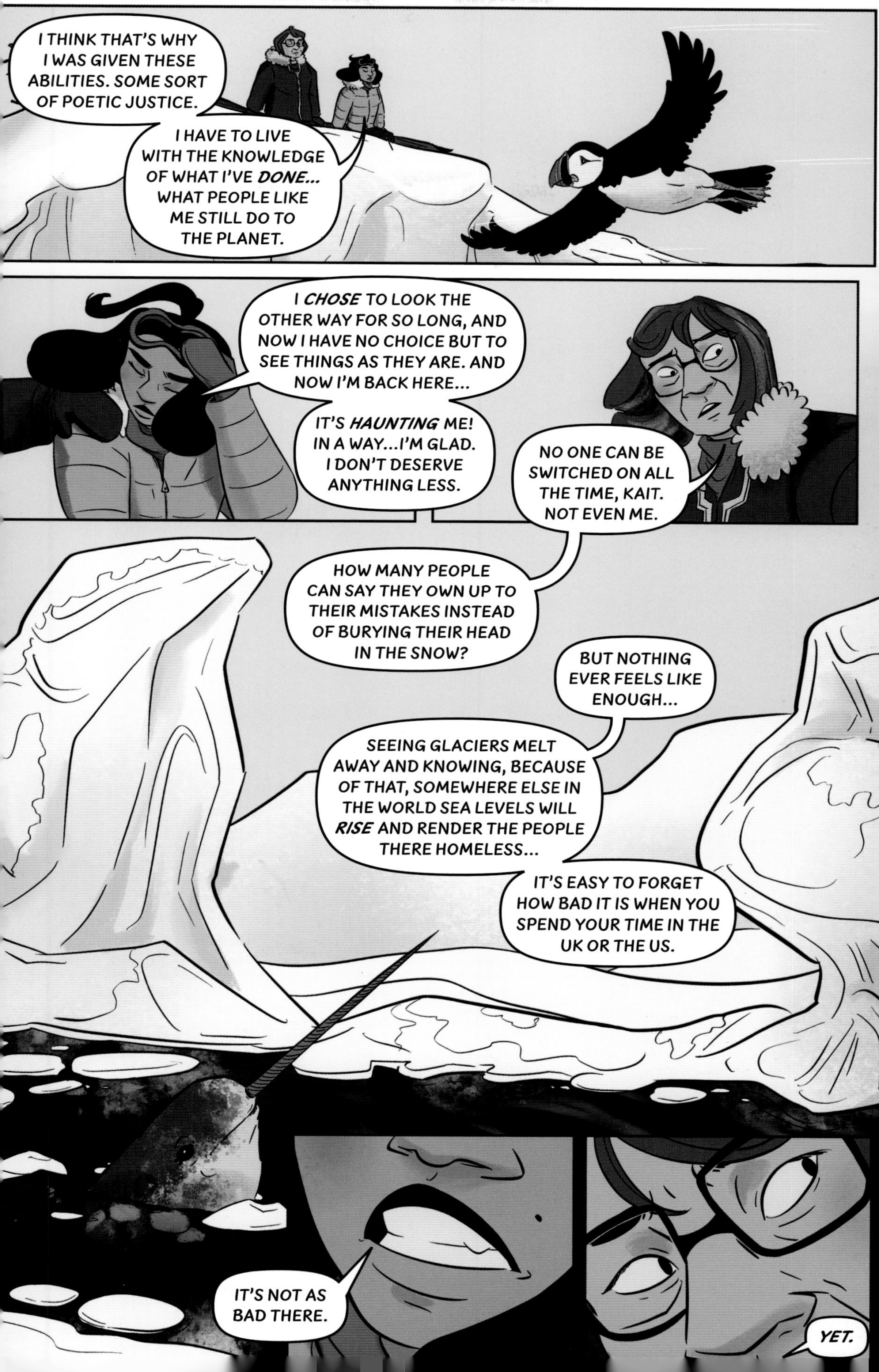
I THINK THAT'S WHY I WAS GIVEN THESE ABILITIES. SOME SORT OF POETIC JUSTICE.
I HAVE TO LIVE WITH THE KNOWLEDGE OF WHAT I'VE *DONE...* WHAT PEOPLE LIKE ME STILL DO TO THE PLANET.
I *CHOSE* TO LOOK THE OTHER WAY FOR SO LONG, AND NOW I HAVE NO CHOICE BUT TO SEE THINGS AS THEY ARE. AND NOW I'M BACK HERE...
IT'S *HAUNTING* ME! IN A WAY...I'M GLAD. I DON'T DESERVE ANYTHING LESS.
NO ONE CAN BE SWITCHED ON ALL THE TIME, KAIT. NOT EVEN ME.
HOW MANY PEOPLE CAN SAY THEY OWN UP TO THEIR MISTAKES INSTEAD OF BURYING THEIR HEAD IN THE SNOW?
BUT NOTHING EVER FEELS LIKE ENOUGH...
SEEING GLACIERS MELT AWAY AND KNOWING, BECAUSE OF THAT, SOMEWHERE ELSE IN THE WORLD SEA LEVELS WILL *RISE* AND RENDER THE PEOPLE THERE HOMELESS...
IT'S EASY TO FORGET HOW BAD IT IS WHEN YOU SPEND YOUR TIME IN THE UK OR THE US.
IT'S NOT AS BAD THERE.
YET.

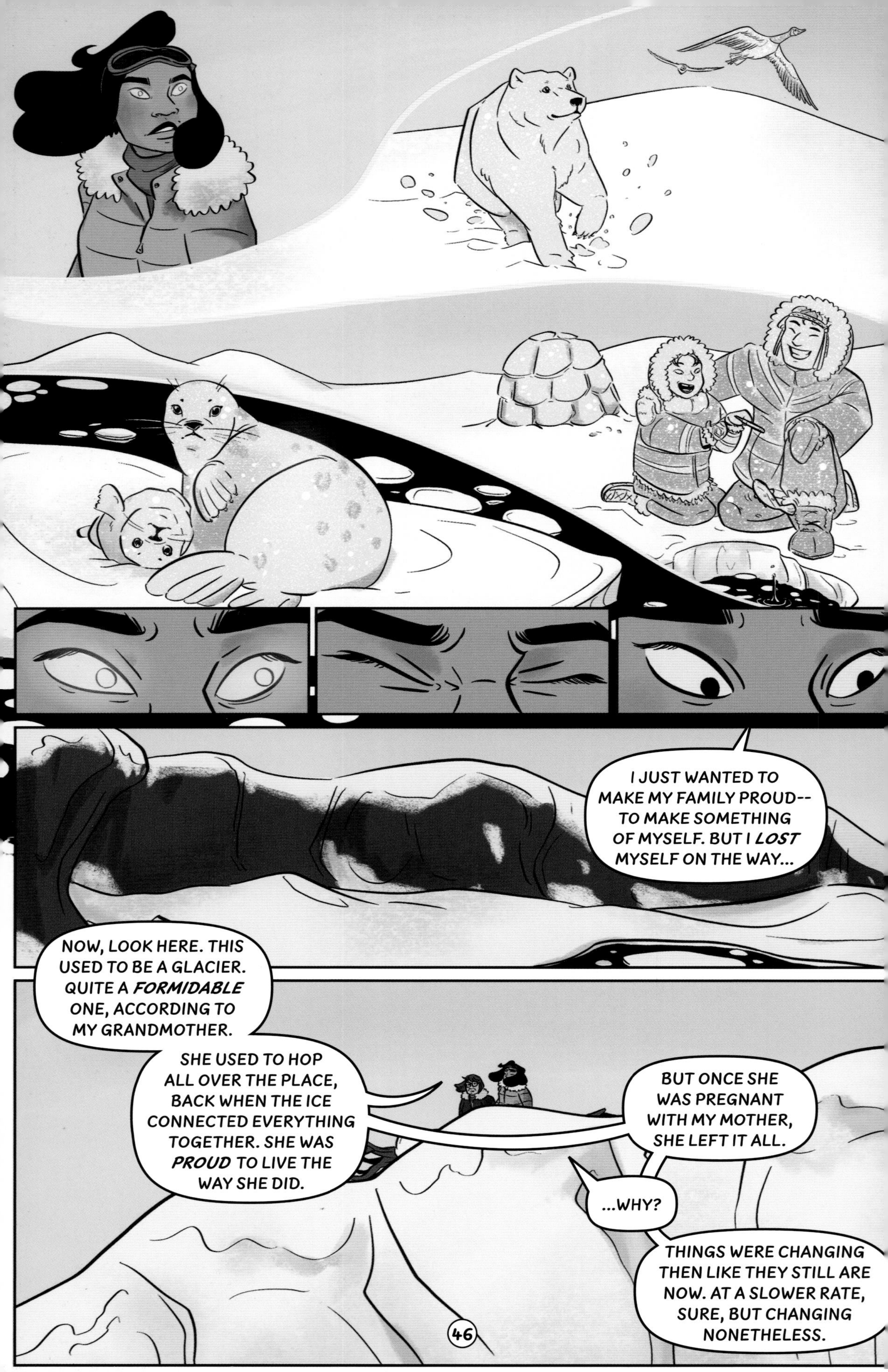

I JUST WANTED TO MAKE MY FAMILY PROUD-- TO MAKE SOMETHING OF MYSELF. BUT I *LOST* MYSELF ON THE WAY...
NOW, LOOK HERE. THIS USED TO BE A GLACIER. QUITE A *FORMIDABLE* ONE, ACCORDING TO MY GRANDMOTHER.
SHE USED TO HOP ALL OVER THE PLACE, BACK WHEN THE ICE CONNECTED EVERYTHING TOGETHER. SHE WAS *PROUD* TO LIVE THE WAY SHE DID.
BUT ONCE SHE WAS PREGNANT WITH MY MOTHER, SHE LEFT IT ALL.
...WHY?
THINGS WERE CHANGING THEN LIKE THEY STILL ARE NOW. AT A SLOWER RATE, SURE, BUT CHANGING NONETHELESS.

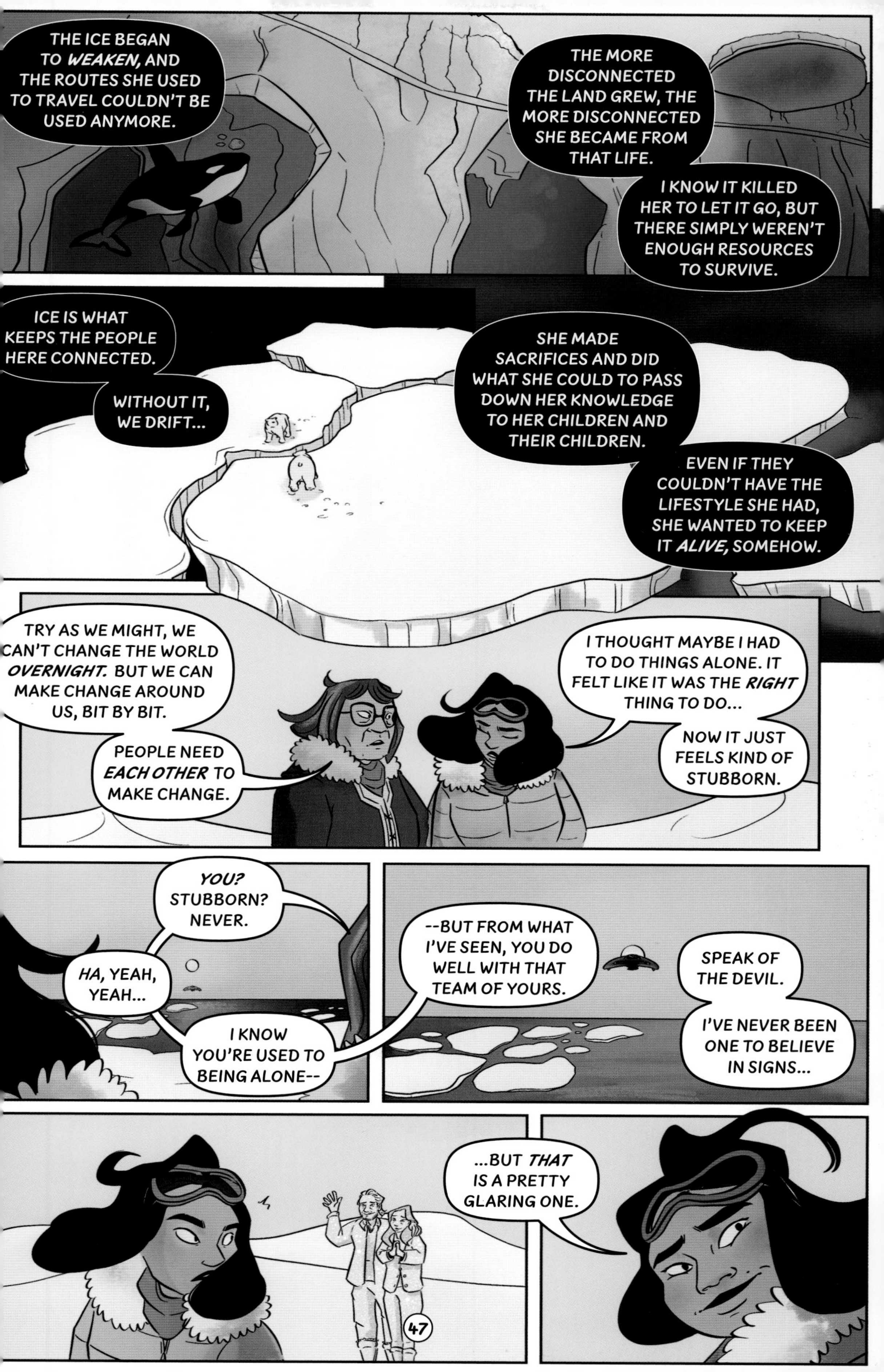
THE ICE BEGAN TO *WEAKEN,* AND THE ROUTES SHE USED TO TRAVEL COULDN'T BE USED ANYMORE.
THE MORE DISCONNECTED THE LAND GREW, THE MORE DISCONNECTED SHE BECAME FROM THAT LIFE.
I KNOW IT KILLED HER TO LET IT GO, BUT THERE SIMPLY WEREN'T ENOUGH RESOURCES TO SURVIVE.
ICE IS WHAT KEEPS THE PEOPLE HERE CONNECTED.
WITHOUT IT, WE DRIFT...
SHE MADE SACRIFICES AND DID WHAT SHE COULD TO PASS DOWN HER KNOWLEDGE TO HER CHILDREN AND THEIR CHILDREN.
EVEN IF THEY COULDN'T HAVE THE LIFESTYLE SHE HAD, SHE WANTED TO KEEP IT *ALIVE,* SOMEHOW.
TRY AS WE MIGHT, WE CAN'T CHANGE THE WORLD *OVERNIGHT.* BUT WE CAN MAKE CHANGE AROUND US, BIT BY BIT.
PEOPLE NEED *EACH OTHER* TO MAKE CHANGE.
I THOUGHT MAYBE I HAD TO DO THINGS ALONE. IT FELT LIKE IT WAS THE *RIGHT* THING TO DO...
NOW IT JUST FEELS KIND OF STUBBORN.
YOU? STUBBORN? NEVER.
HA, YEAH, YEAH...
I KNOW YOU'RE USED TO BEING ALONE--
--BUT FROM WHAT I'VE SEEN, YOU DO WELL WITH THAT TEAM OF YOURS.
SPEAK OF THE DEVIL.
I'VE NEVER BEEN ONE TO BELIEVE IN SIGNS...
...BUT *THAT* IS A PRETTY GLARING ONE.

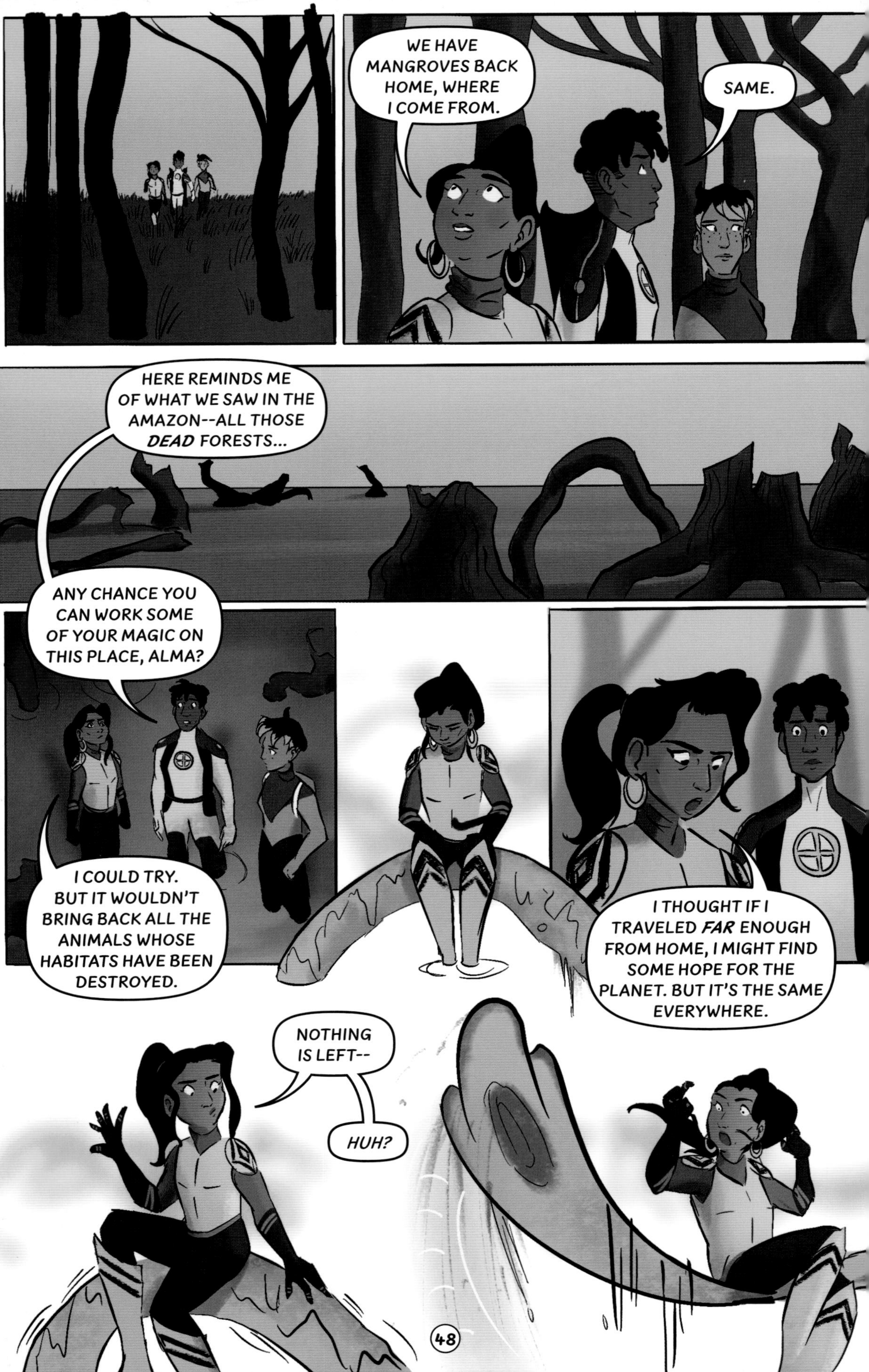

WE HAVE MANGROVES BACK HOME, WHERE I COME FROM.
SAME.
HERE REMINDS ME OF WHAT WE SAW IN THE AMAZON--ALL THOSE *DEAD* FORESTS...
ANY CHANCE YOU CAN WORK SOME OF YOUR MAGIC ON THIS PLACE, ALMA?
I COULD TRY. BUT IT WOULDN'T BRING BACK ALL THE ANIMALS WHOSE HABITATS HAVE BEEN DESTROYED.
I THOUGHT IF I TRAVELED *FAR* ENOUGH FROM HOME, I MIGHT FIND SOME HOPE FOR THE PLANET. BUT IT'S THE SAME EVERYWHERE.
NOTHING IS LEFT--
HUH?

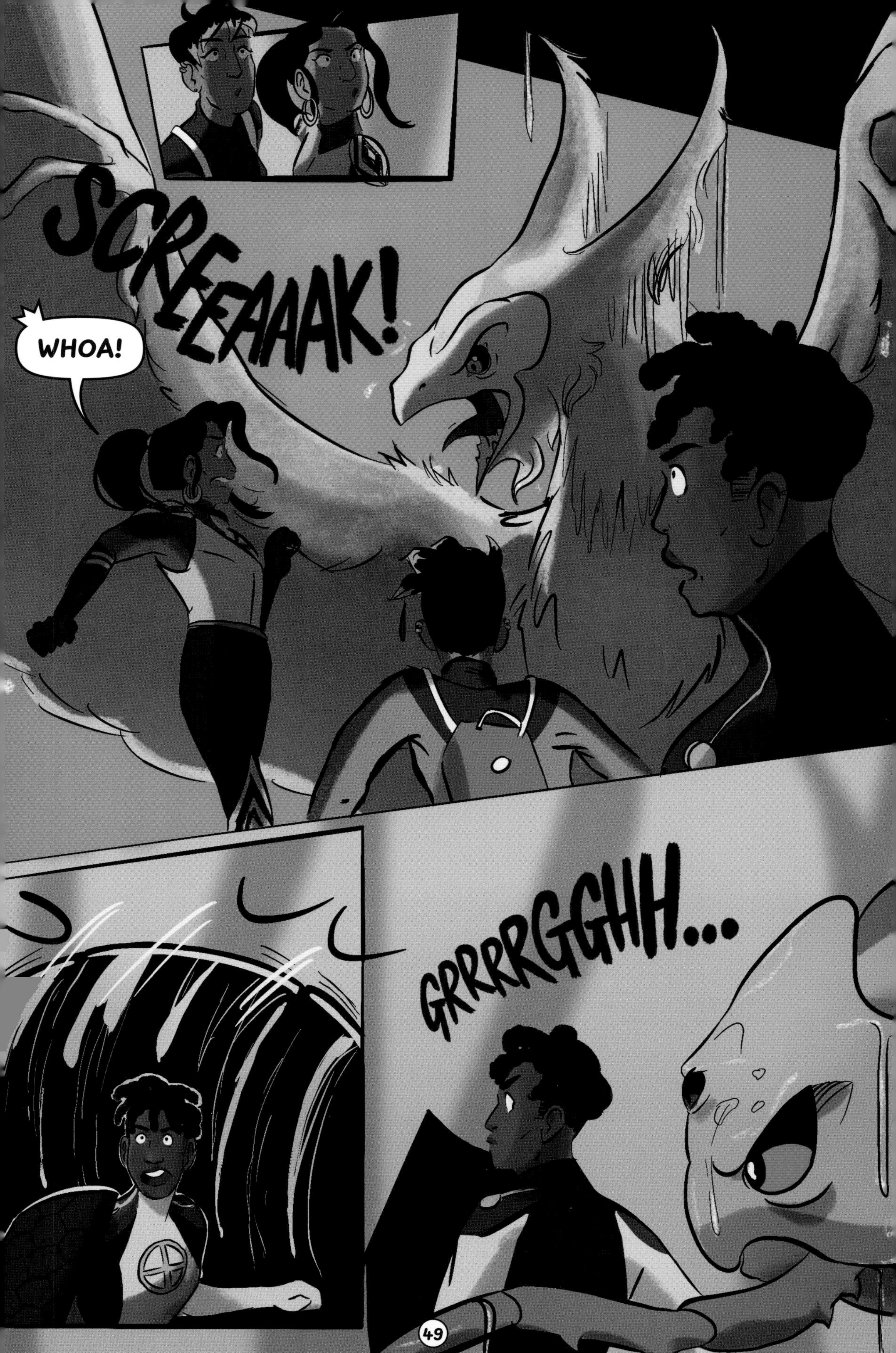
SCREEAAAK!
WHOA!
GRRRRGGHH...

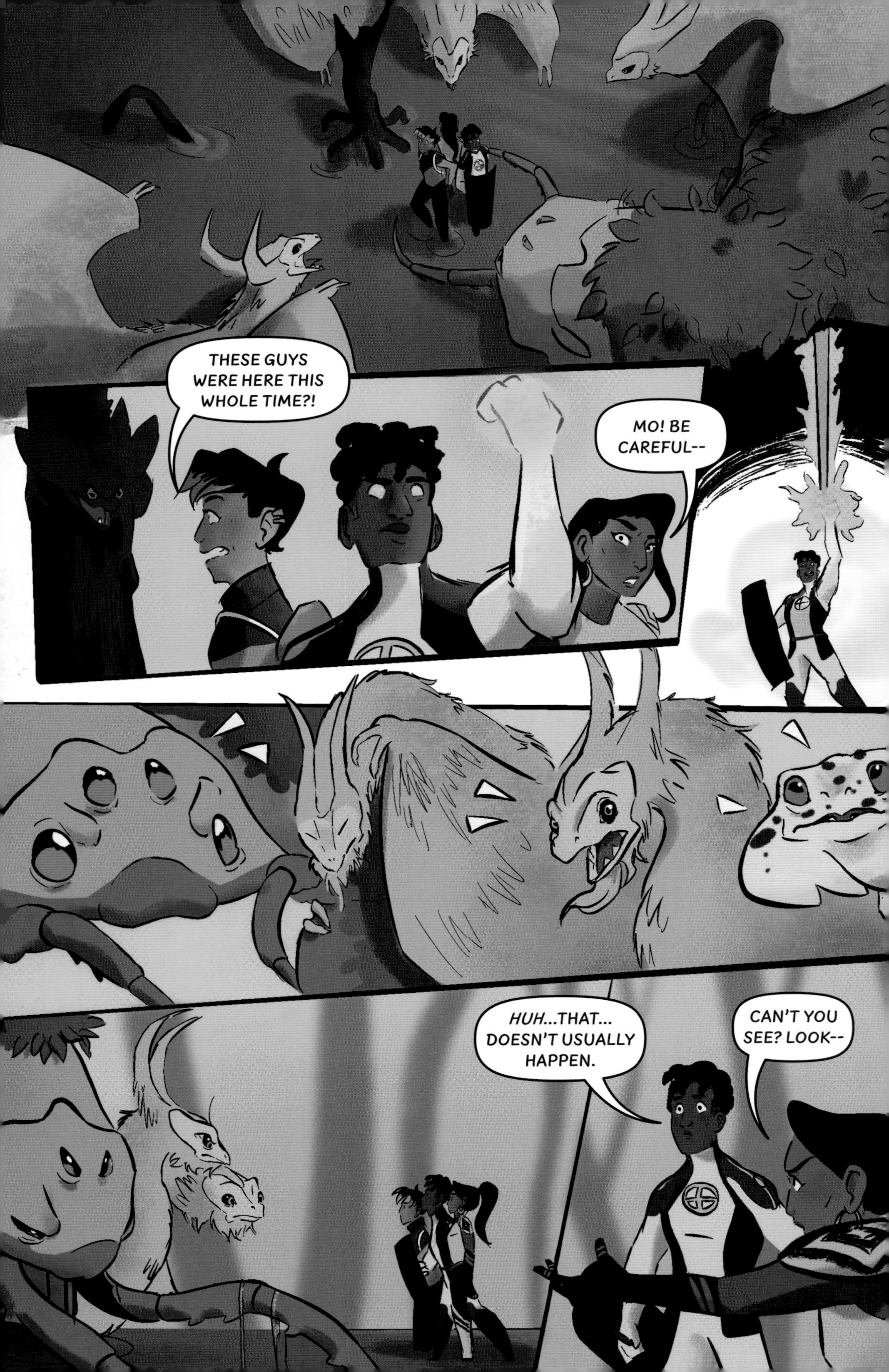
THESE GUYS WERE HERE THIS WHOLE TIME?!
MO! BE CAREFUL--
HUH...THAT... DOESN'T USUALLY HAPPEN.
CAN'T YOU SEE? LOOK--

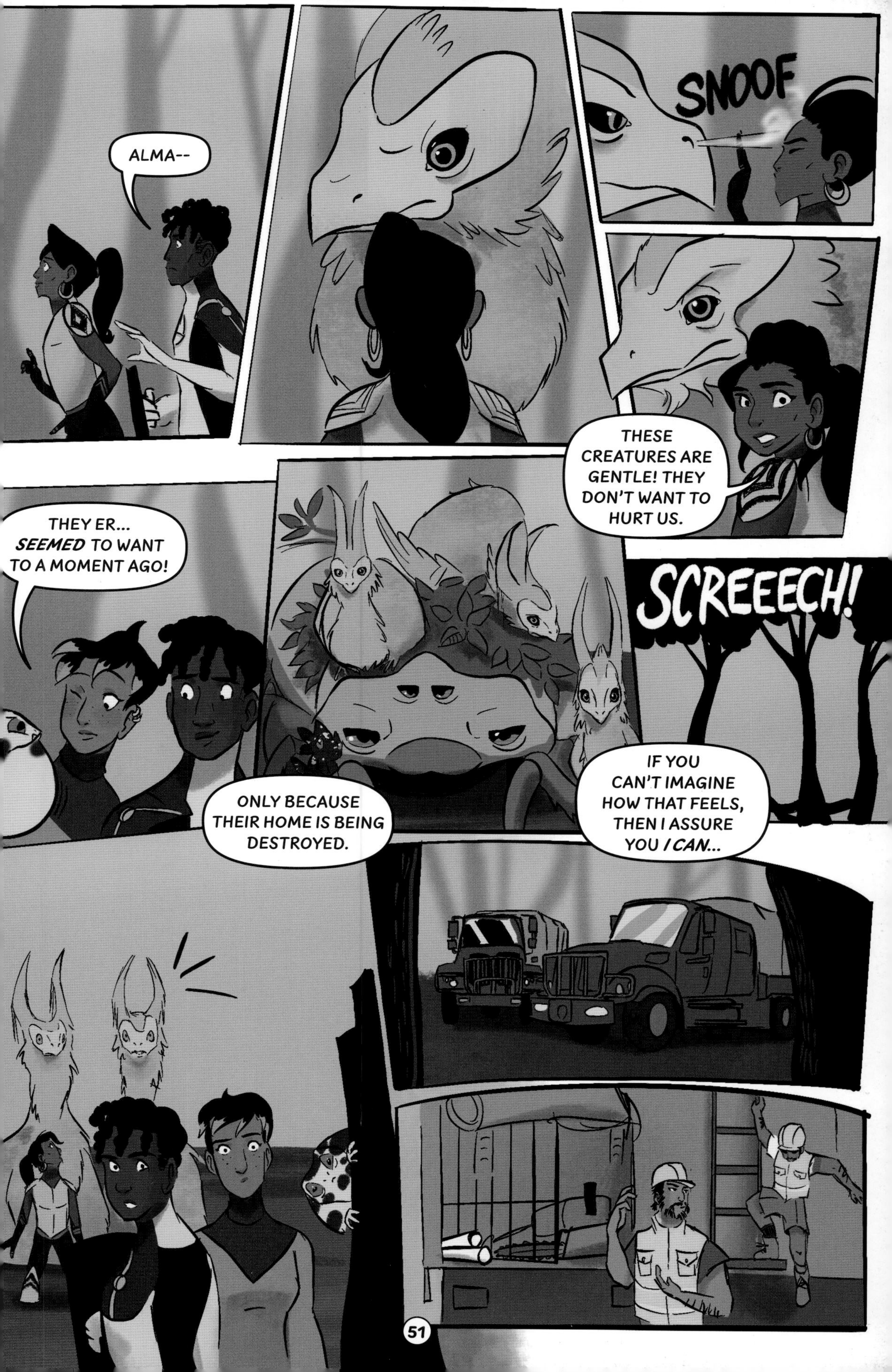
ALMA--
SNOOF
THESE CREATURES ARE GENTLE! THEY DON'T WANT TO HURT US.
THEY ER... *SEEMED* TO WANT TO A MOMENT AGO!
ONLY BECAUSE THEIR HOME IS BEING DESTROYED.
IF YOU CAN'T IMAGINE HOW THAT FEELS, THEN I ASSURE YOU *I CAN*...
SCREEECH!

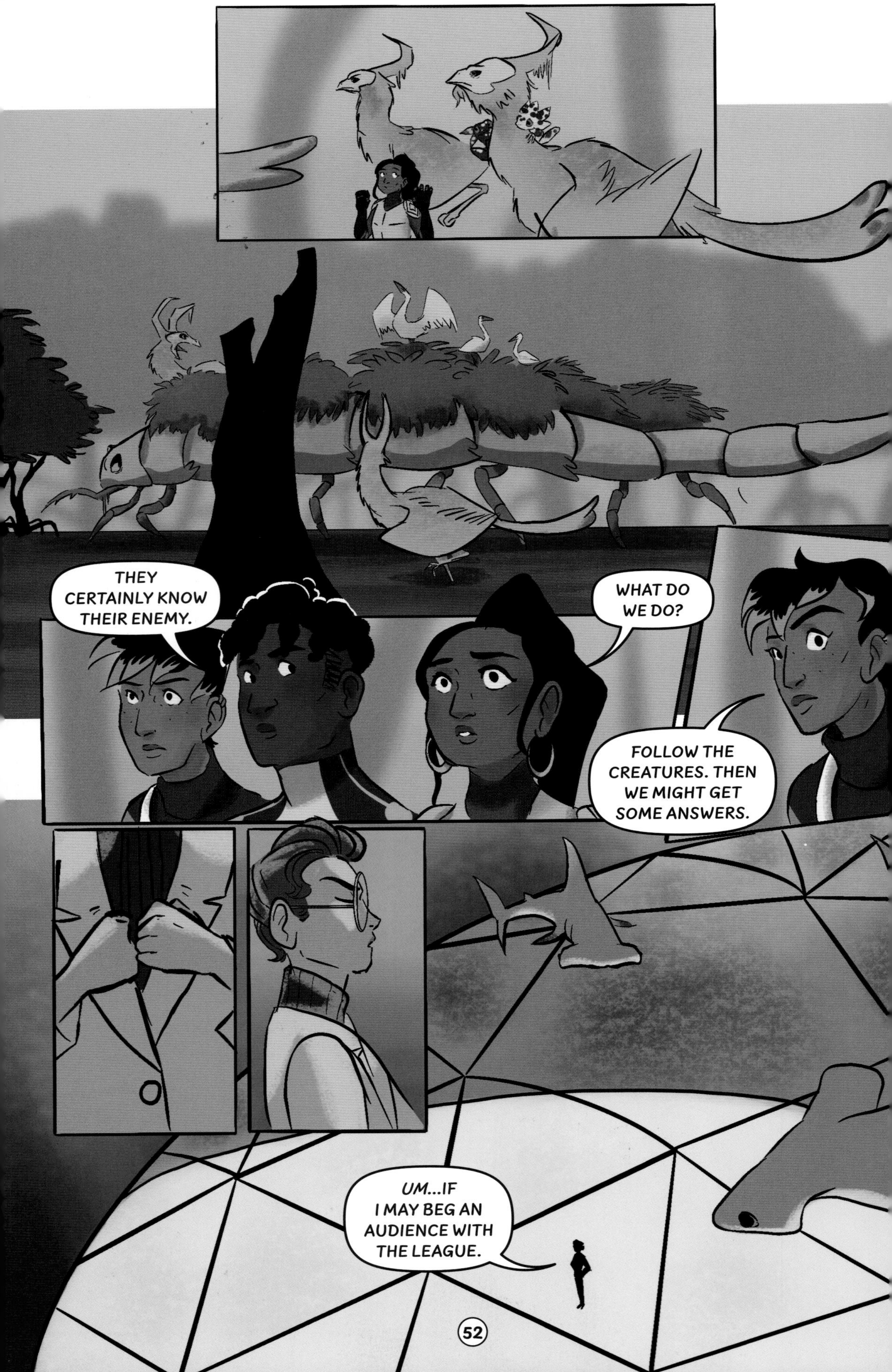
THEY CERTAINLY KNOW THEIR ENEMY.
WHAT DO WE DO?
FOLLOW THE CREATURES. THEN WE MIGHT GET SOME ANSWERS.
UM...IF I MAY BEG AN AUDIENCE WITH THE LEAGUE.

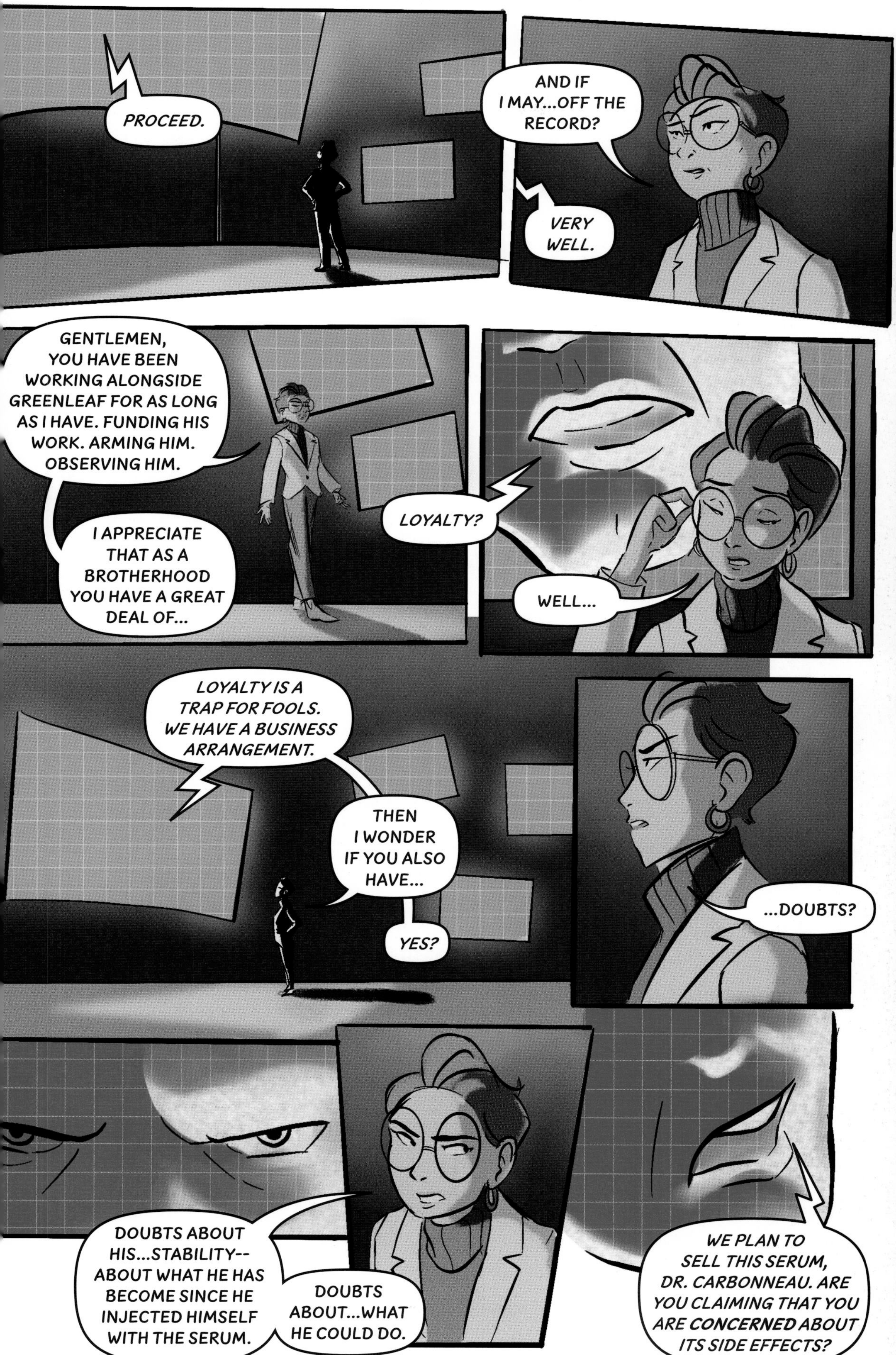
PROCEED.
AND IF I MAY...OFF THE RECORD?
VERY WELL.
GENTLEMEN, YOU HAVE BEEN WORKING ALONGSIDE GREENLEAF FOR AS LONG AS I HAVE. FUNDING HIS WORK. ARMING HIM. OBSERVING HIM.
I APPRECIATE THAT AS A BROTHERHOOD YOU HAVE A GREAT DEAL OF...
LOYALTY?
WELL...
LOYALTY IS A TRAP FOR FOOLS. WE HAVE A BUSINESS ARRANGEMENT.
THEN I WONDER IF YOU ALSO HAVE...
YES?
...DOUBTS?
DOUBTS ABOUT HIS...STABILITY--ABOUT WHAT HE HAS BECOME SINCE HE INJECTED HIMSELF WITH THE SERUM.
DOUBTS ABOUT...WHAT HE COULD DO.
WE PLAN TO SELL THIS SERUM, DR. CARBONNEAU. ARE YOU CLAIMING THAT YOU ARE CONCERNED ABOUT ITS SIDE EFFECTS?

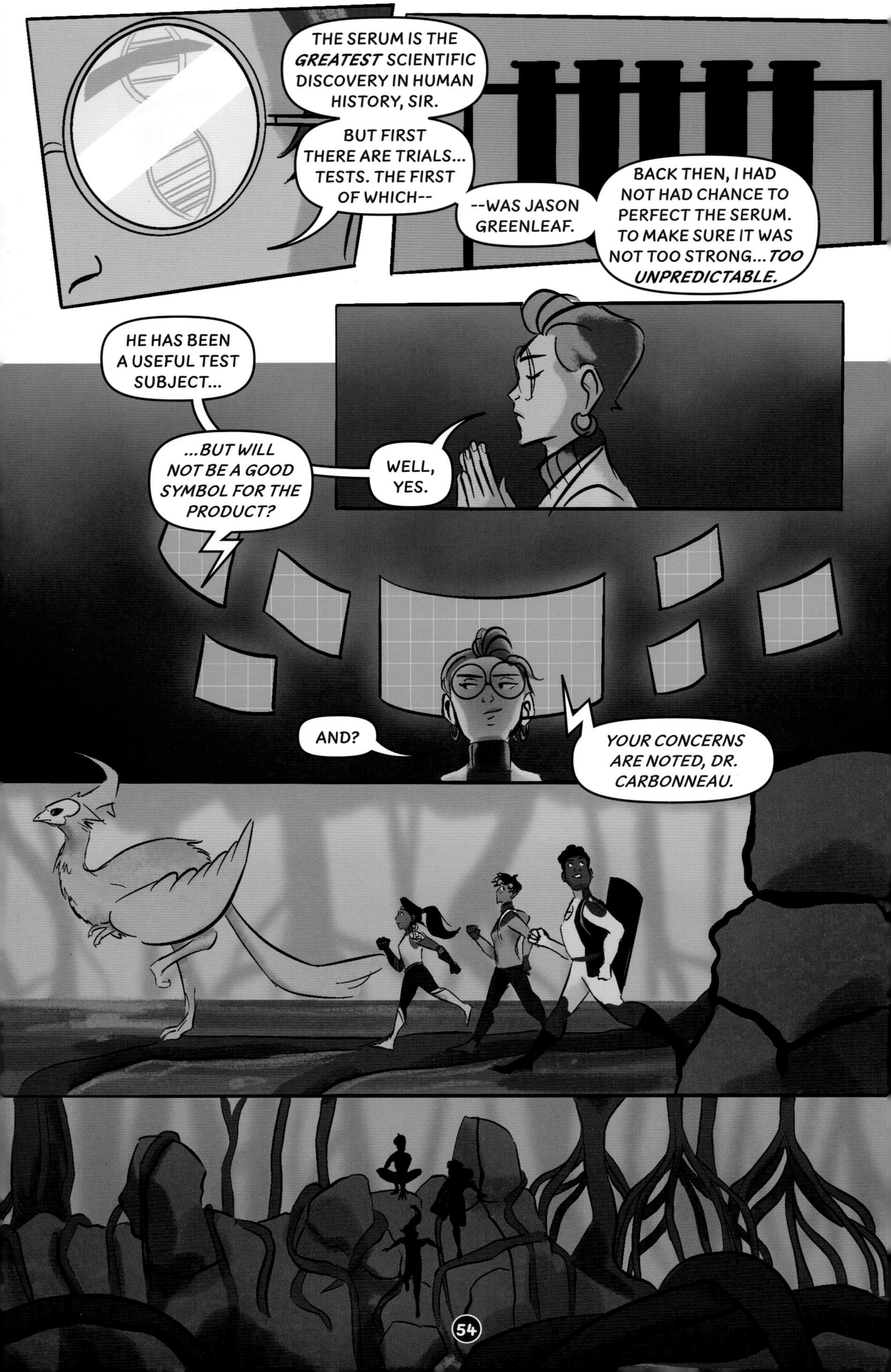
THE SERUM IS THE GREATEST SCIENTIFIC DISCOVERY IN HUMAN HISTORY, SIR.
BUT FIRST THERE ARE TRIALS... TESTS. THE FIRST OF WHICH--
--WAS JASON GREENLEAF.
BACK THEN, I HAD NOT HAD CHANCE TO PERFECT THE SERUM. TO MAKE SURE IT WAS NOT TOO STRONG... TOO UNPREDICTABLE.
HE HAS BEEN A USEFUL TEST SUBJECT...
WELL, YES.
...BUT WILL NOT BE A GOOD SYMBOL FOR THE PRODUCT?
AND?
YOUR CONCERNS ARE NOTED, DR. CARBONNEAU.

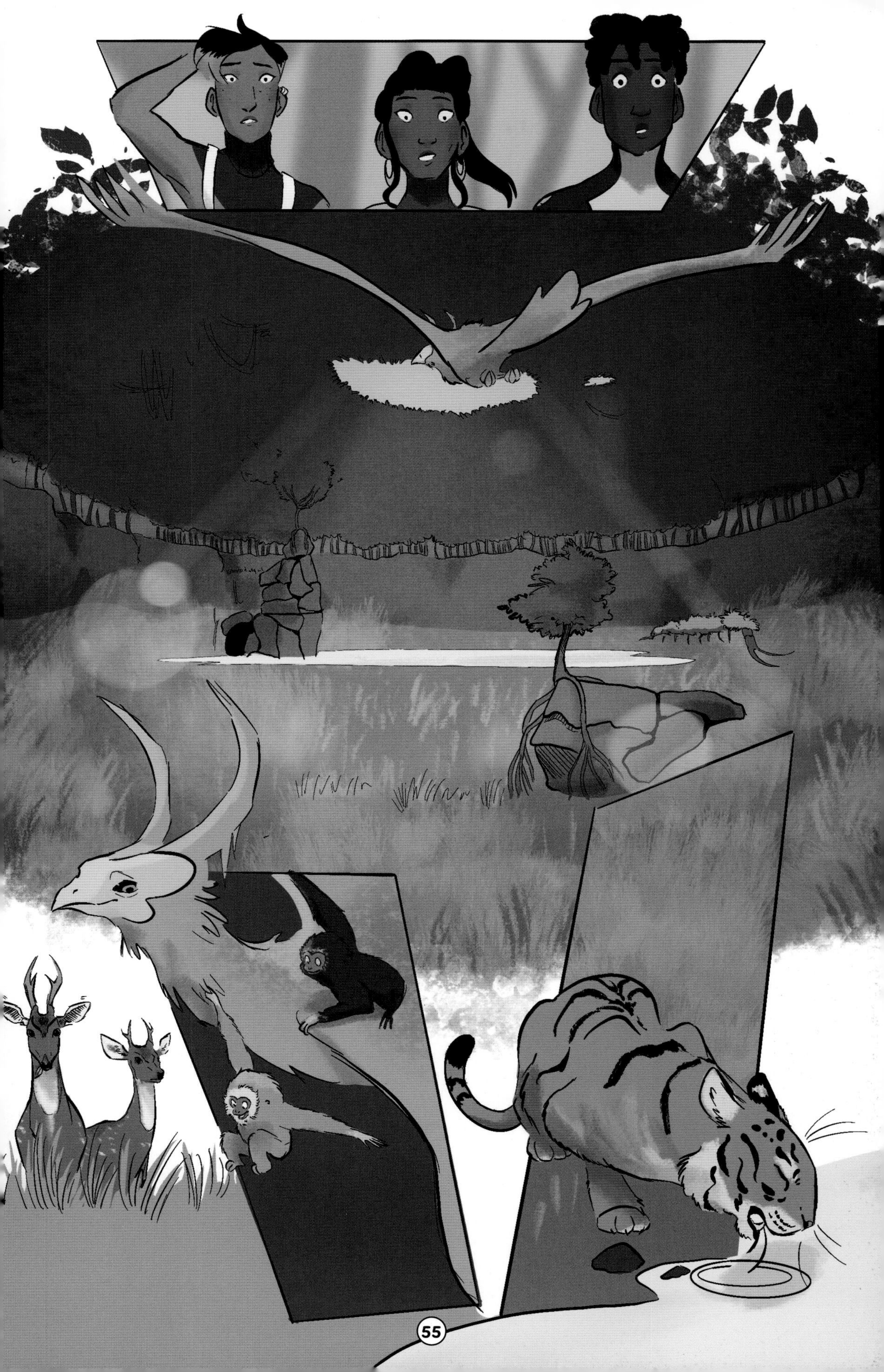

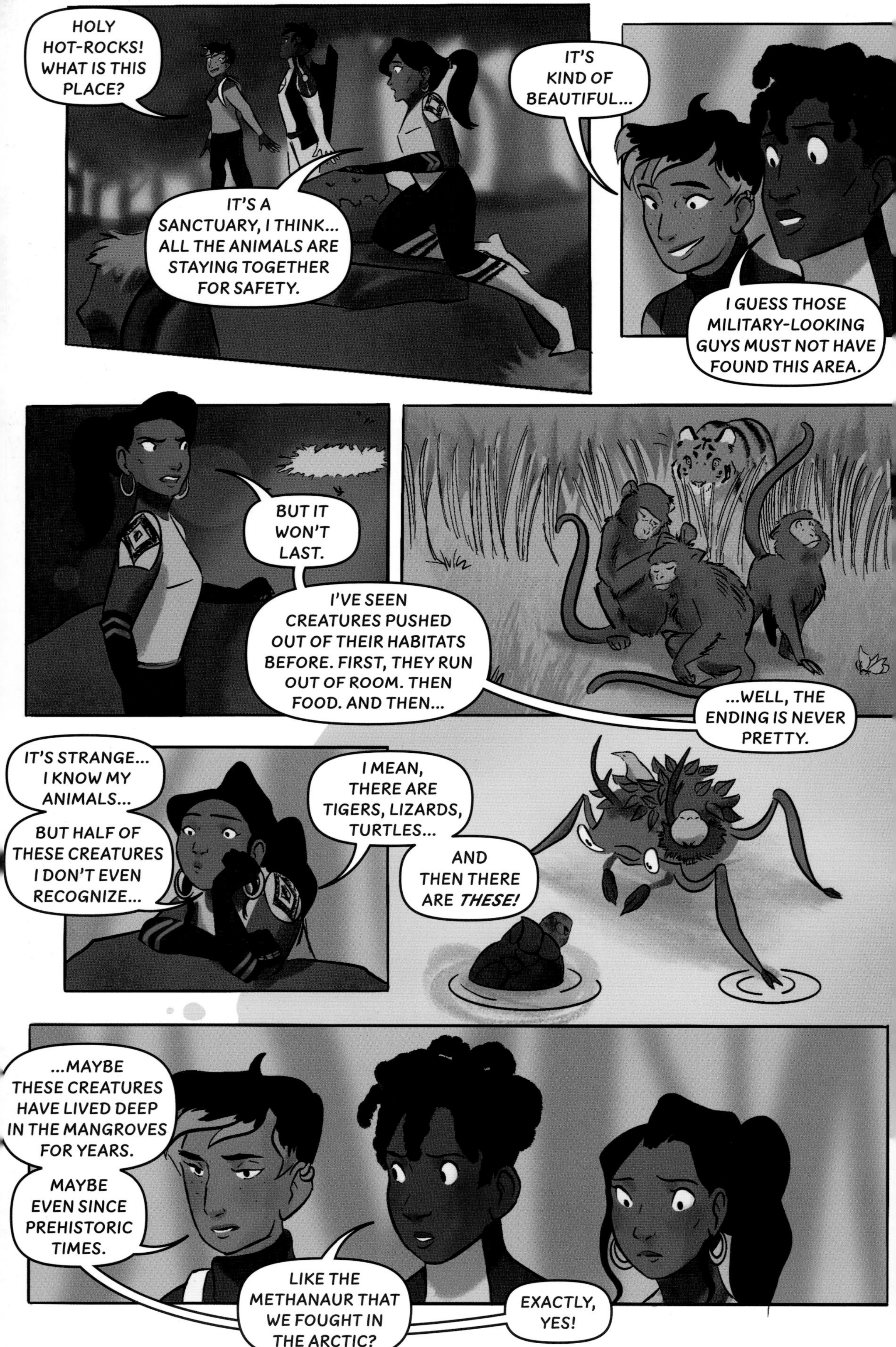
HOLY HOT-ROCKS! WHAT IS THIS PLACE?
IT'S A SANCTUARY, I THINK... ALL THE ANIMALS ARE STAYING TOGETHER FOR SAFETY.
IT'S KIND OF BEAUTIFUL...
I GUESS THOSE MILITARY-LOOKING GUYS MUST NOT HAVE FOUND THIS AREA.
BUT IT WON'T LAST.
I'VE SEEN CREATURES PUSHED OUT OF THEIR HABITATS BEFORE. FIRST, THEY RUN OUT OF ROOM. THEN FOOD. AND THEN...
...WELL, THE ENDING IS NEVER PRETTY.
IT'S STRANGE... I KNOW MY ANIMALS...
BUT HALF OF THESE CREATURES I DON'T EVEN RECOGNIZE...
I MEAN, THERE ARE TIGERS, LIZARDS, TURTLES...
AND THEN THERE ARE *THESE!*
...MAYBE THESE CREATURES HAVE LIVED DEEP IN THE MANGROVES FOR YEARS.
MAYBE EVEN SINCE PREHISTORIC TIMES.
LIKE THE METHANAUR THAT WE FOUGHT IN THE ARCTIC?
EXACTLY, YES!

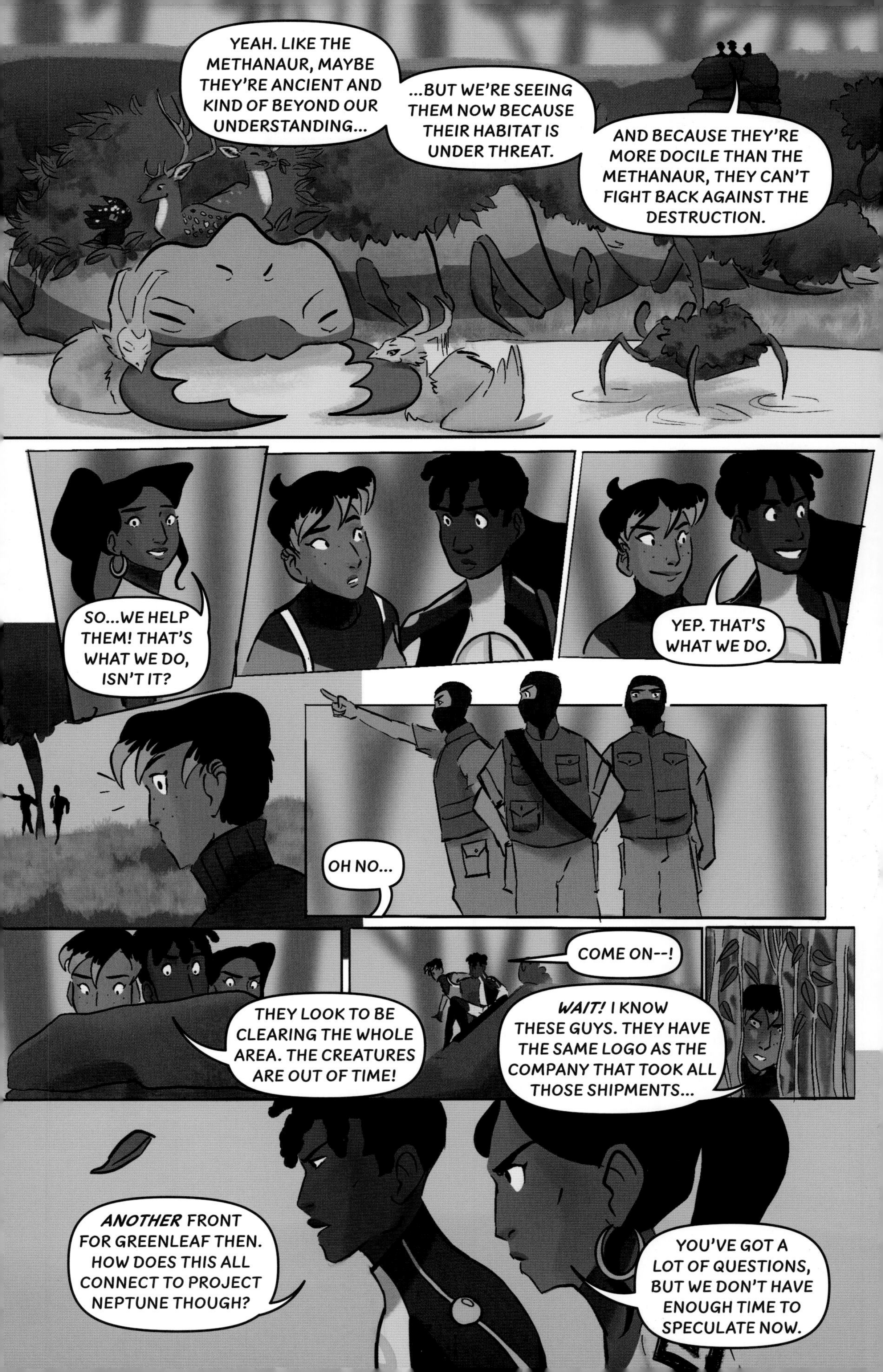
YEAH. LIKE THE METHANAUR, MAYBE THEY'RE ANCIENT AND KIND OF BEYOND OUR UNDERSTANDING...
...BUT WE'RE SEEING THEM NOW BECAUSE THEIR HABITAT IS UNDER THREAT.
AND BECAUSE THEY'RE MORE DOCILE THAN THE METHANAUR, THEY CAN'T FIGHT BACK AGAINST THE DESTRUCTION.
SO...WE HELP THEM! THAT'S WHAT WE DO, ISN'T IT?
YEP. THAT'S WHAT WE DO.
OH NO...
THEY LOOK TO BE CLEARING THE WHOLE AREA. THE CREATURES ARE OUT OF TIME!
COME ON--!
WAIT! I KNOW THESE GUYS. THEY HAVE THE SAME LOGO AS THE COMPANY THAT TOOK ALL THOSE SHIPMENTS...
ANOTHER FRONT FOR GREENLEAF THEN. HOW DOES THIS ALL CONNECT TO PROJECT NEPTUNE THOUGH?
YOU'VE GOT A LOT OF QUESTIONS, BUT WE DON'T HAVE ENOUGH TIME TO SPECULATE NOW.

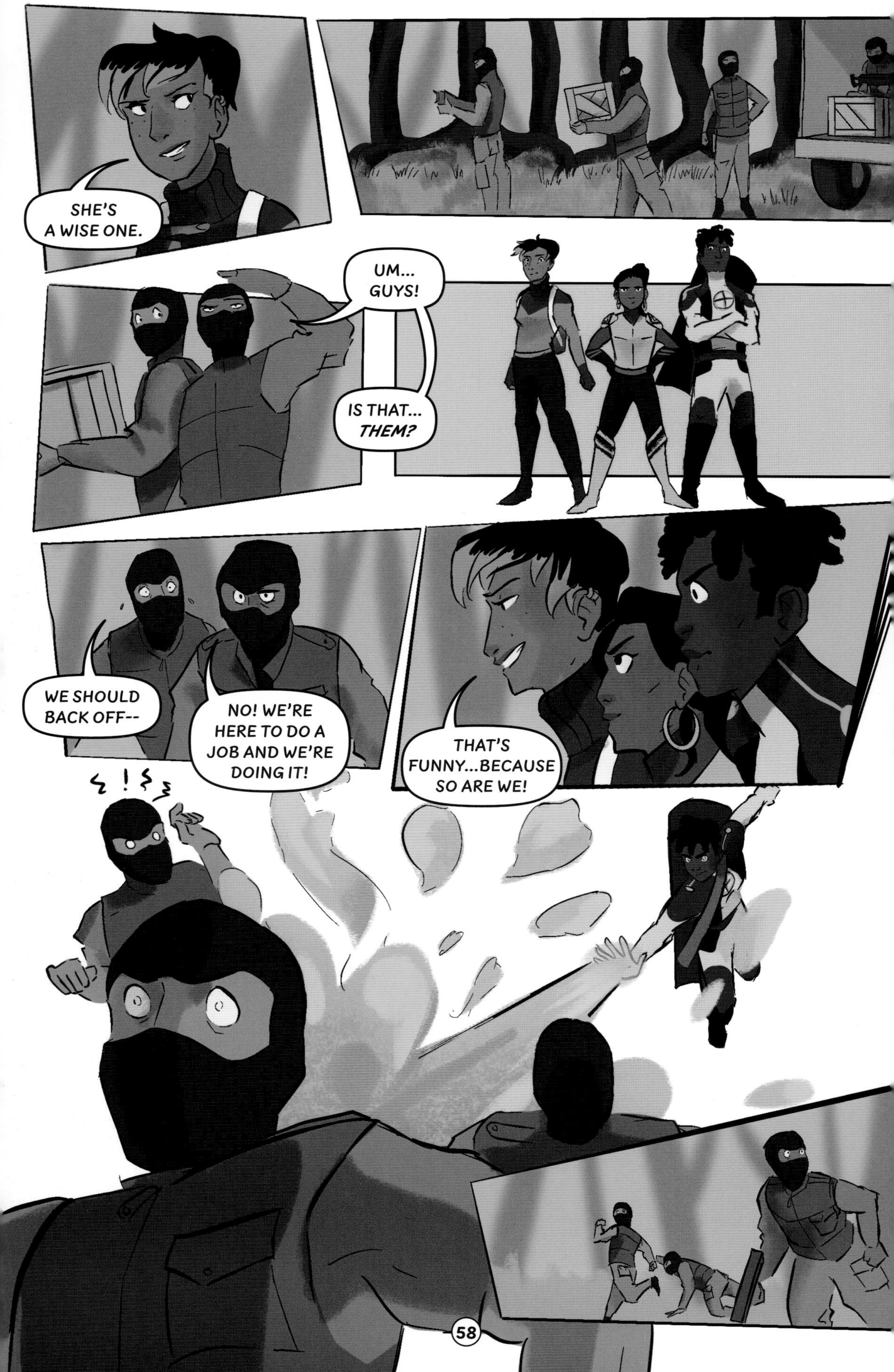
SHE'S A WISE ONE.
UM... GUYS!
IS THAT... *THEM?*
WE SHOULD BACK OFF--
NO! WE'RE HERE TO DO A JOB AND WE'RE DOING IT!
THAT'S FUNNY...BECAUSE SO ARE WE!
!

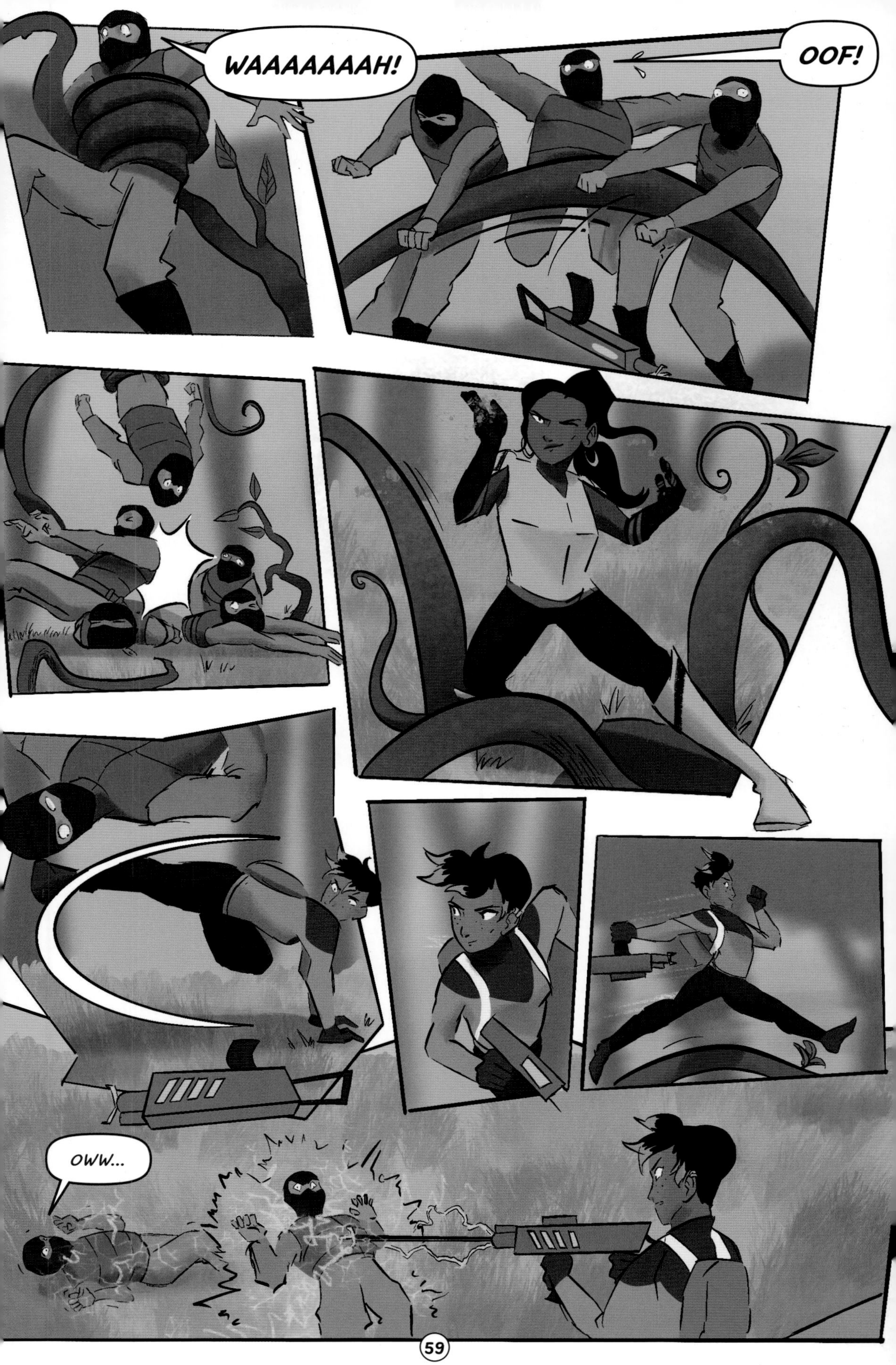
WAAAAAAAH!
OOF!
OWW...

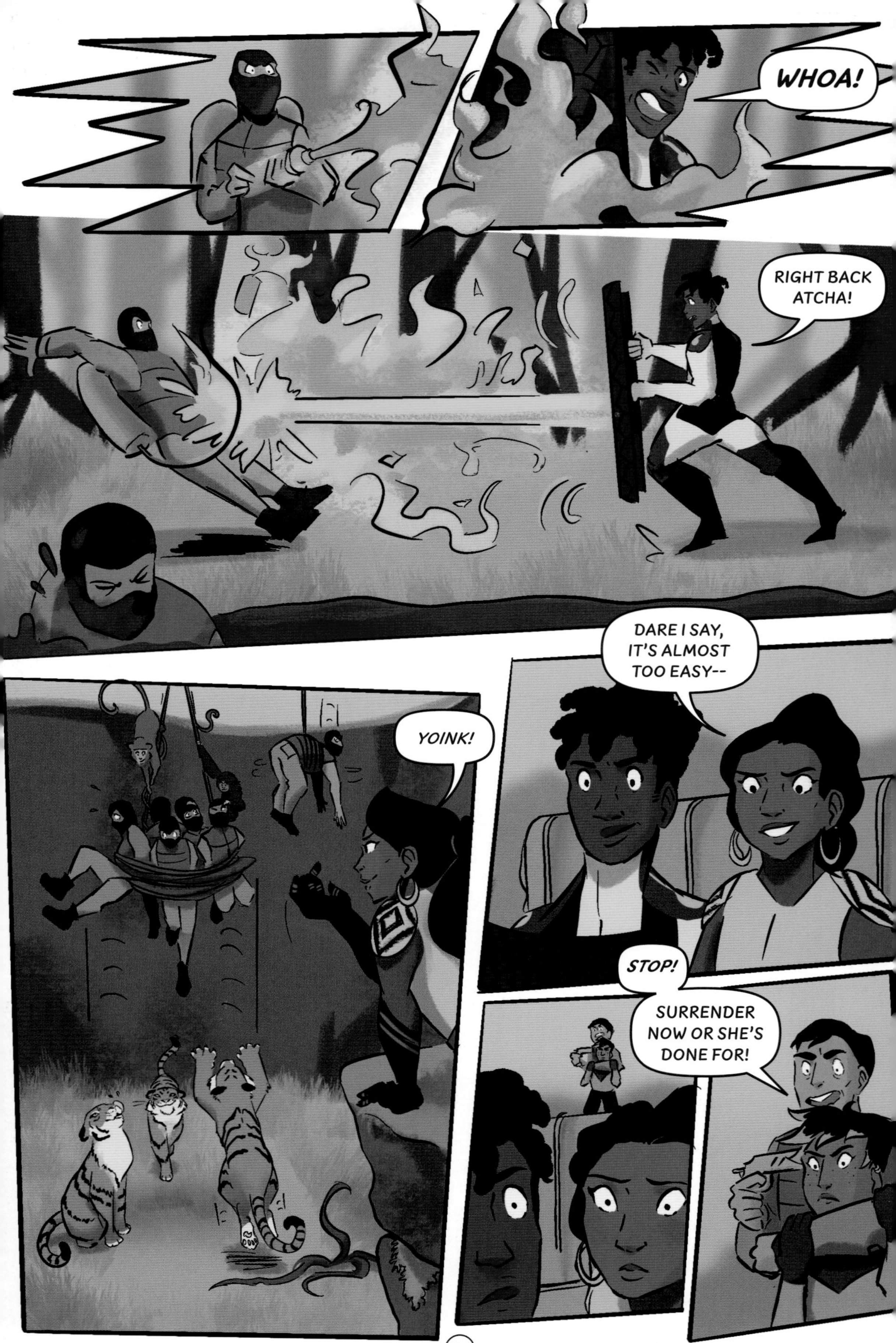
WHOA!
RIGHT BACK ATCHA!
YOINK!
DARE I SAY, IT'S ALMOST TOO EASY--
STOP!
SURRENDER NOW OR SHE'S DONE FOR!

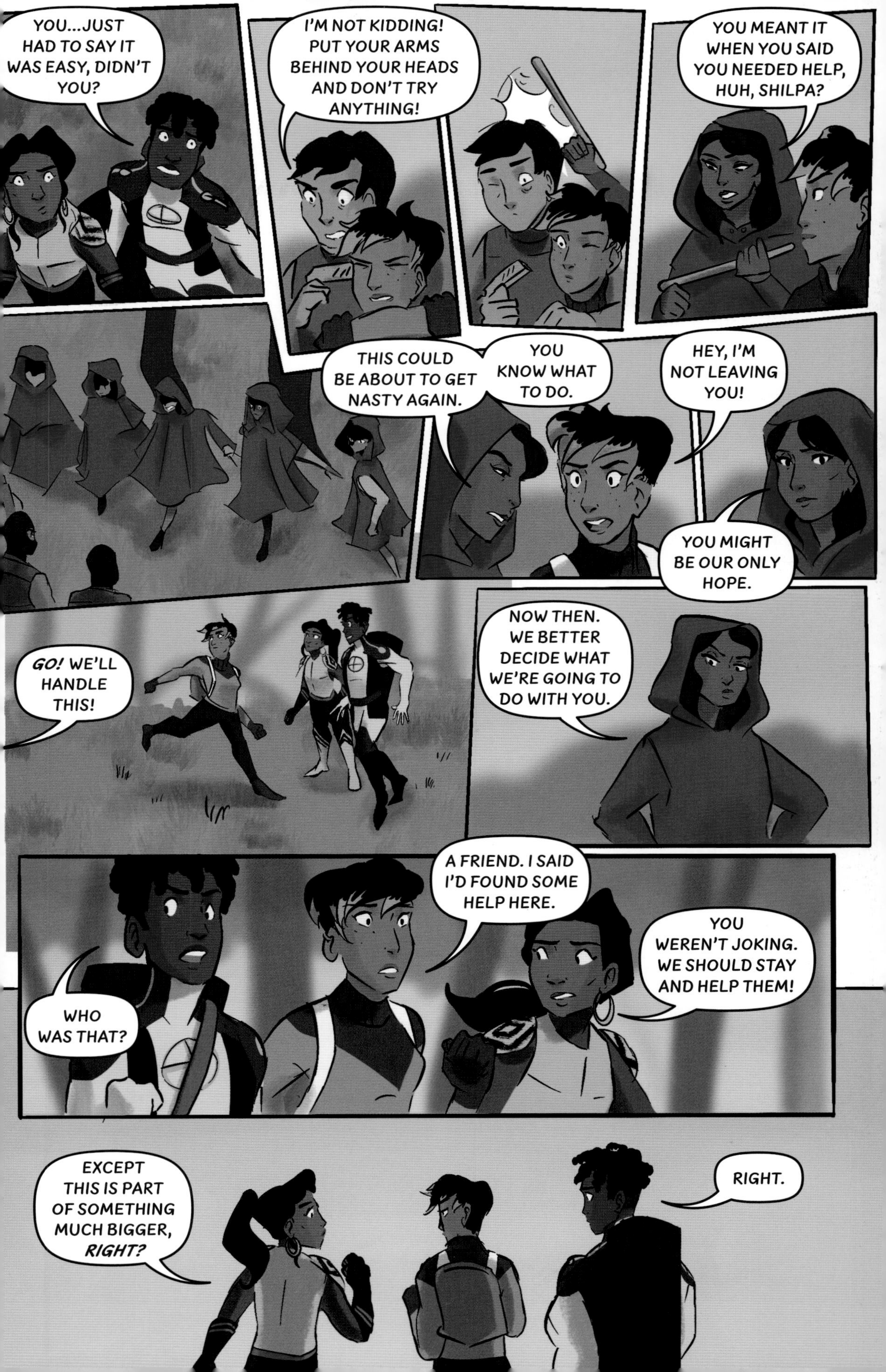
YOU...JUST HAD TO SAY IT WAS EASY, DIDN'T YOU?
I'M NOT KIDDING! PUT YOUR ARMS BEHIND YOUR HEADS AND DON'T TRY ANYTHING!
YOU MEANT IT WHEN YOU SAID YOU NEEDED HELP, HUH, SHILPA?
THIS COULD BE ABOUT TO GET NASTY AGAIN.
YOU KNOW WHAT TO DO.
HEY, I'M NOT LEAVING YOU!
YOU MIGHT BE OUR ONLY HOPE.
GO! WE'LL HANDLE THIS!
NOW THEN. WE BETTER DECIDE WHAT WE'RE GOING TO DO WITH YOU.
WHO WAS THAT?
A FRIEND. I SAID I'D FOUND SOME HELP HERE.
YOU WEREN'T JOKING. WE SHOULD STAY AND HELP THEM!
EXCEPT THIS IS PART OF SOMETHING MUCH BIGGER, RIGHT?
RIGHT.

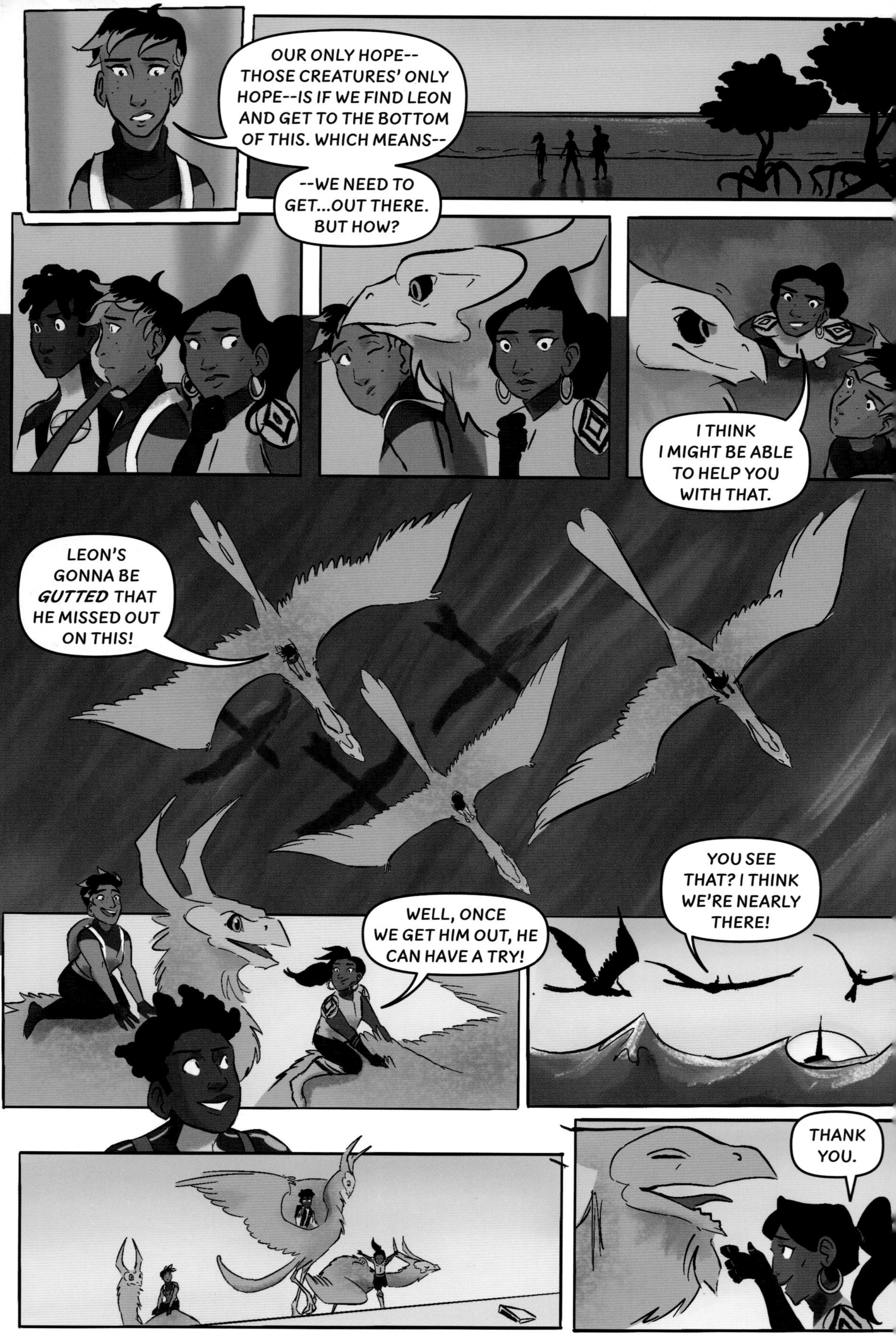
OUR ONLY HOPE-- THOSE CREATURES' ONLY HOPE--IS IF WE FIND LEON AND GET TO THE BOTTOM OF THIS. WHICH MEANS--
--WE NEED TO GET...OUT THERE. BUT HOW?
I THINK I MIGHT BE ABLE TO HELP YOU WITH THAT.
LEON'S GONNA BE *GUTTED* THAT HE MISSED OUT ON THIS!
WELL, ONCE WE GET HIM OUT, HE CAN HAVE A TRY!
YOU SEE THAT? I THINK WE'RE NEARLY THERE!
THANK YOU.

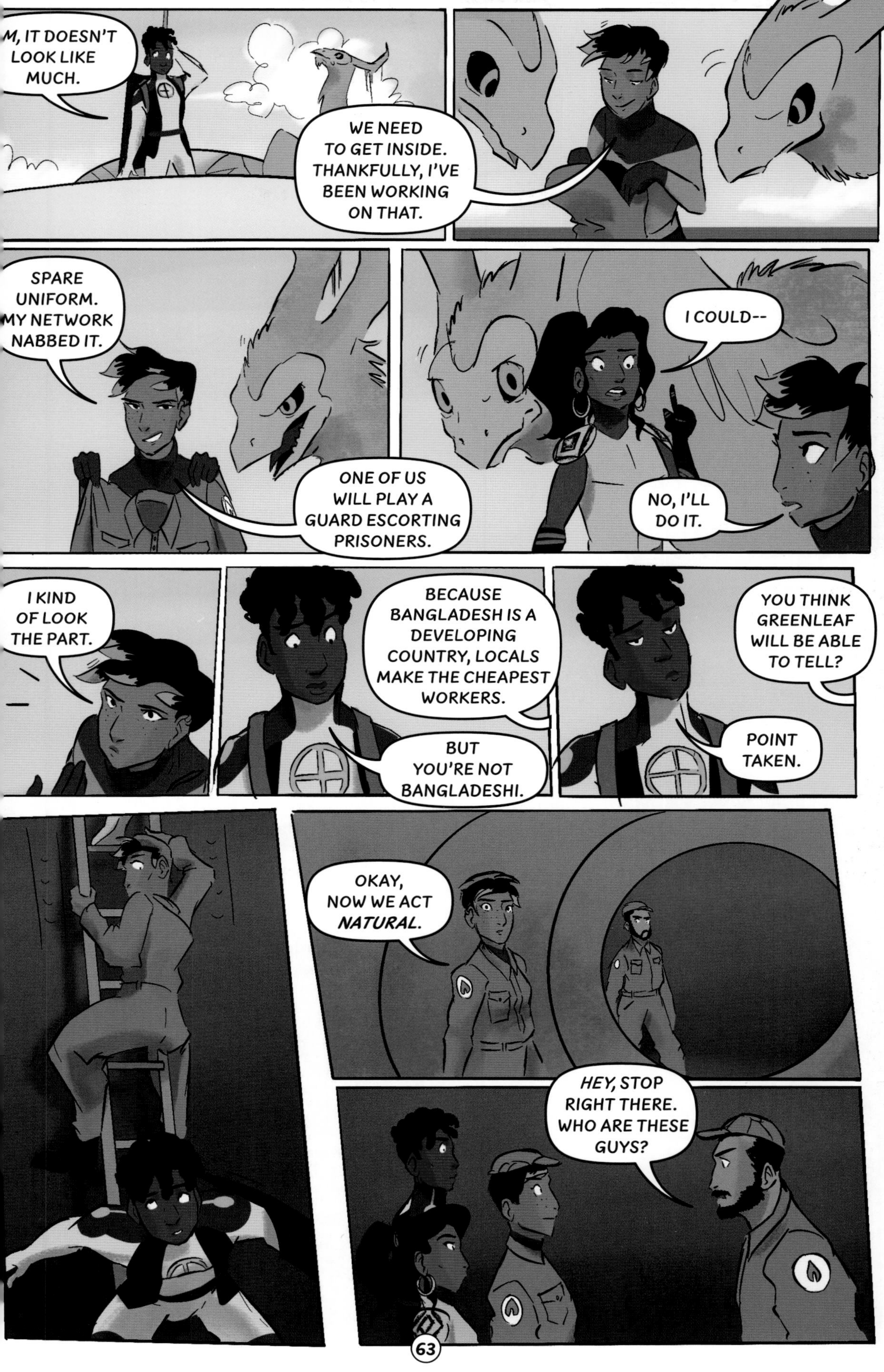
M, IT DOESN'T LOOK LIKE MUCH.
WE NEED TO GET INSIDE. THANKFULLY, I'VE BEEN WORKING ON THAT.
SPARE UNIFORM. MY NETWORK NABBED IT.
ONE OF US WILL PLAY A GUARD ESCORTING PRISONERS.
I COULD--
NO, I'LL DO IT.
I KIND OF LOOK THE PART.
BECAUSE BANGLADESH IS A DEVELOPING COUNTRY, LOCALS MAKE THE CHEAPEST WORKERS.
BUT YOU'RE NOT BANGLADESHI.
YOU THINK GREENLEAF WILL BE ABLE TO TELL?
POINT TAKEN.
OKAY, NOW WE ACT *NATURAL*.
HEY, STOP RIGHT THERE. WHO ARE THESE GUYS?

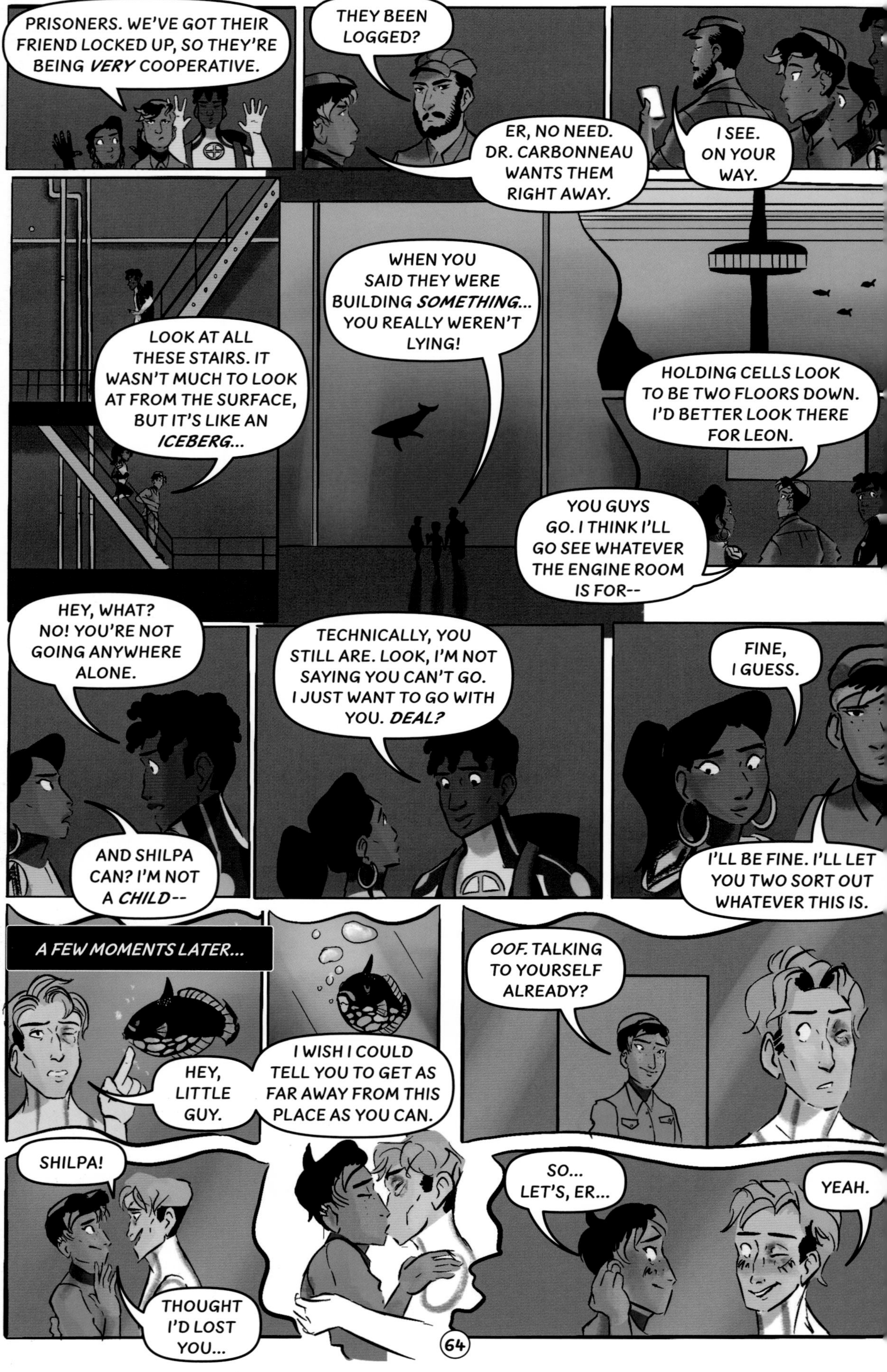
PRISONERS. WE'VE GOT THEIR FRIEND LOCKED UP, SO THEY'RE BEING *VERY* COOPERATIVE.
THEY BEEN LOGGED?
ER, NO NEED. DR. CARBONNEAU WANTS THEM RIGHT AWAY.
I SEE. ON YOUR WAY.
LOOK AT ALL THESE STAIRS. IT WASN'T MUCH TO LOOK AT FROM THE SURFACE, BUT IT'S LIKE AN *ICEBERG*...
WHEN YOU SAID THEY WERE BUILDING *SOMETHING*... YOU REALLY WEREN'T LYING!
HOLDING CELLS LOOK TO BE TWO FLOORS DOWN. I'D BETTER LOOK THERE FOR LEON.
YOU GUYS GO. I THINK I'LL GO SEE WHATEVER THE ENGINE ROOM IS FOR--
HEY, WHAT? NO! YOU'RE NOT GOING ANYWHERE ALONE.
AND SHILPA CAN? I'M NOT A *CHILD*--
TECHNICALLY, YOU STILL ARE. LOOK, I'M NOT SAYING YOU CAN'T GO. I JUST WANT TO GO WITH YOU. *DEAL?*
FINE, I GUESS.
I'LL BE FINE. I'LL LET YOU TWO SORT OUT WHATEVER THIS IS.
A FEW MOMENTS LATER...
HEY, LITTLE GUY.
I WISH I COULD TELL YOU TO GET AS FAR AWAY FROM THIS PLACE AS YOU CAN.
OOF. TALKING TO YOURSELF ALREADY?
SHILPA!
THOUGHT I'D LOST YOU...
SO... LET'S, ER...
YEAH.

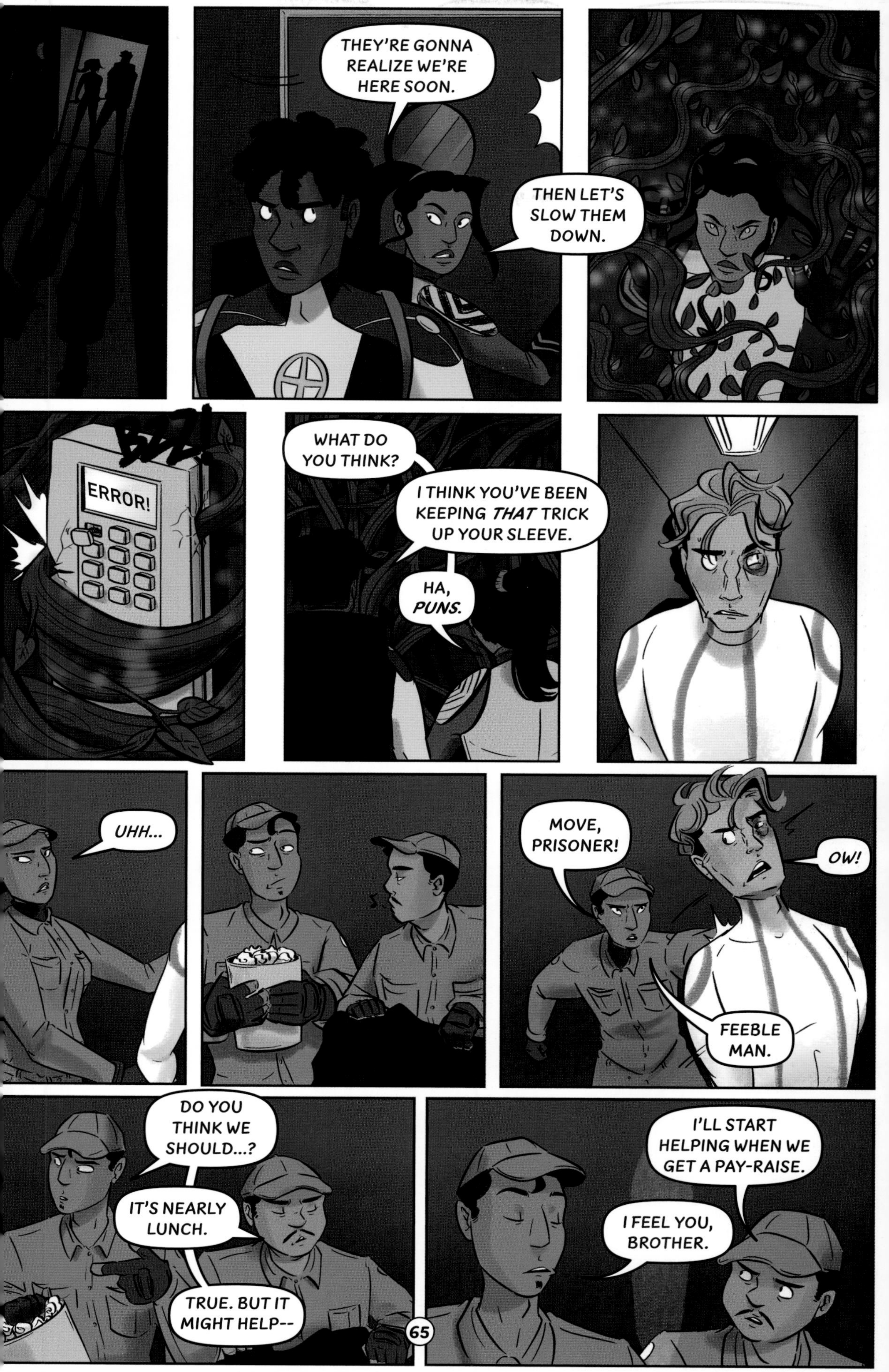
THEY'RE GONNA REALIZE WE'RE HERE SOON.
THEN LET'S SLOW THEM DOWN.
BZZ!
ERROR!
WHAT DO YOU THINK?
I THINK YOU'VE BEEN KEEPING *THAT* TRICK UP YOUR SLEEVE.
HA, *PUNS*.
UHH...
MOVE, PRISONER!
OW!
FEEBLE MAN.
DO YOU THINK WE SHOULD...?
IT'S NEARLY LUNCH.
TRUE. BUT IT MIGHT HELP--
I'LL START HELPING WHEN WE GET A PAY-RAISE.
I FEEL YOU, BROTHER.

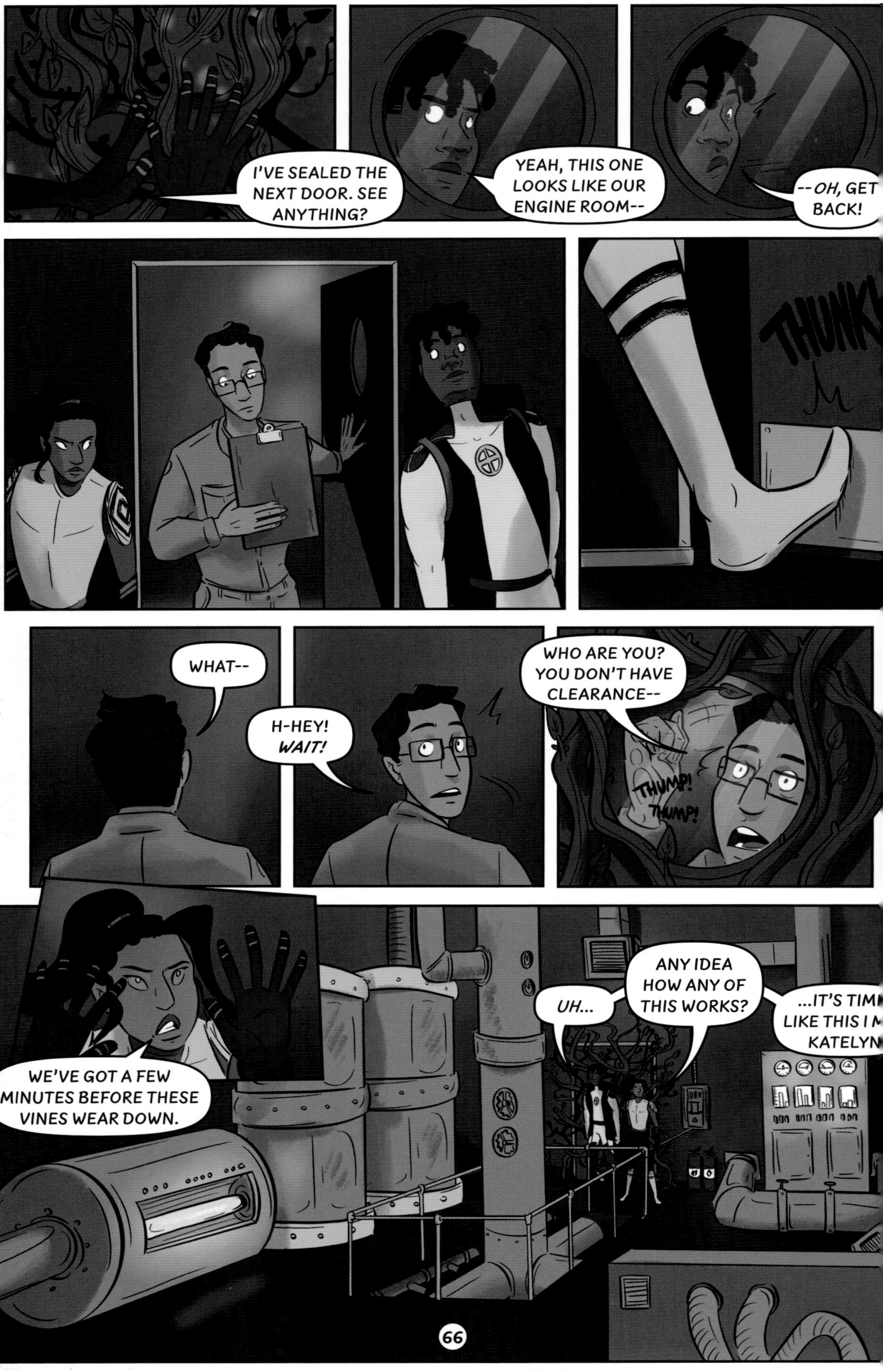
I'VE SEALED THE NEXT DOOR. SEE ANYTHING?
YEAH, THIS ONE LOOKS LIKE OUR ENGINE ROOM--
--*OH*, GET BACK!
THUNK
WHAT--
H-HEY! *WAIT!*
WHO ARE YOU? YOU DON'T HAVE CLEARANCE--
THUMP! THUMP!
WE'VE GOT A FEW MINUTES BEFORE THESE VINES WEAR DOWN.
UH...
ANY IDEA HOW ANY OF THIS WORKS?
...IT'S TIM
LIKE THIS I
KATELYN

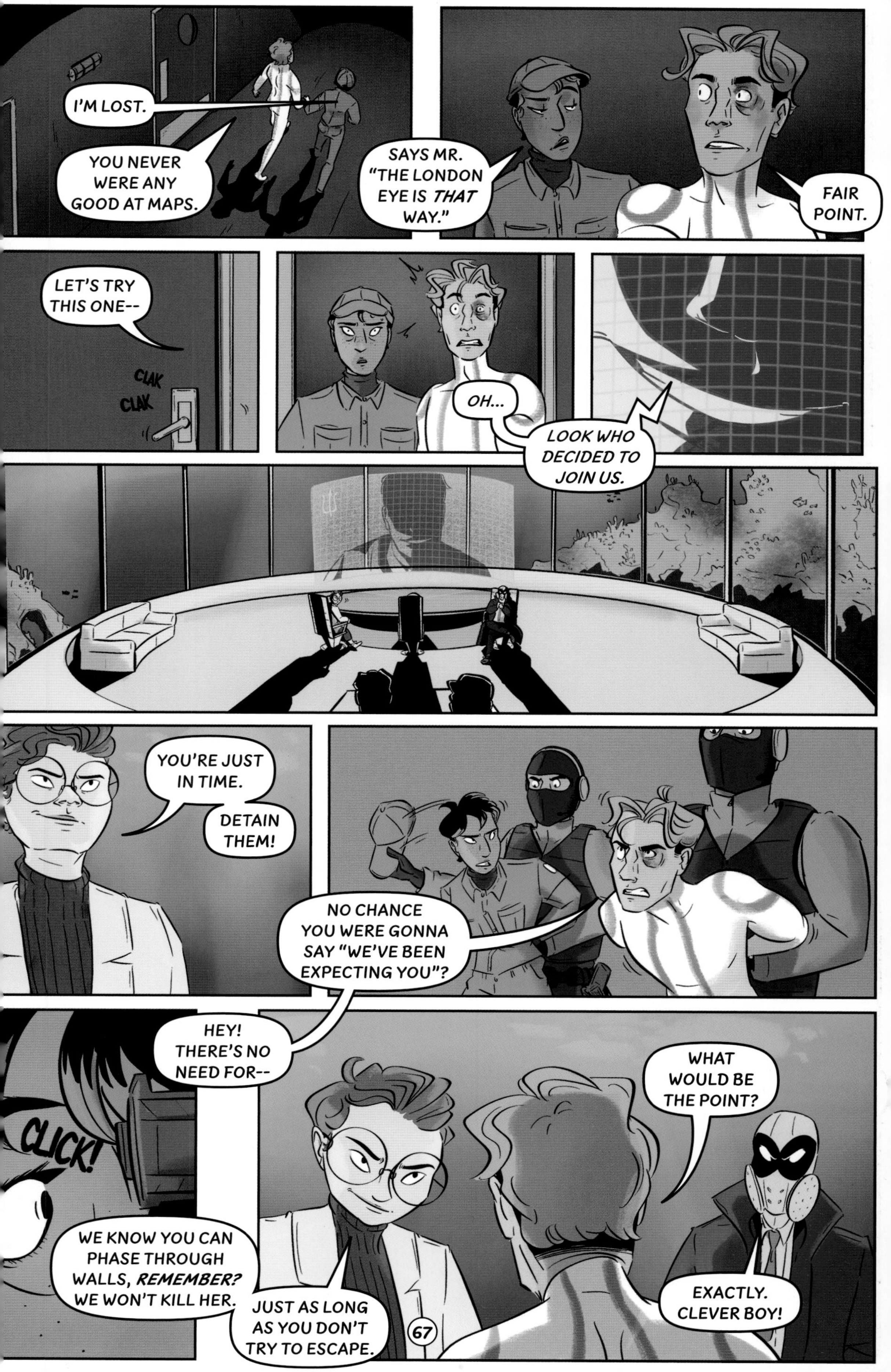

I'M LOST.
YOU NEVER WERE ANY GOOD AT MAPS.
SAYS MR. "THE LONDON EYE IS *THAT* WAY."
FAIR POINT.
LET'S TRY THIS ONE--
CLAK
CLAK
OH...
LOOK WHO DECIDED TO JOIN US.
YOU'RE JUST IN TIME.
DETAIN THEM!
NO CHANCE YOU WERE GONNA SAY "WE'VE BEEN EXPECTING YOU"?
HEY! THERE'S NO NEED FOR--
CLICK!
WHAT WOULD BE THE POINT?
WE KNOW YOU CAN PHASE THROUGH WALLS, *REMEMBER?* WE WON'T KILL HER.
JUST AS LONG AS YOU DON'T TRY TO ESCAPE.
EXACTLY. CLEVER BOY!

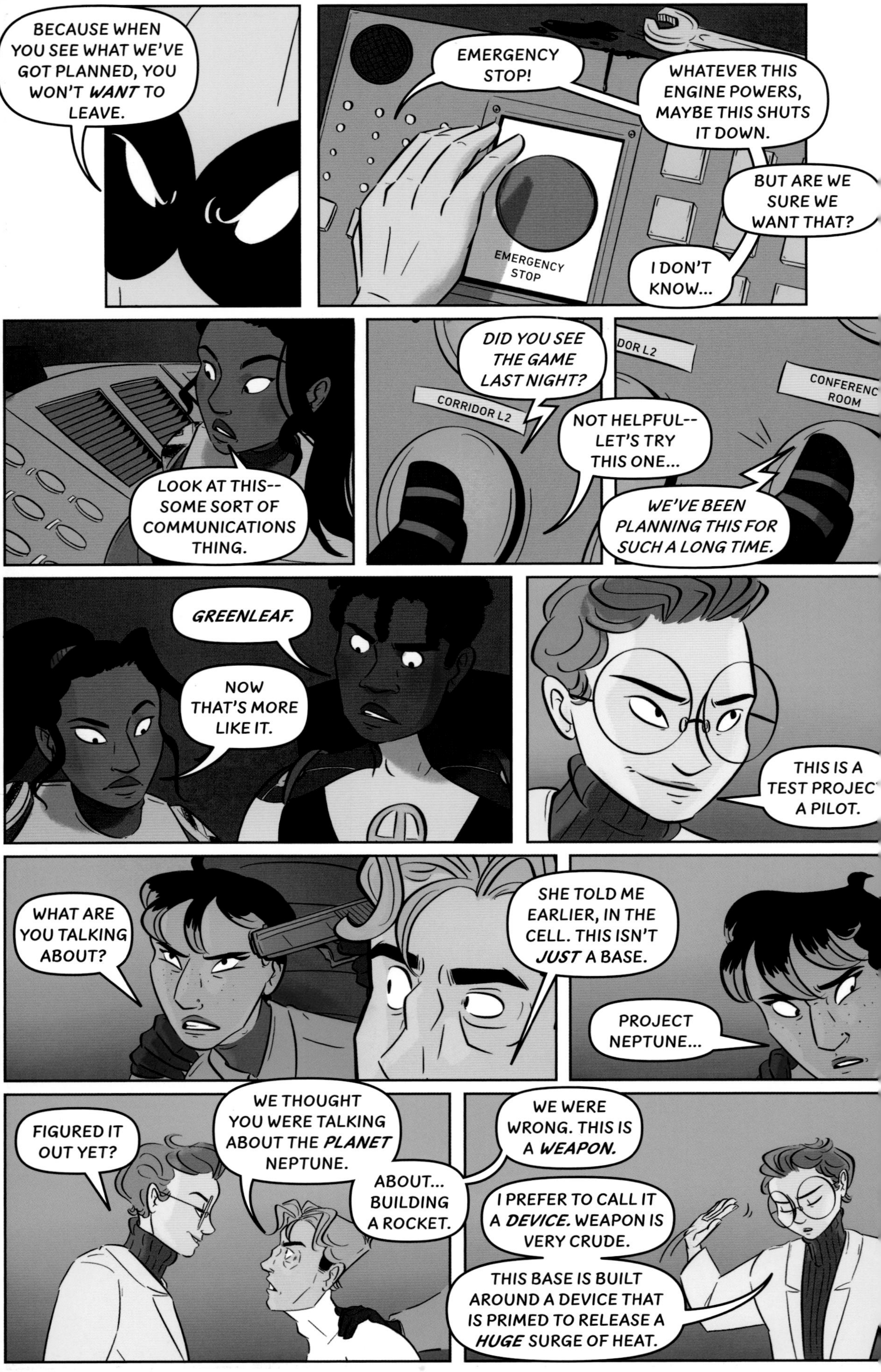

BECAUSE WHEN YOU SEE WHAT WE'VE GOT PLANNED, YOU WON'T *WANT* TO LEAVE.
EMERGENCY STOP!
WHATEVER THIS ENGINE POWERS, MAYBE THIS SHUTS IT DOWN.
EMERGENCY STOP
BUT ARE WE SURE WE WANT THAT?
I DON'T KNOW...
LOOK AT THIS-- SOME SORT OF COMMUNICATIONS THING.
CORRIDOR L2
DID YOU SEE THE GAME LAST NIGHT?
NOT HELPFUL-- LET'S TRY THIS ONE...
DOR L2
CONFERENC ROOM
WE'VE BEEN PLANNING THIS FOR SUCH A LONG TIME.
GREENLEAF.
NOW THAT'S MORE LIKE IT.
THIS IS A TEST PROJEC A PILOT.
WHAT ARE YOU TALKING ABOUT?
SHE TOLD ME EARLIER, IN THE CELL. THIS ISN'T *JUST* A BASE.
PROJECT NEPTUNE...
FIGURED IT OUT YET?
WE THOUGHT YOU WERE TALKING ABOUT THE *PLANET* NEPTUNE.
ABOUT... BUILDING A ROCKET.
WE WERE WRONG. THIS IS A ***WEAPON.***
I PREFER TO CALL IT A *DEVICE.* WEAPON IS VERY CRUDE.
THIS BASE IS BUILT AROUND A DEVICE THAT IS PRIMED TO RELEASE A *HUGE* SURGE OF HEAT.

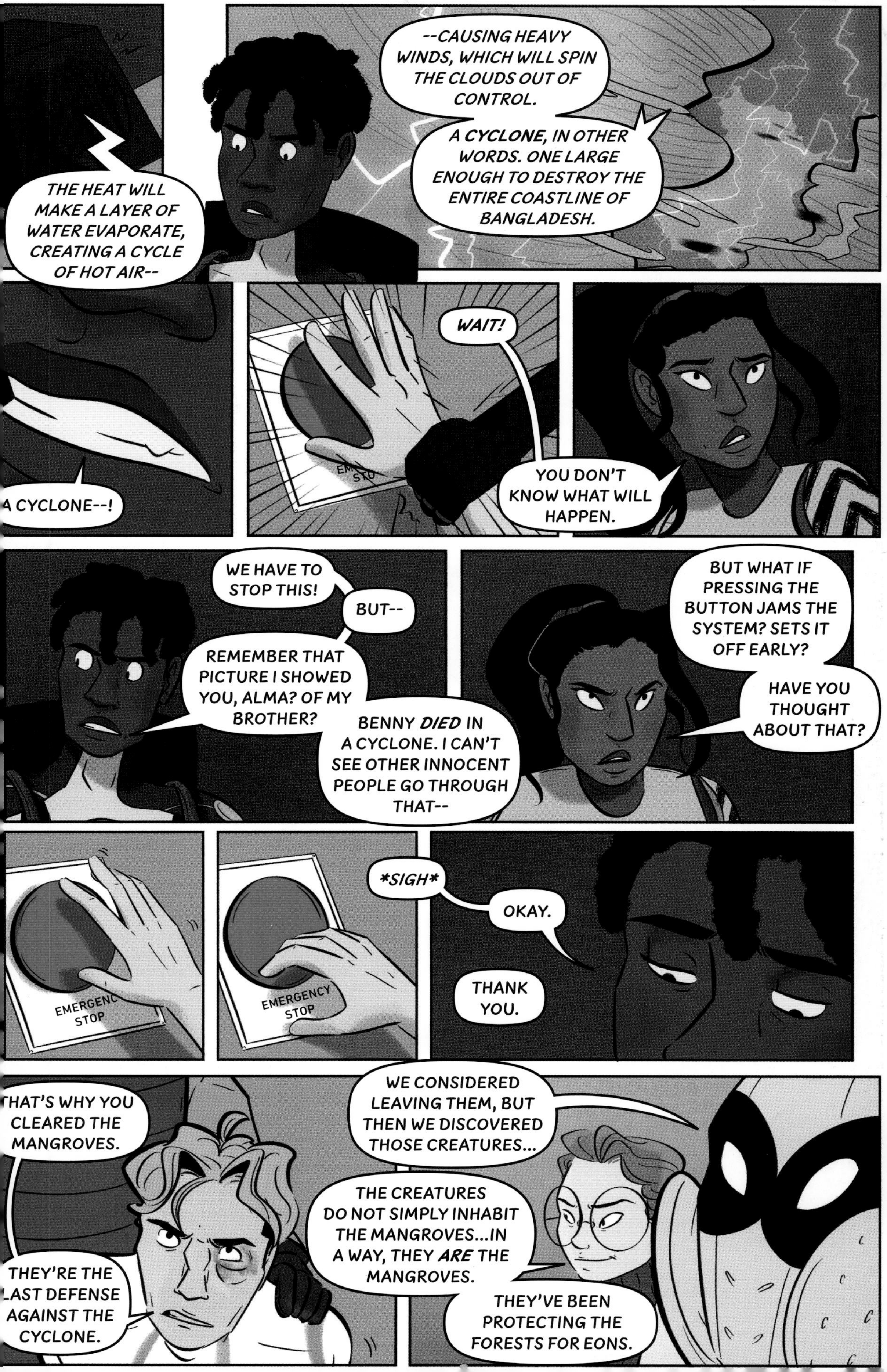

THE HEAT WILL MAKE A LAYER OF WATER EVAPORATE, CREATING A CYCLE OF HOT AIR--
--CAUSING HEAVY WINDS, WHICH WILL SPIN THE CLOUDS OUT OF CONTROL.
A CYCLONE, IN OTHER WORDS. ONE LARGE ENOUGH TO DESTROY THE ENTIRE COASTLINE OF BANGLADESH.
A CYCLONE--!
WAIT!
YOU DON'T KNOW WHAT WILL HAPPEN.
WE HAVE TO STOP THIS!
BUT--
REMEMBER THAT PICTURE I SHOWED YOU, ALMA? OF MY BROTHER?
BENNY DIED IN A CYCLONE. I CAN'T SEE OTHER INNOCENT PEOPLE GO THROUGH THAT--
BUT WHAT IF PRESSING THE BUTTON JAMS THE SYSTEM? SETS IT OFF EARLY?
HAVE YOU THOUGHT ABOUT THAT?
EMERGENC STOP
EMERGENCY STOP
SIGH
OKAY.
THANK YOU.
THAT'S WHY YOU CLEARED THE MANGROVES.
THEY'RE THE LAST DEFENSE AGAINST THE CYCLONE.
WE CONSIDERED LEAVING THEM, BUT THEN WE DISCOVERED THOSE CREATURES...
THE CREATURES DO NOT SIMPLY INHABIT THE MANGROVES...IN A WAY, THEY ARE THE MANGROVES.
THEY'VE BEEN PROTECTING THE FORESTS FOR EONS.

THEY WERE BEAUTIFUL.

BEAUTIFUL AND UNTOUCHED, AND YOU HAD TO GET YOUR *FILTHY* HANDS ON THEM!

MAY I REMIND YOU THAT WE'RE THE ONES W THE BIGGER WEAPONS, S I'D WATCH YOUR TONGU IF I WERE YOU.

SO THAT'S ALL THIS IS NOW? REVENGE AND DESTRUCTION?

THIS IS JUST A *TEST* PROJECT. WE HAVE THOUSANDS OF SITES LIKE THIS IN DEVELOPMENT ALL AROUND THE WORLD. DEVICES OF ALL DIFFERENT KINDS.

ENOUGH OF THEM USED OVER A LONG ENOUGH PERIOD OF TIME AND SEA LEVELS WILL RISE ACROSS THE *ENTIRE* PLANET, FLOODING TOWNS AND CITIES.

NEW YORK? WHO REMEMBERS NEW YORK? THAT AMERICAN *HELLHOLE* WILL BE THE FIRST TO GO.

WE DIDN'T CALL IT PROJECT NEPTUN BECAUSE WE'RE GOI INTO *SPACE*.

BUT BECAUSE WE'RE CREATING A NEW WATERY DOMAIN FITTING FOR NEPTUNE, GOD OF THE SEA.

SO...THE ENTIRE PLANET, UNDERWATER... BUT THAT MEANS HUMANS WON'T BE ABLE TO SURVIVE!

UNLESS YOU'RE A SUPERHUMAN...

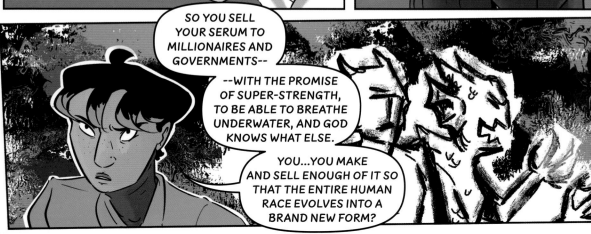

SO YOU SELL YOUR SERUM TO MILLIONAIRES AND GOVERNMENTS--

--WITH THE PROMISE OF SUPER-STRENGTH, TO BE ABLE TO BREATHE UNDERWATER, AND GOD KNOWS WHAT ELSE.

YOU...YOU MAKE AND SELL ENOUGH OF IT SO THAT THE ENTIRE HUMAN RACE EVOLVES INTO A BRAND NEW FORM?

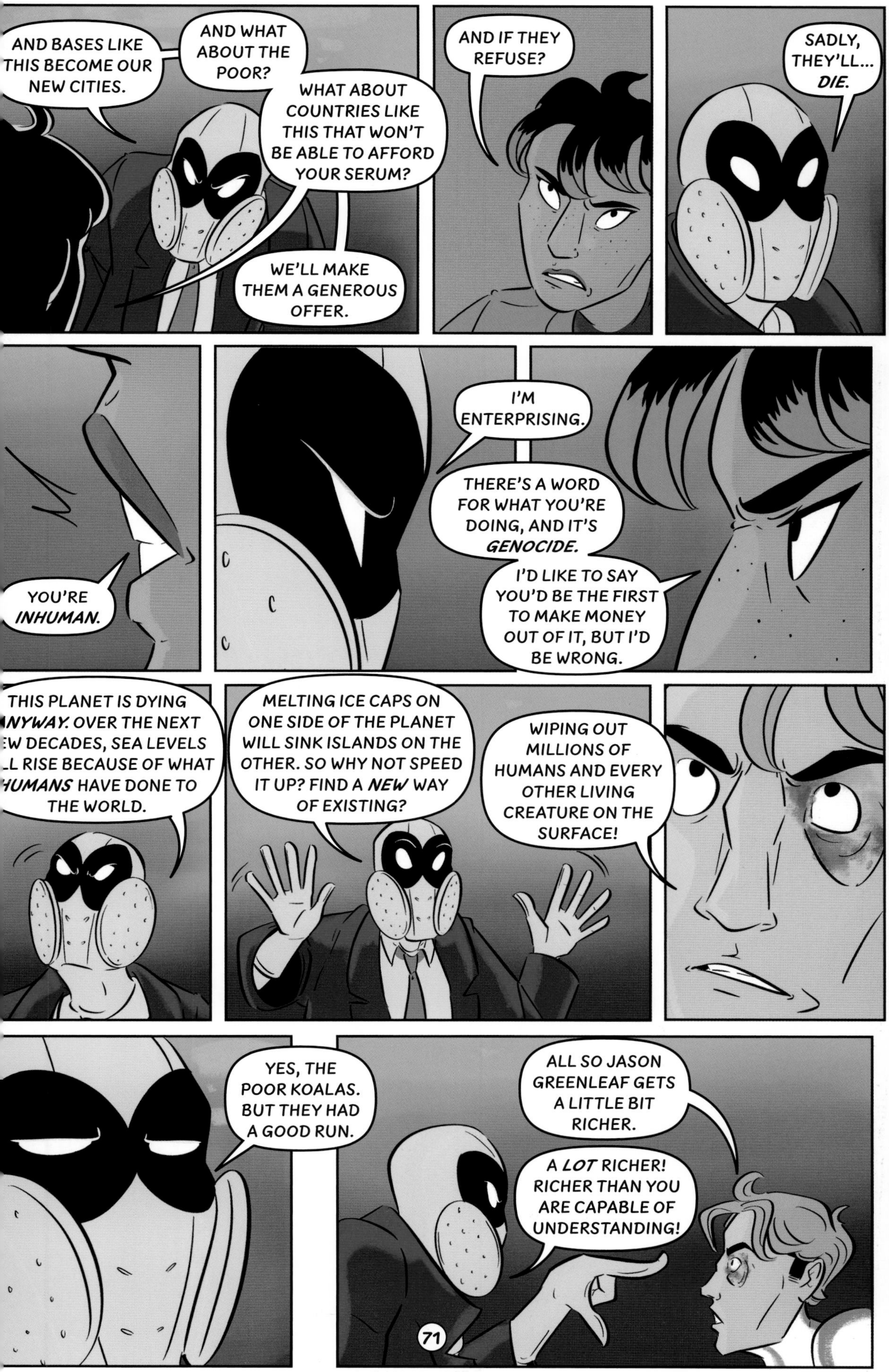
AND BASES LIKE THIS BECOME OUR NEW CITIES.
AND WHAT ABOUT THE POOR?
WHAT ABOUT COUNTRIES LIKE THIS THAT WON'T BE ABLE TO AFFORD YOUR SERUM?
WE'LL MAKE THEM A GENEROUS OFFER.
AND IF THEY REFUSE?
SADLY, THEY'LL... *DIE*.
YOU'RE *INHUMAN*.
I'M ENTERPRISING.
THERE'S A WORD FOR WHAT YOU'RE DOING, AND IT'S *GENOCIDE*.
I'D LIKE TO SAY YOU'D BE THE FIRST TO MAKE MONEY OUT OF IT, BUT I'D BE WRONG.
THIS PLANET IS DYING NYWAY. OVER THE NEXT W DECADES, SEA LEVELS L RISE BECAUSE OF WHAT HUMANS HAVE DONE TO THE WORLD.
MELTING ICE CAPS ON ONE SIDE OF THE PLANET WILL SINK ISLANDS ON THE OTHER. SO WHY NOT SPEED IT UP? FIND A *NEW* WAY OF EXISTING?
WIPING OUT MILLIONS OF HUMANS AND EVERY OTHER LIVING CREATURE ON THE SURFACE!
YES, THE POOR KOALAS. BUT THEY HAD A GOOD RUN.
ALL SO JASON GREENLEAF GETS A LITTLE BIT RICHER.
A *LOT* RICHER! RICHER THAN YOU ARE CAPABLE OF UNDERSTANDING!

ALL THOSE PLANS YOU FOILED...

ALL THOSE TIMES I TRIED TO CHANGE THE WORLD IN A *KINDER*, GENTLER WAY.

LIKE BURNING DOWN THE RAINFOREST?

APART FROM THAT.

BUT NOW, AT LAST, I'M ONE STEP AHEAD OF YOU. WHAT ARE YOU NOW-- YOU RENEGADES?

YOU'RE JUST A MOTLEY CREW OF ANGRY YOUTHS WHO PROBABLY COULDN'T EVEN CHANGE A FUSE. *I'VE WON--*

BEEP!

ATTENTION! UNAUTHORIZED AIRCRAFT APPROACHING LANDING PAD.

WHAT THE HELL?!

SHOW EXTERNAL CAMERA.

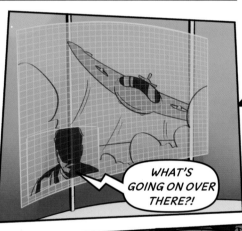

WHAT'S GOING ON OVER THERE?!

WHOOOSH!

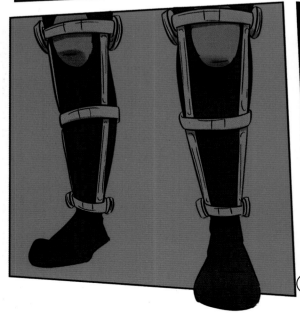

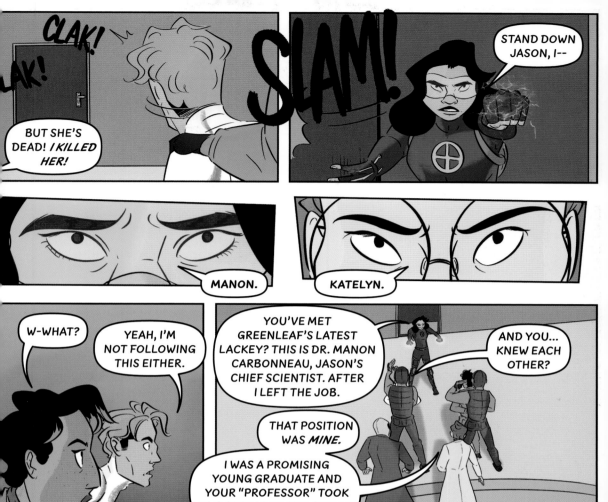

CLAK!
CLAK!

SLAM!

BUT SHE'S DEAD! *I KILLED HER!*

STAND DOWN JASON, I--

MANON.

KATELYN.

W-WHAT?

YEAH, I'M NOT FOLLOWING THIS EITHER.

YOU'VE MET GREENLEAF'S LATEST LACKEY? THIS IS DR. MANON CARBONNEAU, JASON'S CHIEF SCIENTIST. AFTER I LEFT THE JOB.

AND YOU... KNEW EACH OTHER?

THAT POSITION WAS *MINE.*

I WAS A PROMISING YOUNG GRADUATE AND YOUR "PROFESSOR" TOOK OUR RESEARCH AND PASSED IT OFF AS HER OWN!

SHE THREW ME UNDER THE BUS--ALL SO SHE COULD BE GREENLEAF'S GOLDEN GIRL!

THAT'S YOUR TWISTED VERSION OF EVENTS.

NO--SHILPA, DON'T...

BUT SHILPA'S RIGHT, YOU CAN'T LET HER--

MANON'S RIGHT. EVERY WORD OF WHAT SHE SAID IS *TRUE.*

I WAS A WHOLE OTHER PERSON BACK THEN. COLD. MANIPULATIVE.

I DON'T BELIEVE IT. EVEN AFTER ALL YOU'VE TOLD US.

WELL START BELIEVING IT! BECAUSE I WAS. I WISH I WASN'T, BUT THE PAST CAN'T BE CHANGED. I MADE MISTAKES. AND SHE WAS ONE OF THEM.

I'VE SEEN SO MANY GHOSTS TODAY, BUT THIS IS THE WORST.

73

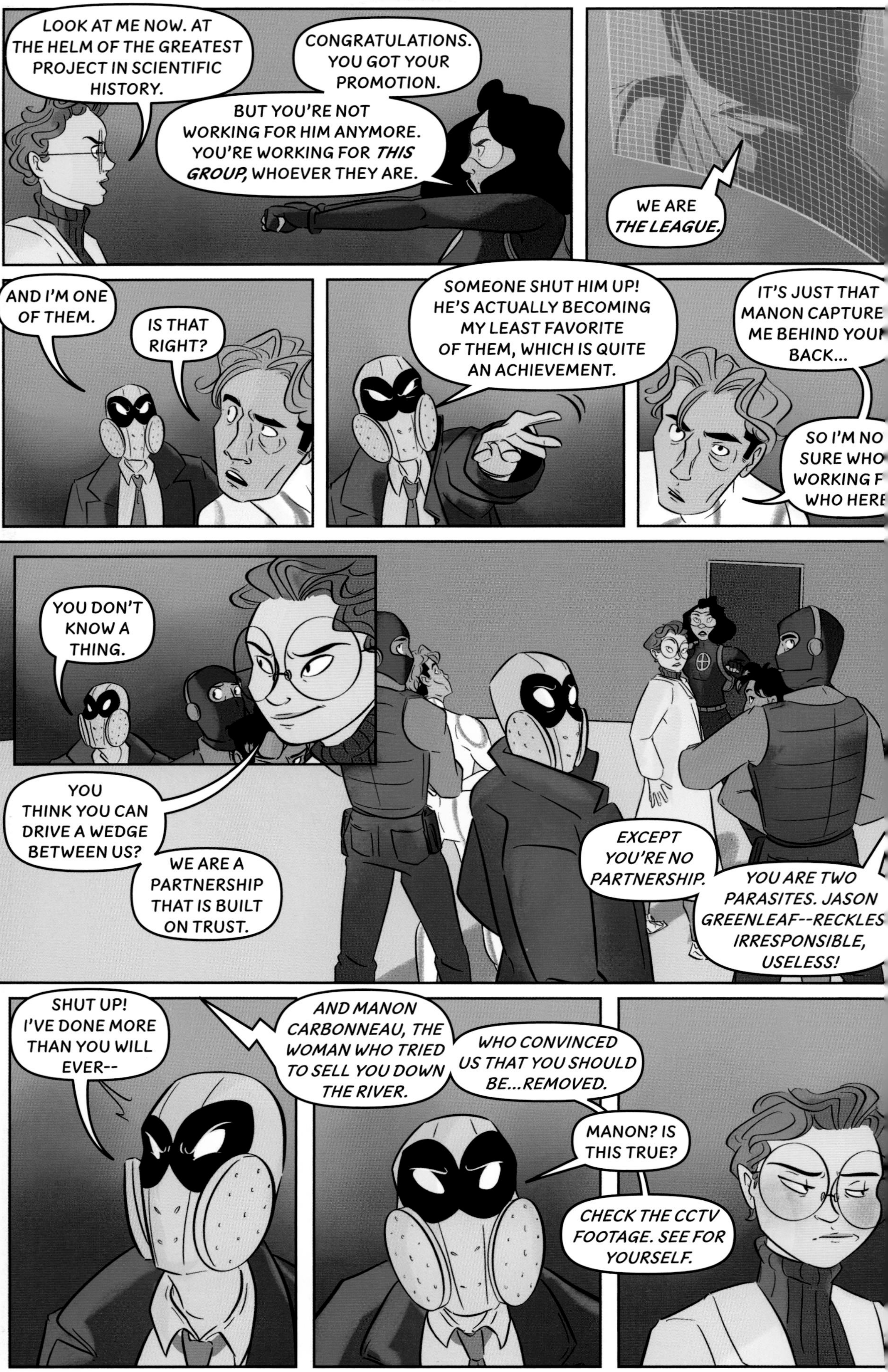
LOOK AT ME NOW. AT THE HELM OF THE GREATEST PROJECT IN SCIENTIFIC HISTORY.
CONGRATULATIONS. YOU GOT YOUR PROMOTION.
BUT YOU'RE NOT WORKING FOR HIM ANYMORE. YOU'RE WORKING FOR *THIS GROUP,* WHOEVER THEY ARE.
WE ARE *THE LEAGUE.*
AND I'M ONE OF THEM.
IS THAT RIGHT?
SOMEONE SHUT HIM UP! HE'S ACTUALLY BECOMING MY LEAST FAVORITE OF THEM, WHICH IS QUITE AN ACHIEVEMENT.
IT'S JUST THAT MANON CAPTURE ME BEHIND YOU BACK...
SO I'M NO SURE WHO WORKING F WHO HERE
YOU DON'T KNOW A THING.
YOU THINK YOU CAN DRIVE A WEDGE BETWEEN US?
WE ARE A PARTNERSHIP THAT IS BUILT ON TRUST.
EXCEPT YOU'RE NO PARTNERSHIP.
YOU ARE TWO PARASITES. JASON GREENLEAF--RECKLES IRRESPONSIBLE, USELESS!
SHUT UP! I'VE DONE MORE THAN YOU WILL EVER--
AND MANON CARBONNEAU, THE WOMAN WHO TRIED TO SELL YOU DOWN THE RIVER.
WHO CONVINCED US THAT YOU SHOULD BE...REMOVED.
MANON? IS THIS TRUE?
CHECK THE CCTV FOOTAGE. SEE FOR YOURSELF.

BUT SUCH POLITICS DO NOT MATTER.

WITH THE BASE INFILTRATED, AN EARLY DEMONSTRATION IS IN ORDER, I THINK.

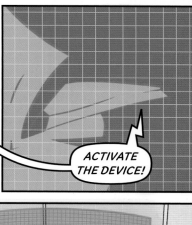

ACTIVATE THE DEVICE!

I WOULD SAY "UNTIL THE NEXT TIME"--BUT I SENSE THIS FAREWELL MAY BE RATHER FINAL.

CALL TERMINATED

DEVICE ACTIVE

OH DEAR. LOOKS LIKE YOU'VE BEEN LEFT IN THE DUST...

ALL OF YOU.

LIKE RATS LEAVING A SINKING SHIP. NO LOYALTY.

YOU'RE A FINE ONE TO TALK ABOUT LOYALTY-- STABBING YOUR OWN BUSINESS PARTNER IN THE BACK.

AND YOU'RE A FINE ONE TO TALK ABOUT BACKSTABBING.

YEAH, THIS WEAPON IS ABOUT TO GO OFF AND EVERYONE'S LEAVING, WHICH--I THINK-- MEANS IT'S GOING TO TAKE THE BASE WITH IT.

STOP IT!

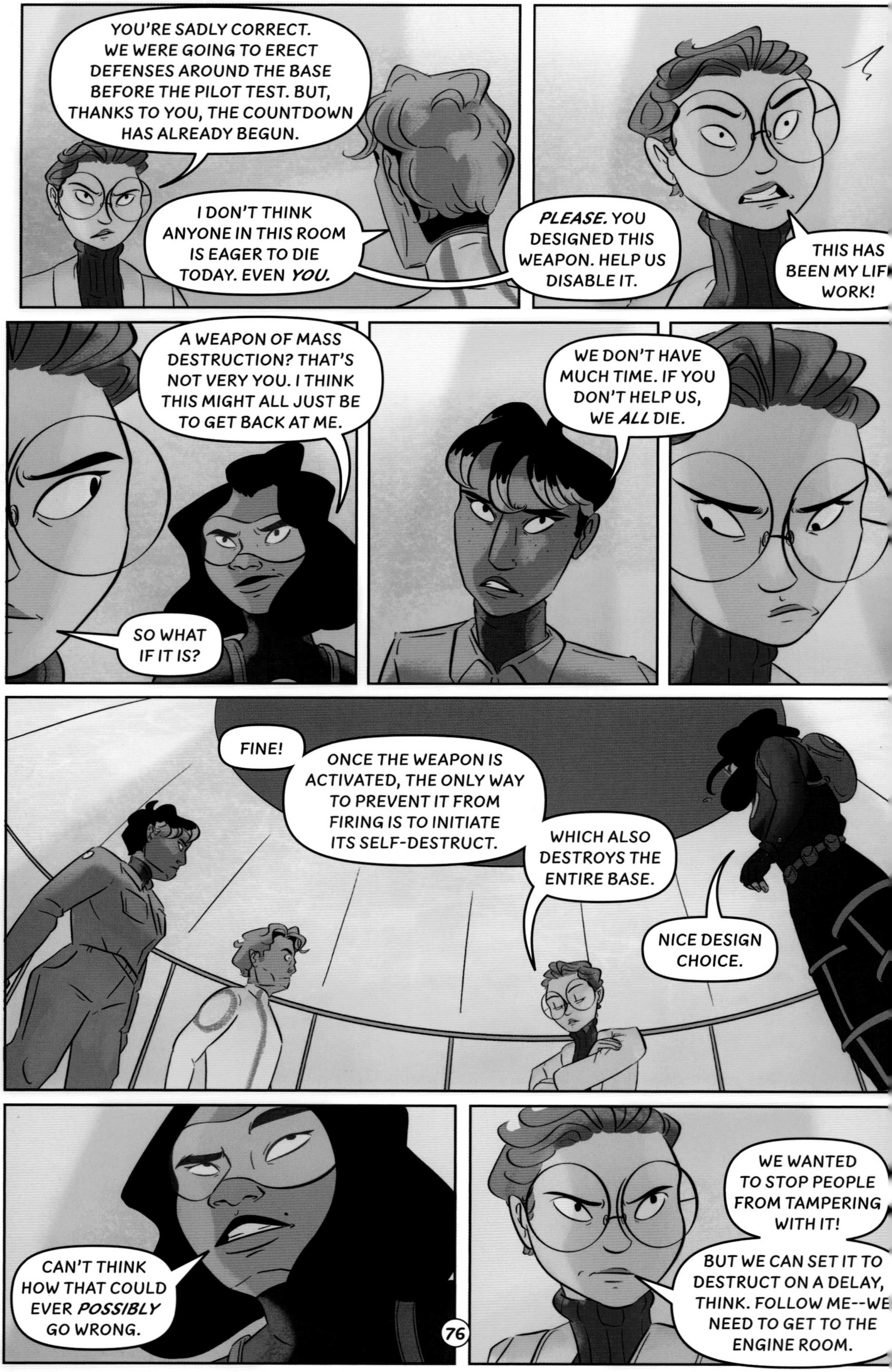

YOU'RE SADLY CORRECT. WE WERE GOING TO ERECT DEFENSES AROUND THE BASE BEFORE THE PILOT TEST. BUT, THANKS TO YOU, THE COUNTDOWN HAS ALREADY BEGUN.
I DON'T THINK ANYONE IN THIS ROOM IS EAGER TO DIE TODAY. EVEN *YOU.*
PLEASE. YOU DESIGNED THIS WEAPON. HELP US DISABLE IT.
THIS HAS BEEN MY LIF WORK!
A WEAPON OF MASS DESTRUCTION? THAT'S NOT VERY YOU. I THINK THIS MIGHT ALL JUST BE TO GET BACK AT ME.
SO WHAT IF IT IS?
WE DON'T HAVE MUCH TIME. IF YOU DON'T HELP US, WE *ALL* DIE.
FINE!
ONCE THE WEAPON IS ACTIVATED, THE ONLY WAY TO PREVENT IT FROM FIRING IS TO INITIATE ITS SELF-DESTRUCT.
WHICH ALSO DESTROYS THE ENTIRE BASE.
NICE DESIGN CHOICE.
CAN'T THINK HOW THAT COULD EVER *POSSIBLY* GO WRONG.
WE WANTED TO STOP PEOPLE FROM TAMPERING WITH IT!
BUT WE CAN SET IT TO DESTRUCT ON A DELAY, THINK. FOLLOW ME--WE NEED TO GET TO THE ENGINE ROOM.

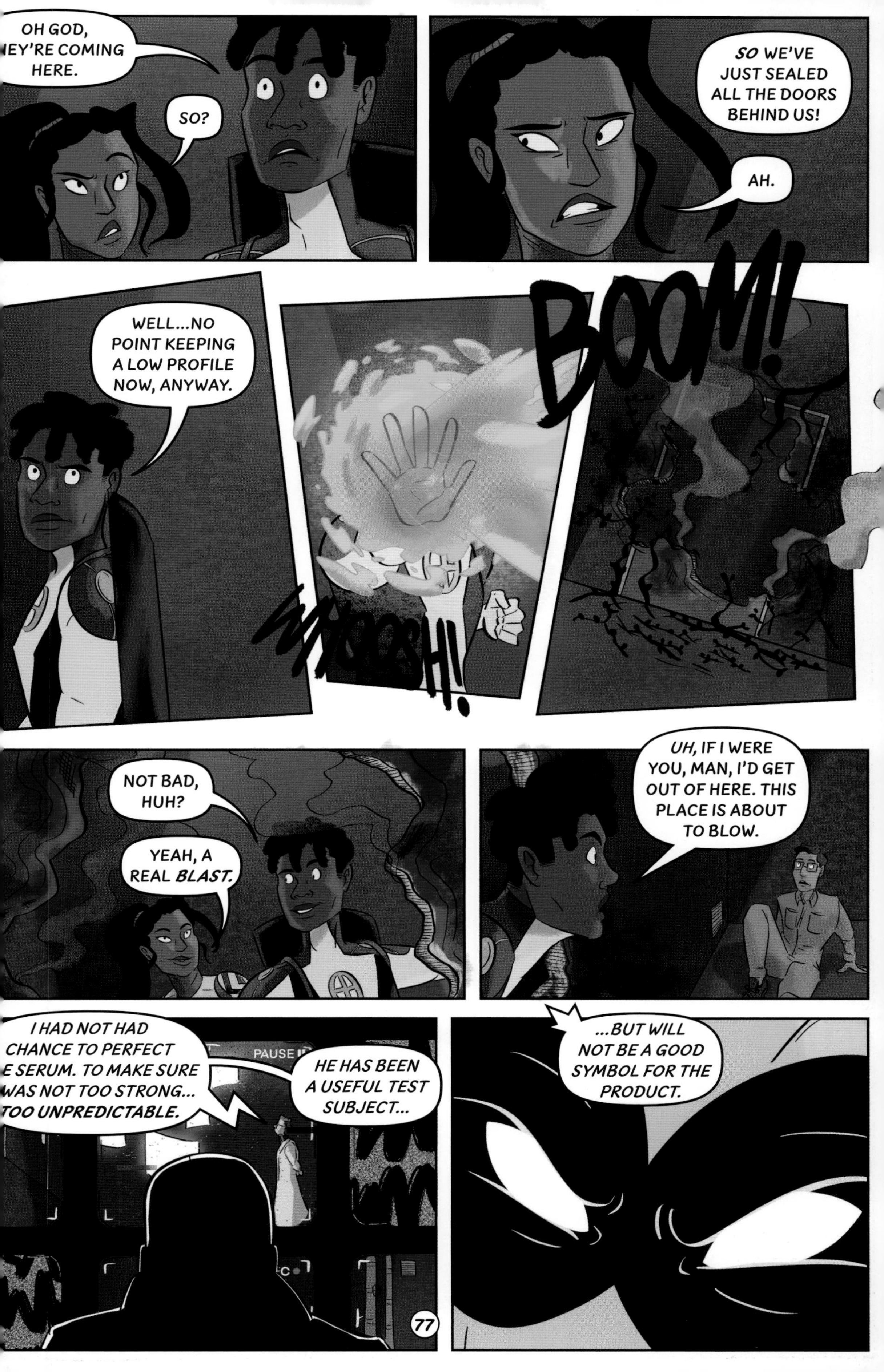
OH GOD,
EY'RE COMING HERE.
SO?
SO WE'VE JUST SEALED ALL THE DOORS BEHIND US!
AH.
WELL...NO POINT KEEPING A LOW PROFILE NOW, ANYWAY.
WHOOSH!!
BOOM!
NOT BAD, HUH?
YEAH, A REAL BLAST.
UH, IF I WERE YOU, MAN, I'D GET OUT OF HERE. THIS PLACE IS ABOUT TO BLOW.
I HAD NOT HAD CHANCE TO PERFECT E SERUM. TO MAKE SURE WAS NOT TOO STRONG... TOO UNPREDICTABLE.
PAUSE
HE HAS BEEN A USEFUL TEST SUBJECT...
...BUT WILL NOT BE A GOOD SYMBOL FOR THE PRODUCT.

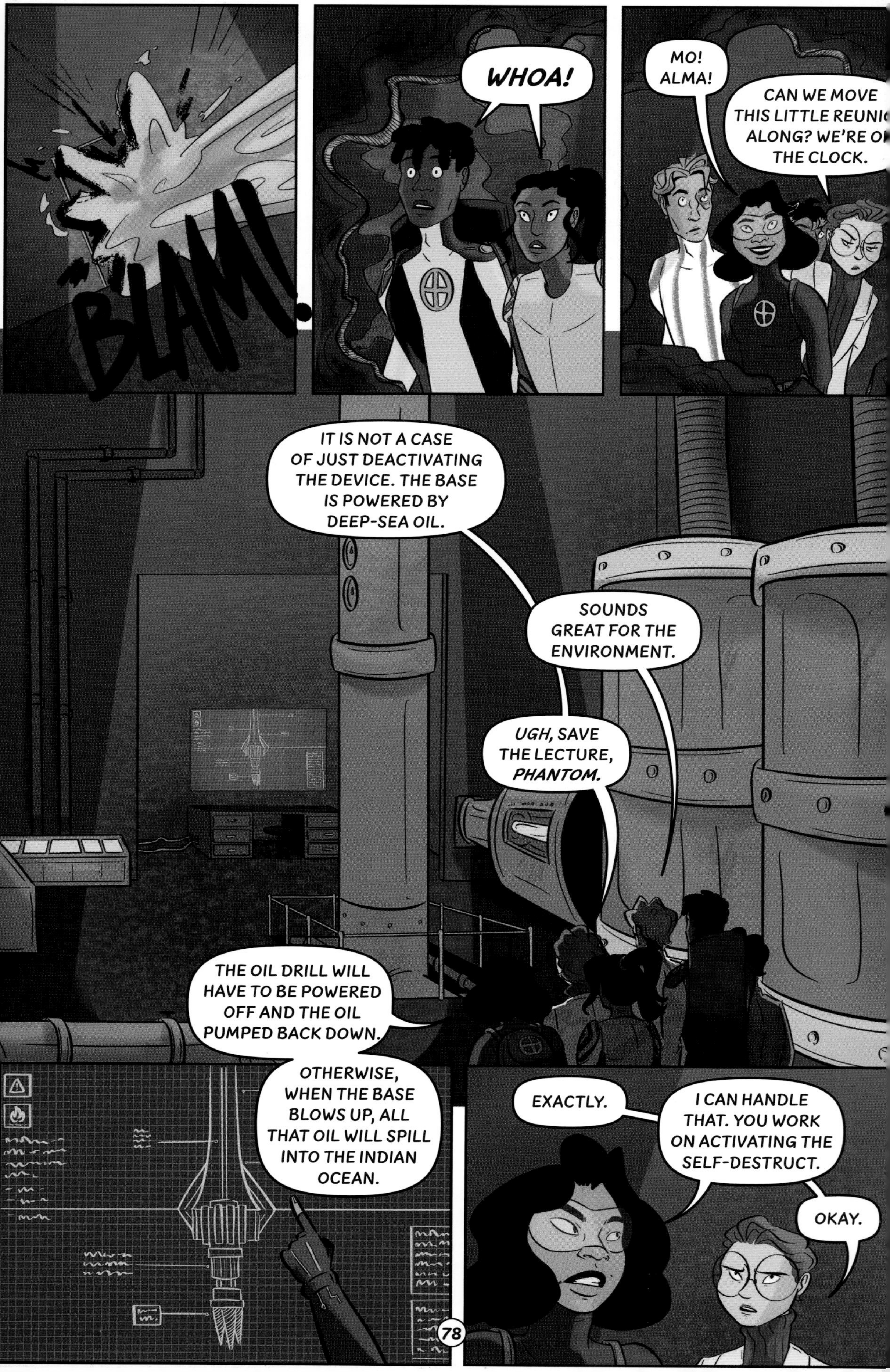
BLAM!
WHOA!
MO! ALMA!
CAN WE MOVE THIS LITTLE REUNI
ALONG? WE'RE O
THE CLOCK.
IT IS NOT A CASE OF JUST DEACTIVATING THE DEVICE. THE BASE IS POWERED BY DEEP-SEA OIL.
SOUNDS GREAT FOR THE ENVIRONMENT.
UGH, SAVE THE LECTURE, PHANTOM.
THE OIL DRILL WILL HAVE TO BE POWERED OFF AND THE OIL PUMPED BACK DOWN.
OTHERWISE, WHEN THE BASE BLOWS UP, ALL THAT OIL WILL SPILL INTO THE INDIAN OCEAN.
EXACTLY.
I CAN HANDLE THAT. YOU WORK ON ACTIVATING THE SELF-DESTRUCT.
OKAY.

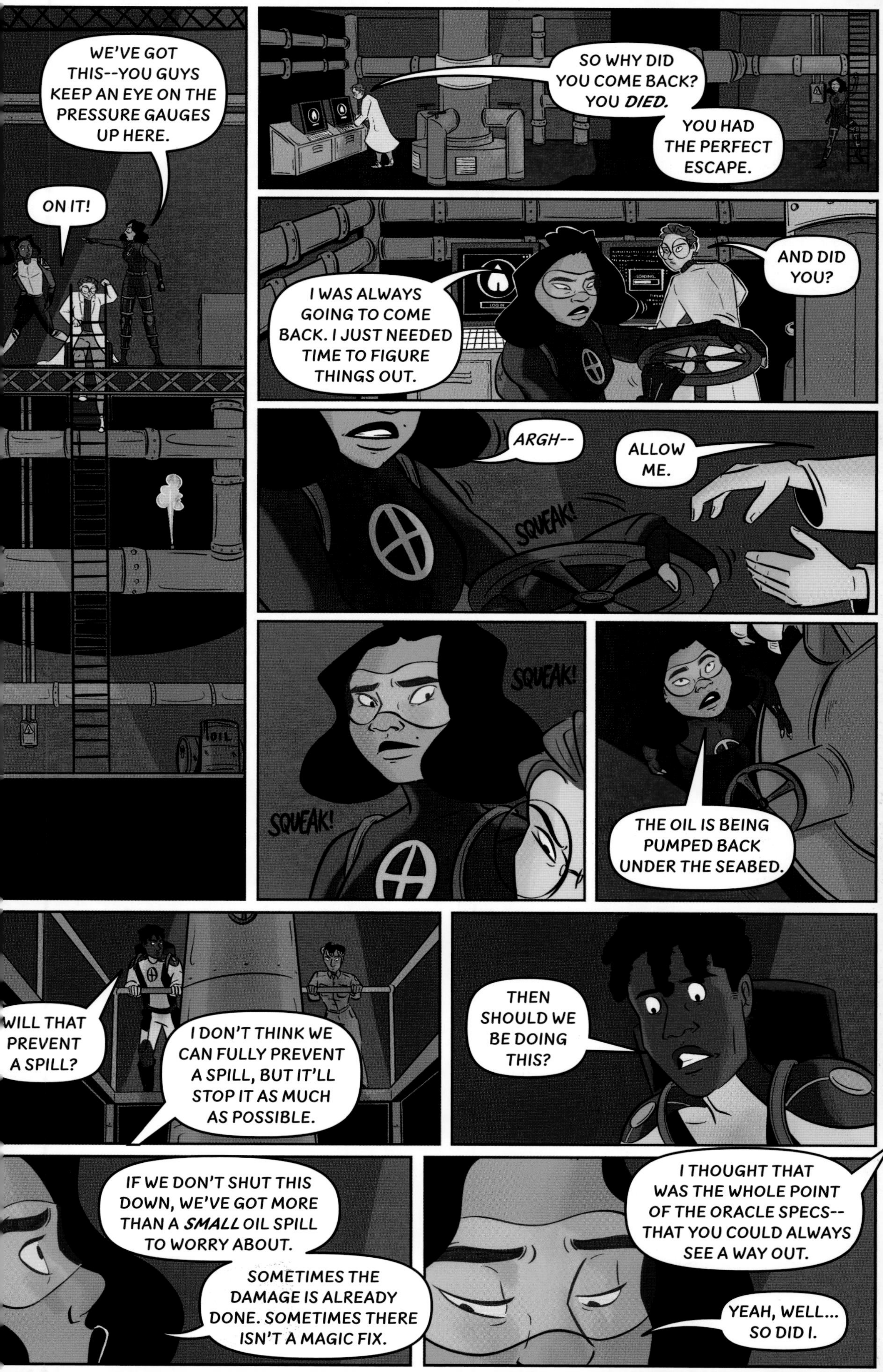
WE'VE GOT THIS--YOU GUYS KEEP AN EYE ON THE PRESSURE GAUGES UP HERE.
ON IT!
OIL
SO WHY DID YOU COME BACK? YOU *DIED.*
YOU HAD THE PERFECT ESCAPE.
I WAS ALWAYS GOING TO COME BACK. I JUST NEEDED TIME TO FIGURE THINGS OUT.
AND DID YOU?
ARGH--
ALLOW ME.
SQUEAK!
SQUEAK!
SQUEAK!
THE OIL IS BEING PUMPED BACK UNDER THE SEABED.
WILL THAT PREVENT A SPILL?
I DON'T THINK WE CAN FULLY PREVENT A SPILL, BUT IT'LL STOP IT AS MUCH AS POSSIBLE.
THEN SHOULD WE BE DOING THIS?
IF WE DON'T SHUT THIS DOWN, WE'VE GOT MORE THAN A *SMALL* OIL SPILL TO WORRY ABOUT.
SOMETIMES THE DAMAGE IS ALREADY DONE. SOMETIMES THERE ISN'T A MAGIC FIX.
I THOUGHT THAT WAS THE WHOLE POINT OF THE ORACLE SPECS--THAT YOU COULD ALWAYS SEE A WAY OUT.
YEAH, WELL... SO DID I.

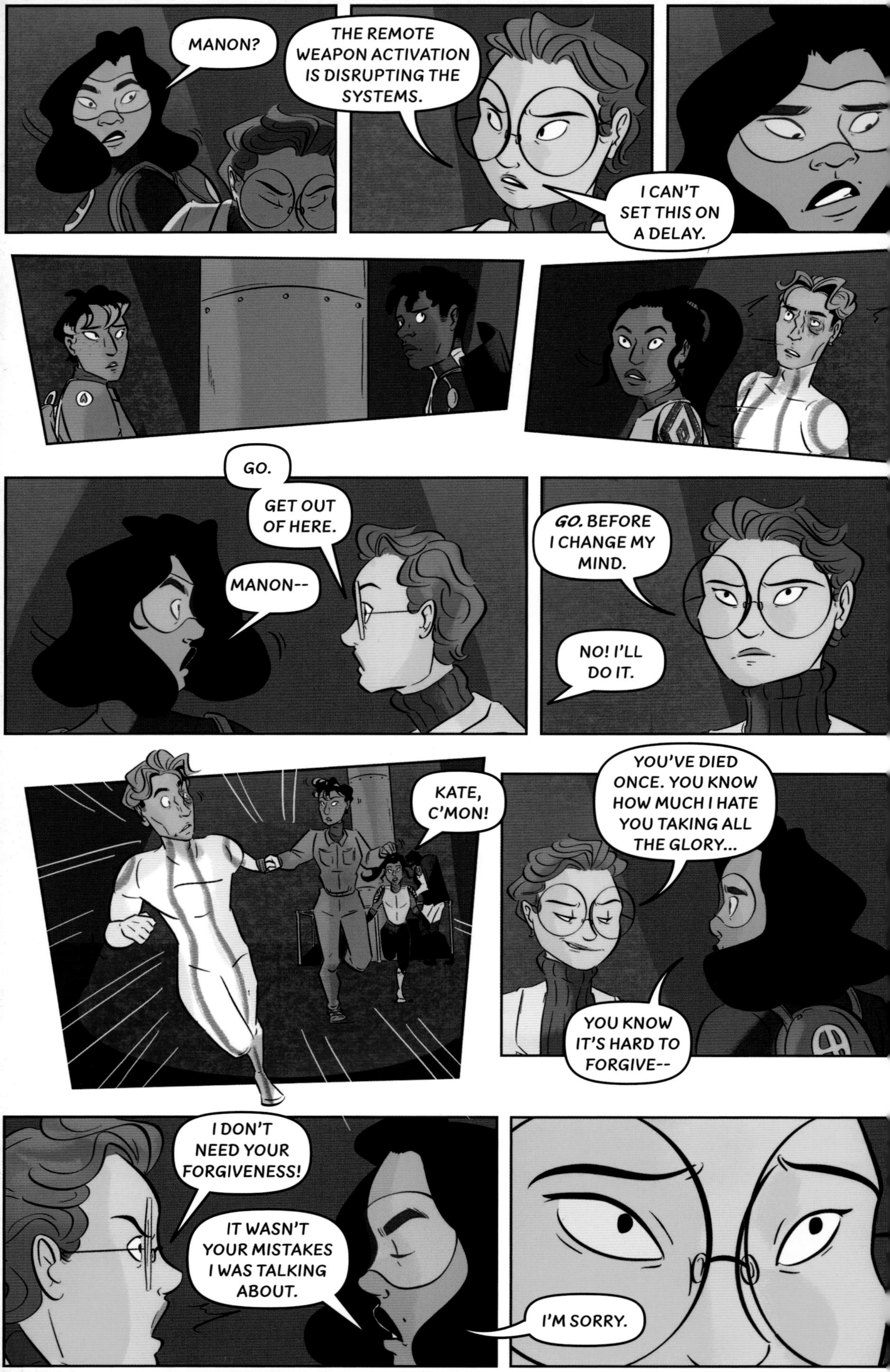
MANON?
THE REMOTE WEAPON ACTIVATION IS DISRUPTING THE SYSTEMS.
I CAN'T SET THIS ON A DELAY.
GO.
GET OUT OF HERE.
MANON--
GO. BEFORE I CHANGE MY MIND.
NO! I'LL DO IT.
KATE, C'MON!
YOU'VE DIED ONCE. YOU KNOW HOW MUCH I HATE YOU TAKING ALL THE GLORY...
YOU KNOW IT'S HARD TO FORGIVE--
I DON'T NEED YOUR FORGIVENESS!
IT WASN'T YOUR MISTAKES I WAS TALKING ABOUT.
I'M SORRY.

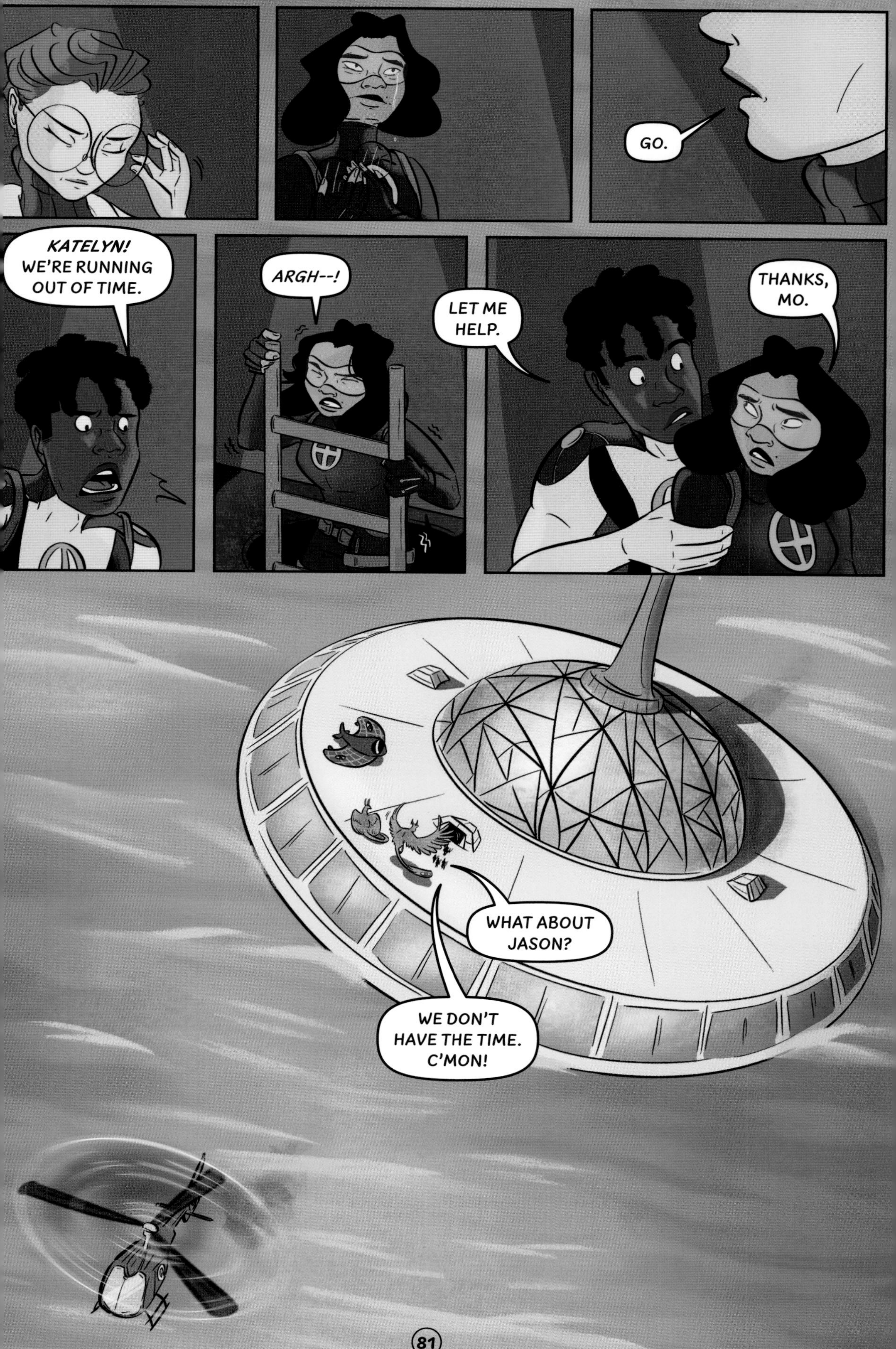
GO.
KATELYN! WE'RE RUNNING OUT OF TIME.
ARGH--!
LET ME HELP.
THANKS, MO.
WHAT ABOUT JASON?
WE DON'T HAVE THE TIME. C'MON!

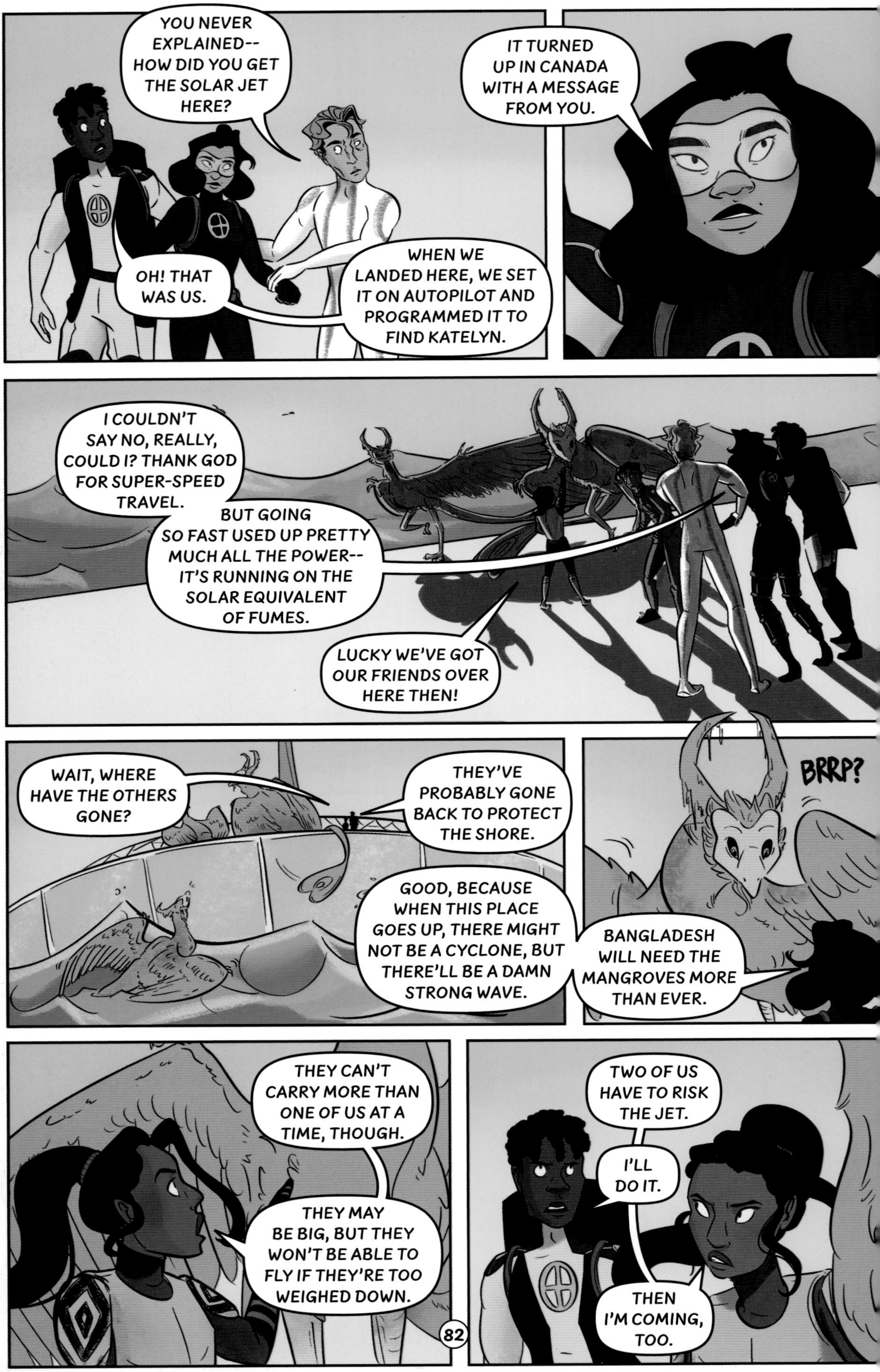
YOU NEVER EXPLAINED-- HOW DID YOU GET THE SOLAR JET HERE?
OH! THAT WAS US.
WHEN WE LANDED HERE, WE SET IT ON AUTOPILOT AND PROGRAMMED IT TO FIND KATELYN.
IT TURNED UP IN CANADA WITH A MESSAGE FROM YOU.
I COULDN'T SAY NO, REALLY, COULD I? THANK GOD FOR SUPER-SPEED TRAVEL.
BUT GOING SO FAST USED UP PRETTY MUCH ALL THE POWER-- IT'S RUNNING ON THE SOLAR EQUIVALENT OF FUMES.
LUCKY WE'VE GOT OUR FRIENDS OVER HERE THEN!
WAIT, WHERE HAVE THE OTHERS GONE?
THEY'VE PROBABLY GONE BACK TO PROTECT THE SHORE.
GOOD, BECAUSE WHEN THIS PLACE GOES UP, THERE MIGHT NOT BE A CYCLONE, BUT THERE'LL BE A DAMN STRONG WAVE.
BRRP?
BANGLADESH WILL NEED THE MANGROVES MORE THAN EVER.
THEY CAN'T CARRY MORE THAN ONE OF US AT A TIME, THOUGH.
THEY MAY BE BIG, BUT THEY WON'T BE ABLE TO FLY IF THEY'RE TOO WEIGHED DOWN.
TWO OF US HAVE TO RISK THE JET.
I'LL DO IT.
THEN I'M COMING, TOO.

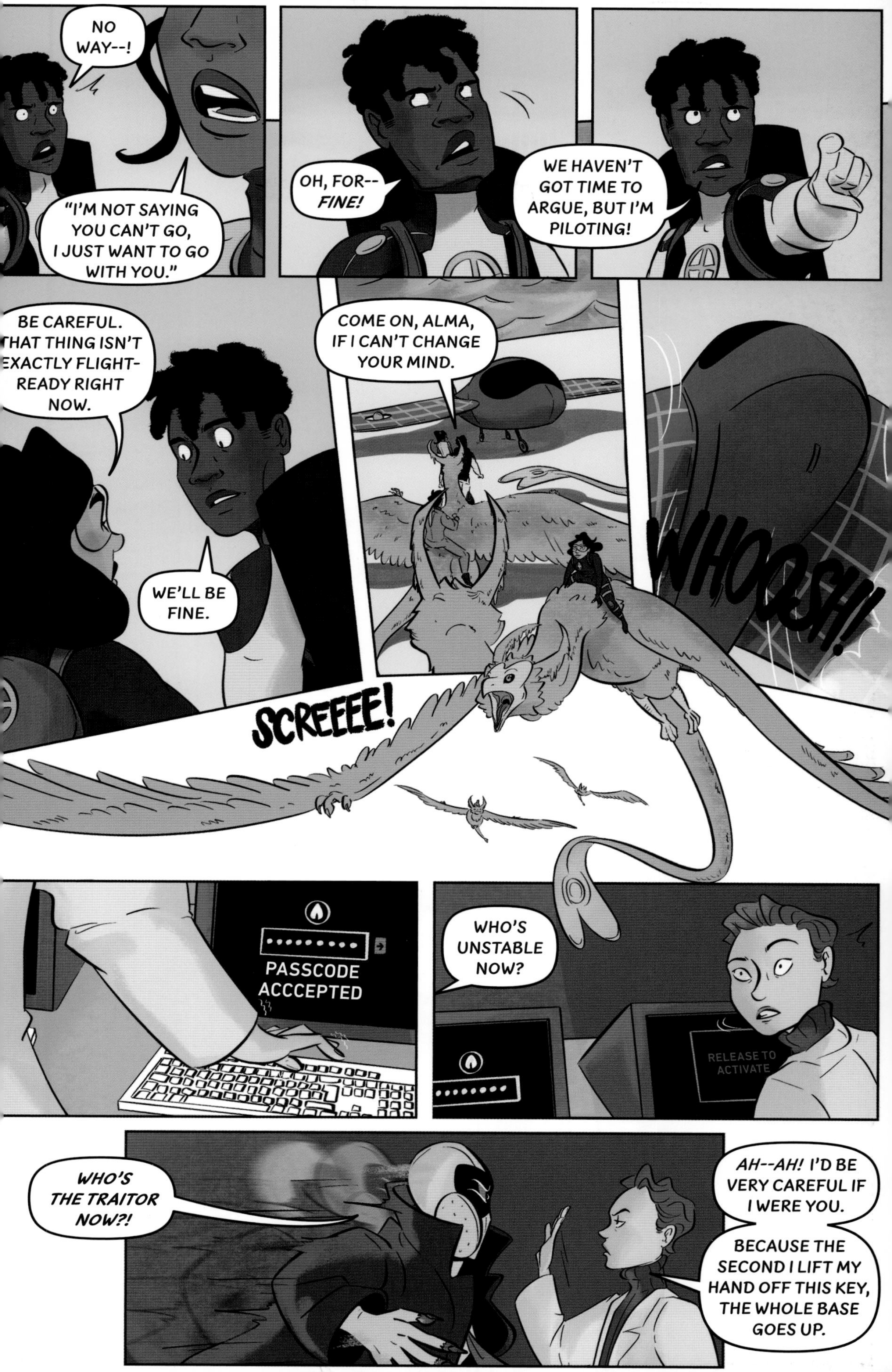
NO WAY--!
"I'M NOT SAYING YOU CAN'T GO, I JUST WANT TO GO WITH YOU."
OH, FOR-- *FINE!*
WE HAVEN'T GOT TIME TO ARGUE, BUT I'M PILOTING!
BE CAREFUL. THAT THING ISN'T EXACTLY FLIGHT-READY RIGHT NOW.
WE'LL BE FINE.
COME ON, ALMA, IF I CAN'T CHANGE YOUR MIND.
WHOOSH!!
SCREEEE!
PASSCODE ACCCEPTED
WHO'S UNSTABLE NOW?
RELEASE TO ACTIVATE
WHO'S THE TRAITOR NOW?!
AH--AH! I'D BE VERY CAREFUL IF I WERE YOU.
BECAUSE THE SECOND I LIFT MY HAND OFF THIS KEY, THE WHOLE BASE GOES UP.

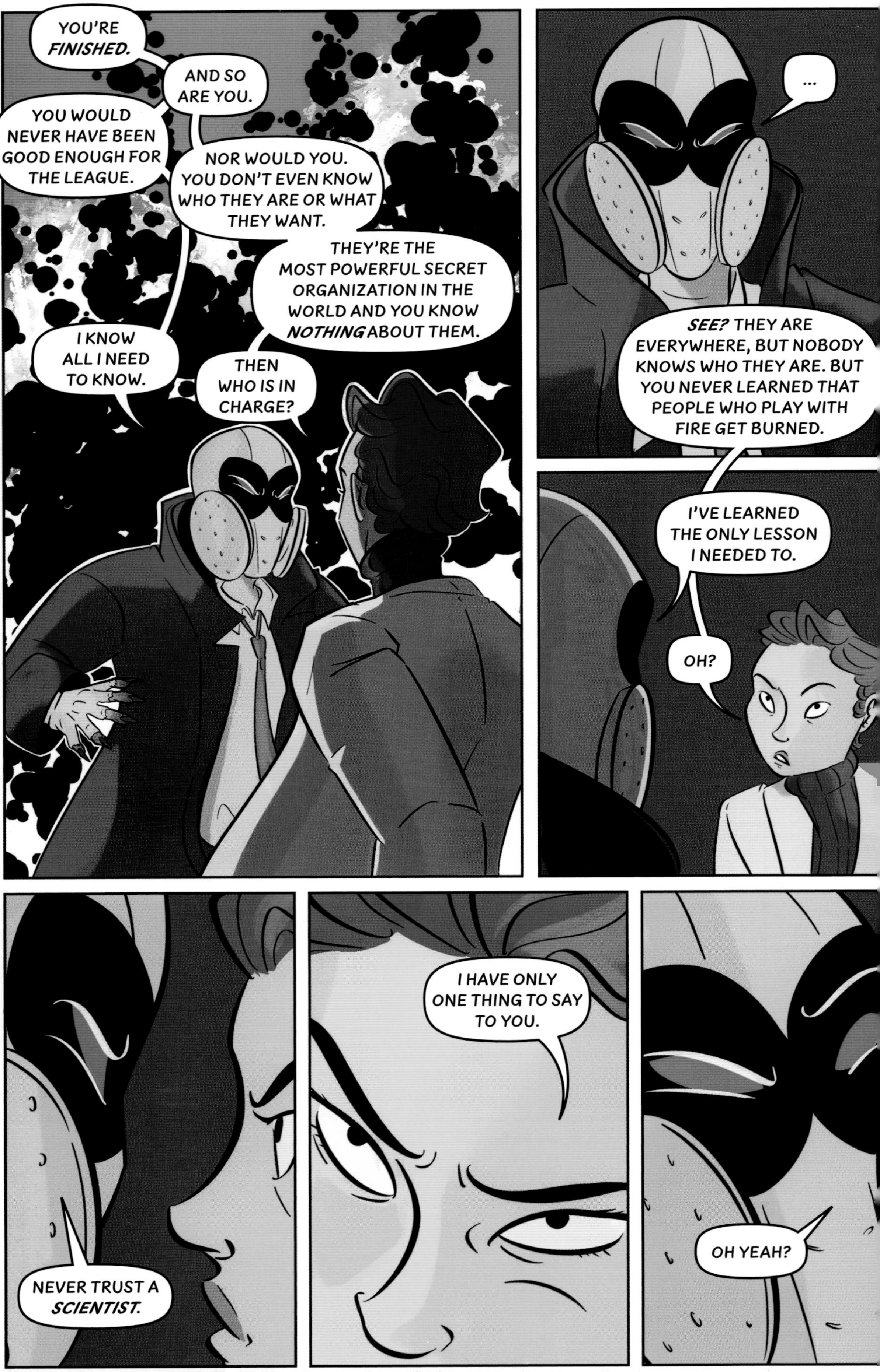
YOU'RE *FINISHED.*
AND SO ARE YOU.
YOU WOULD NEVER HAVE BEEN GOOD ENOUGH FOR THE LEAGUE.
NOR WOULD YOU. YOU DON'T EVEN KNOW WHO THEY ARE OR WHAT THEY WANT.
THEY'RE THE MOST POWERFUL SECRET ORGANIZATION IN THE WORLD AND YOU KNOW *NOTHING* ABOUT THEM.
I KNOW ALL I NEED TO KNOW.
THEN WHO IS IN CHARGE?
...
SEE? THEY ARE EVERYWHERE, BUT NOBODY KNOWS WHO THEY ARE. BUT YOU NEVER LEARNED THAT PEOPLE WHO PLAY WITH FIRE GET BURNED.
I'VE LEARNED THE ONLY LESSON I NEEDED TO.
OH?
I HAVE ONLY ONE THING TO SAY TO YOU.
OH YEAH?
NEVER TRUST A *SCIENTIST.*

TEN.

WHAT?

NINE.

OH, GOD--!

EIGHT!

FASTER! COME ON!

SWOOSH!

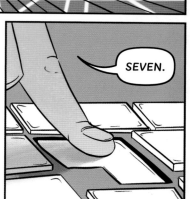

SEVEN.

VROOOM.

RUMBLE RUMBLE

ARE WE GOING TO MAKE IT?

I DON'T KNOW! I JUST NEED TO FOCUS...

SIX...

HUFF! HUFF!

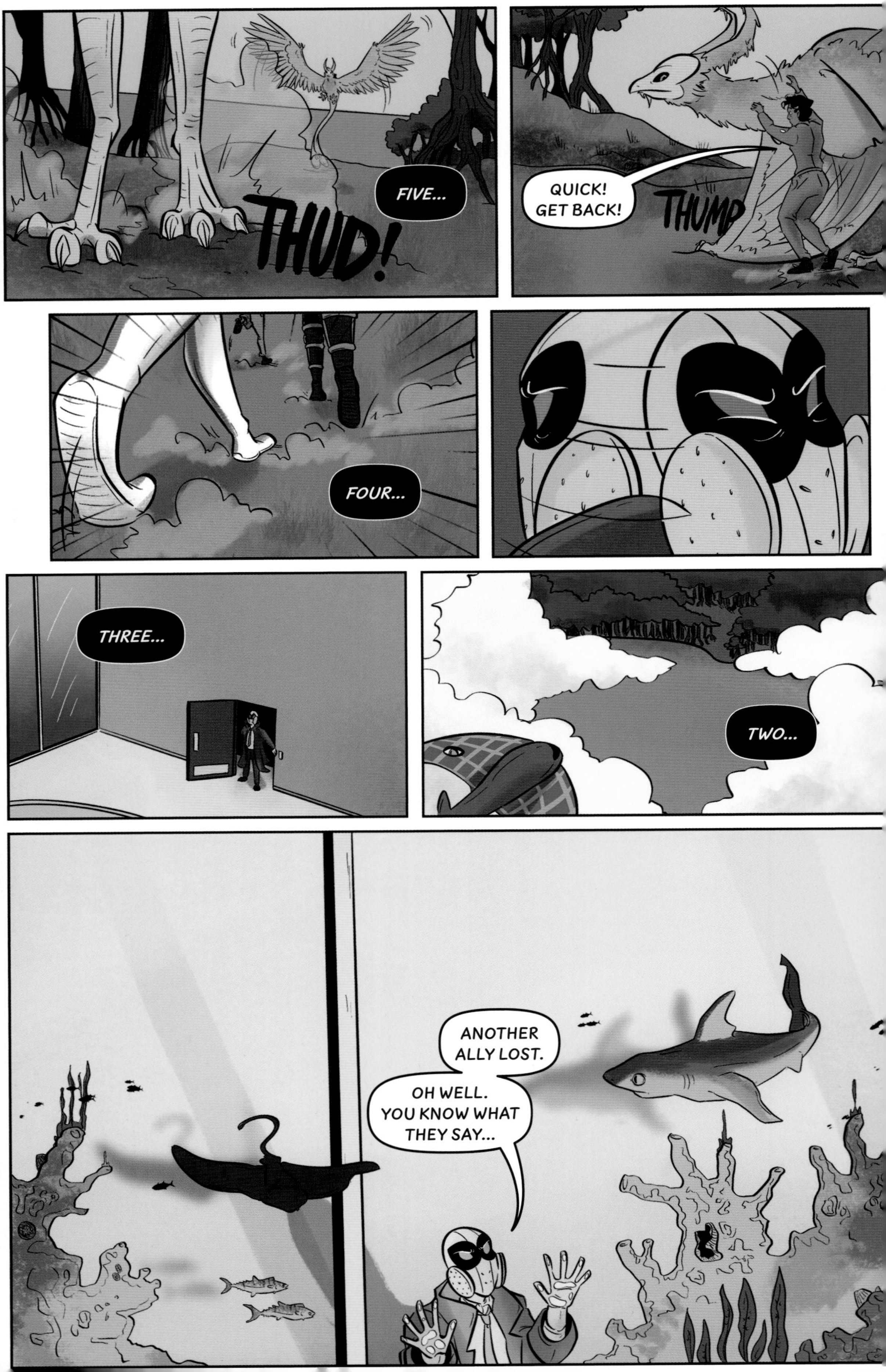
FIVE...
THUD!
QUICK! GET BACK!
THUMP
FOUR...
THREE...
TWO...
ANOTHER ALLY LOST.
OH WELL. YOU KNOW WHAT THEY SAY...

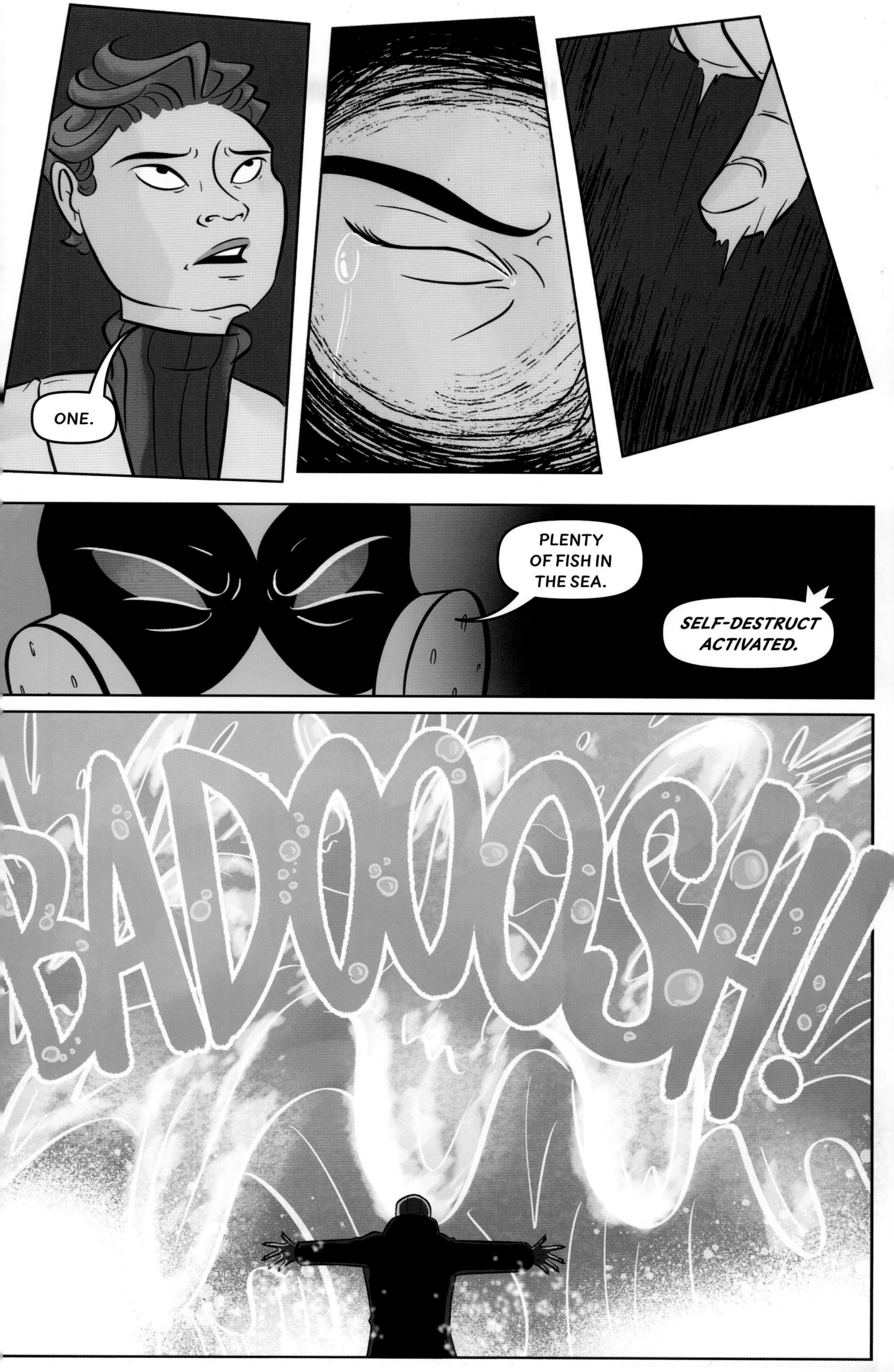
ONE.
PLENTY OF FISH IN THE SEA.
SELF-DESTRUCT ACTIVATED.
BADOOOSH!!

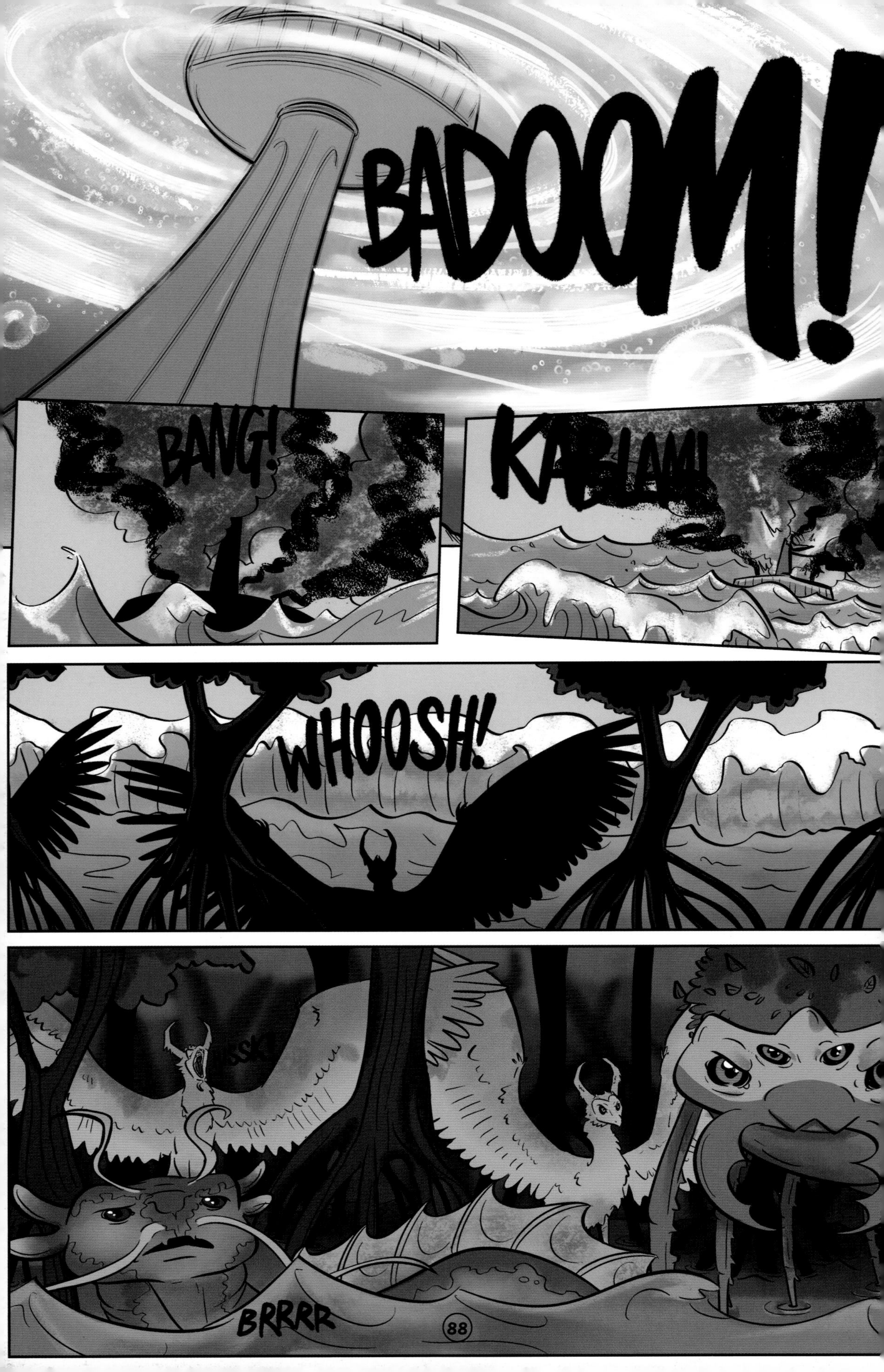
BADOOM!
BANG!
KABLAM!
WHOOSH!
BRRRR

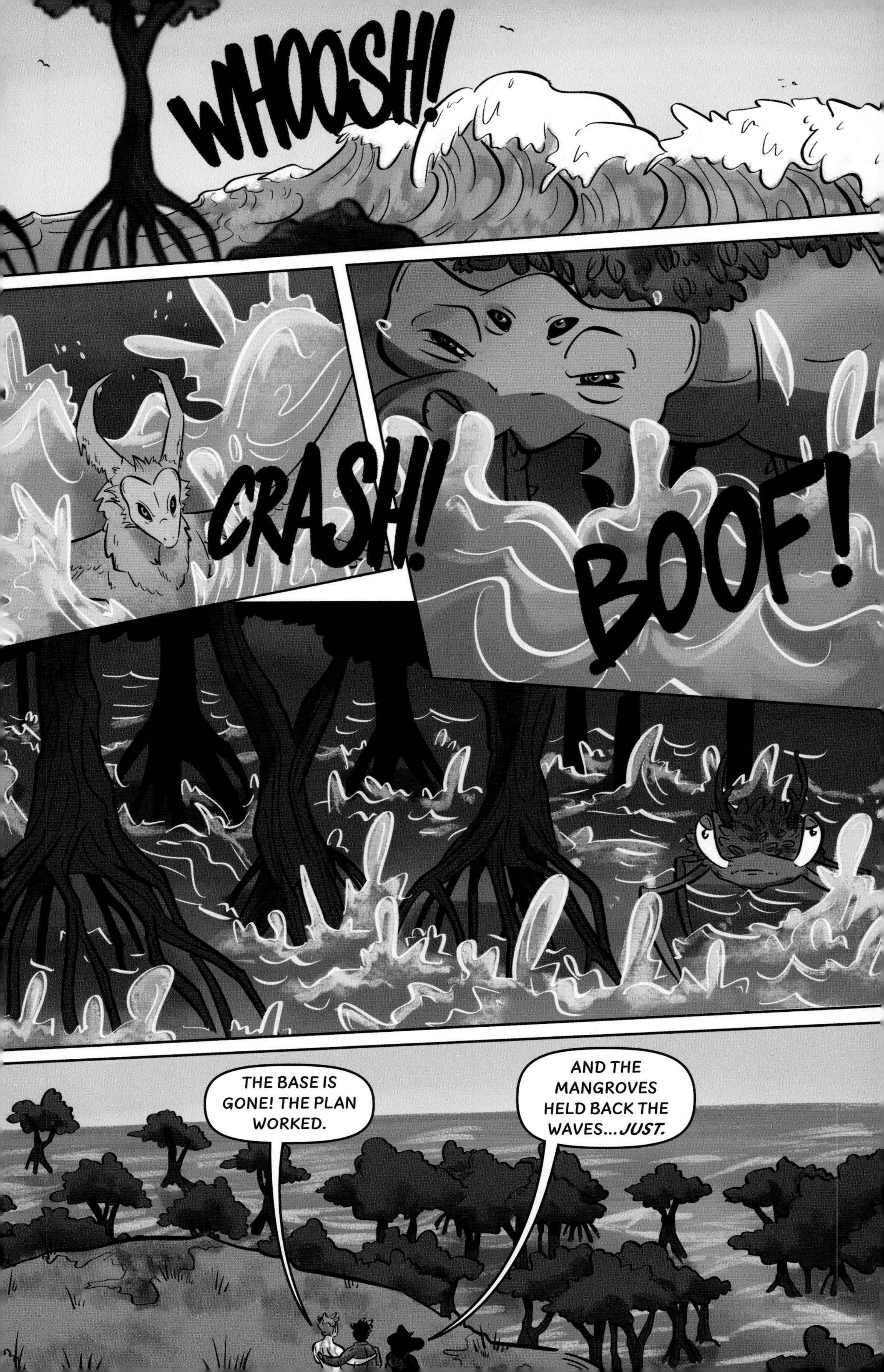
WHOOSH!
CRASH!
BOOF!
THE BASE IS GONE! THE PLAN WORKED.
AND THE MANGROVES HELD BACK THE WAVES... *JUST.*

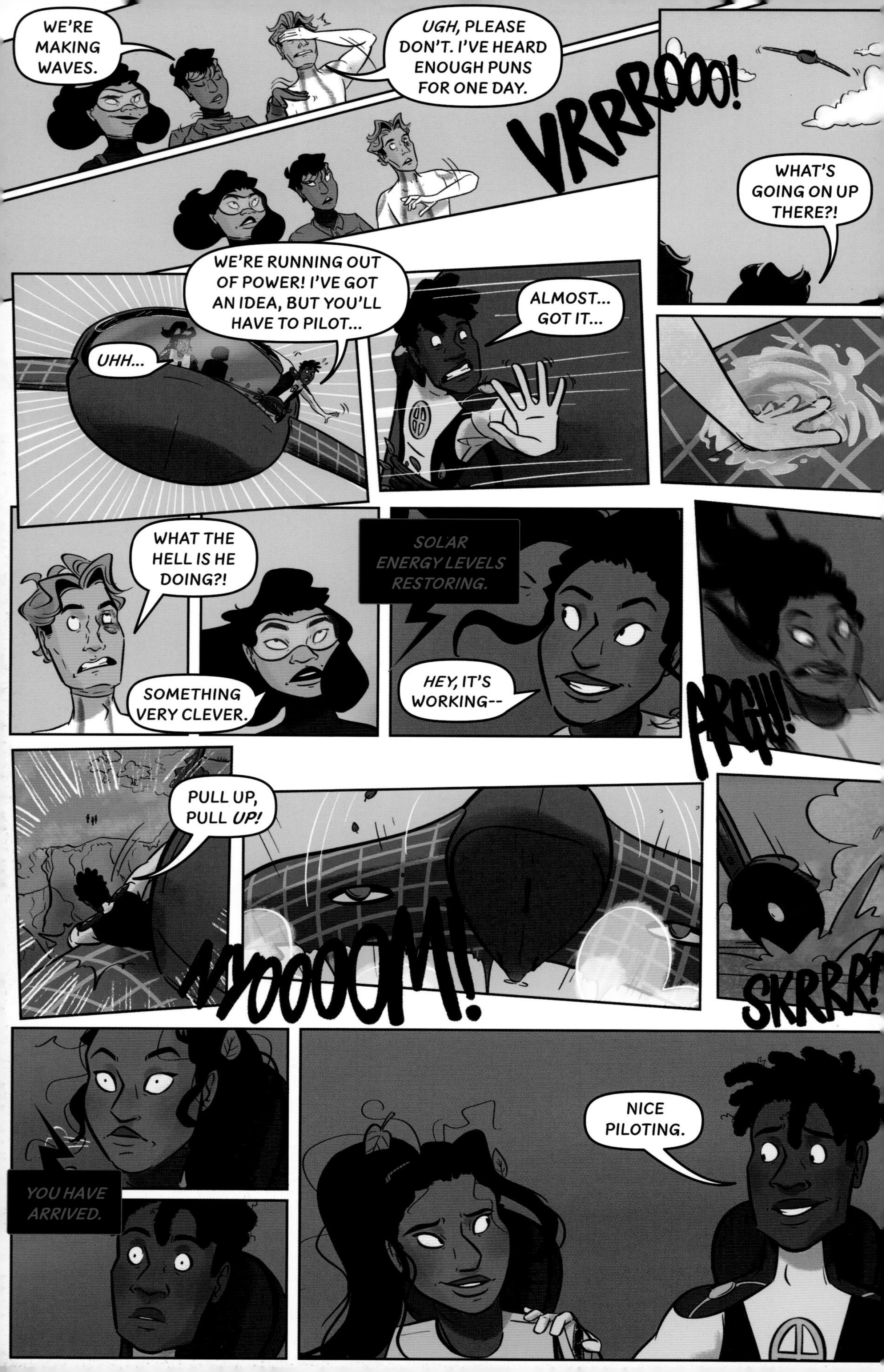

WE'RE MAKING WAVES.
UGH, PLEASE DON'T. I'VE HEARD ENOUGH PUNS FOR ONE DAY.
VRRROOO!
WHAT'S GOING ON UP THERE?!
WE'RE RUNNING OUT OF POWER! I'VE GOT AN IDEA, BUT YOU'LL HAVE TO PILOT...
UHH...
ALMOST... GOT IT...
WHAT THE HELL IS HE DOING?!
SOMETHING VERY CLEVER.
SOLAR ENERGY LEVELS RESTORING.
HEY, IT'S WORKING--
ARGH!
PULL UP, PULL UP!
MYOOOOM!
SKRRR!
YOU HAVE ARRIVED.
NICE PILOTING.

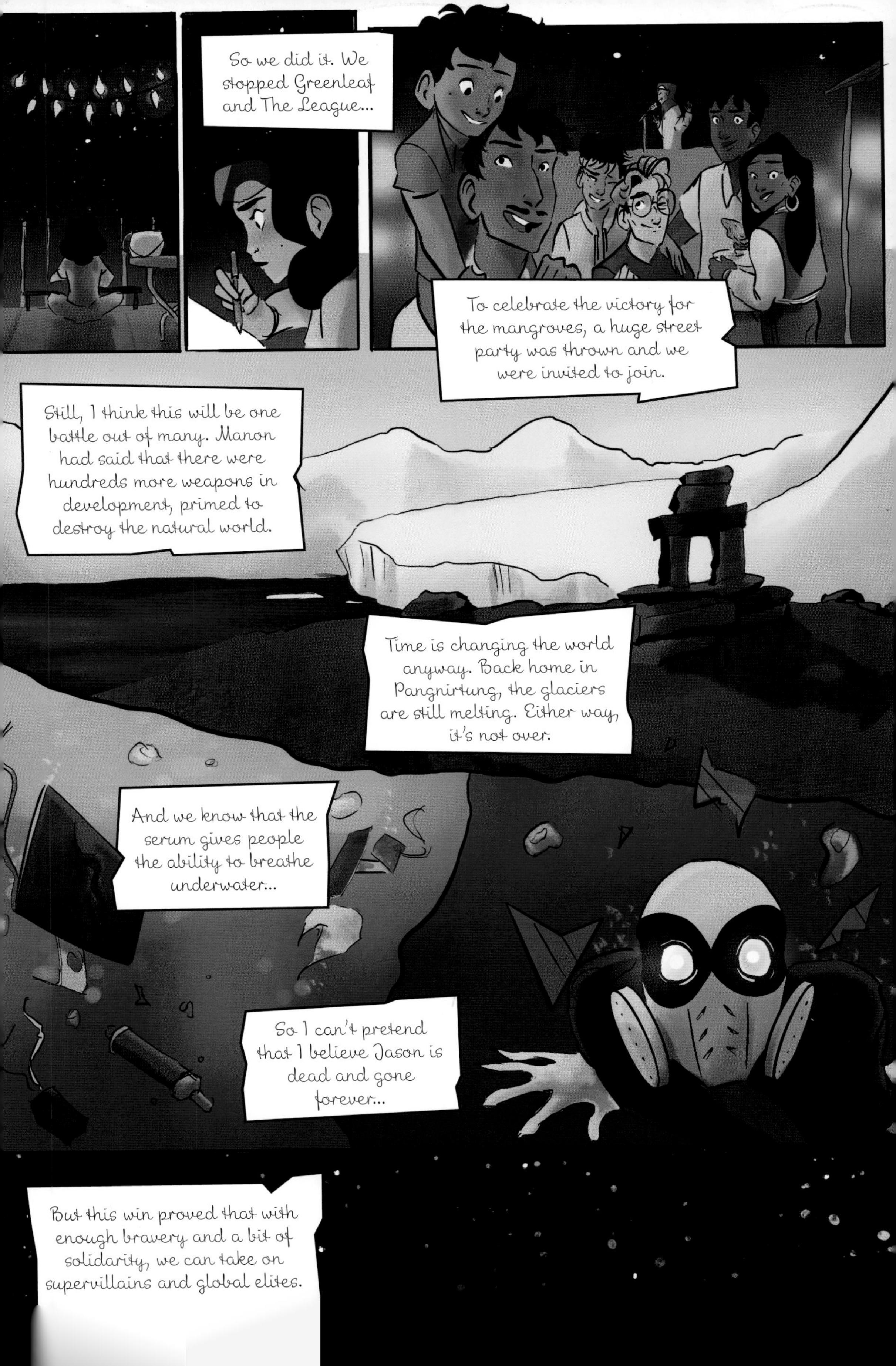
So we did it. We stopped Greenleaf and The League...
To celebrate the victory for the mangroves, a huge street party was thrown and we were invited to join.
Still, I think this will be one battle out of many. Manon had said that there were hundreds more weapons in development, primed to destroy the natural world.
Time is changing the world anyway. Back home in Pangnirtung, the glaciers are still melting. Either way, it's not over.
And we know that the serum gives people the ability to breathe underwater...
So I can't pretend that I believe Jason is dead and gone forever...
But this win proved that with enough bravery and a bit of solidarity, we can take on supervillains and global elites.

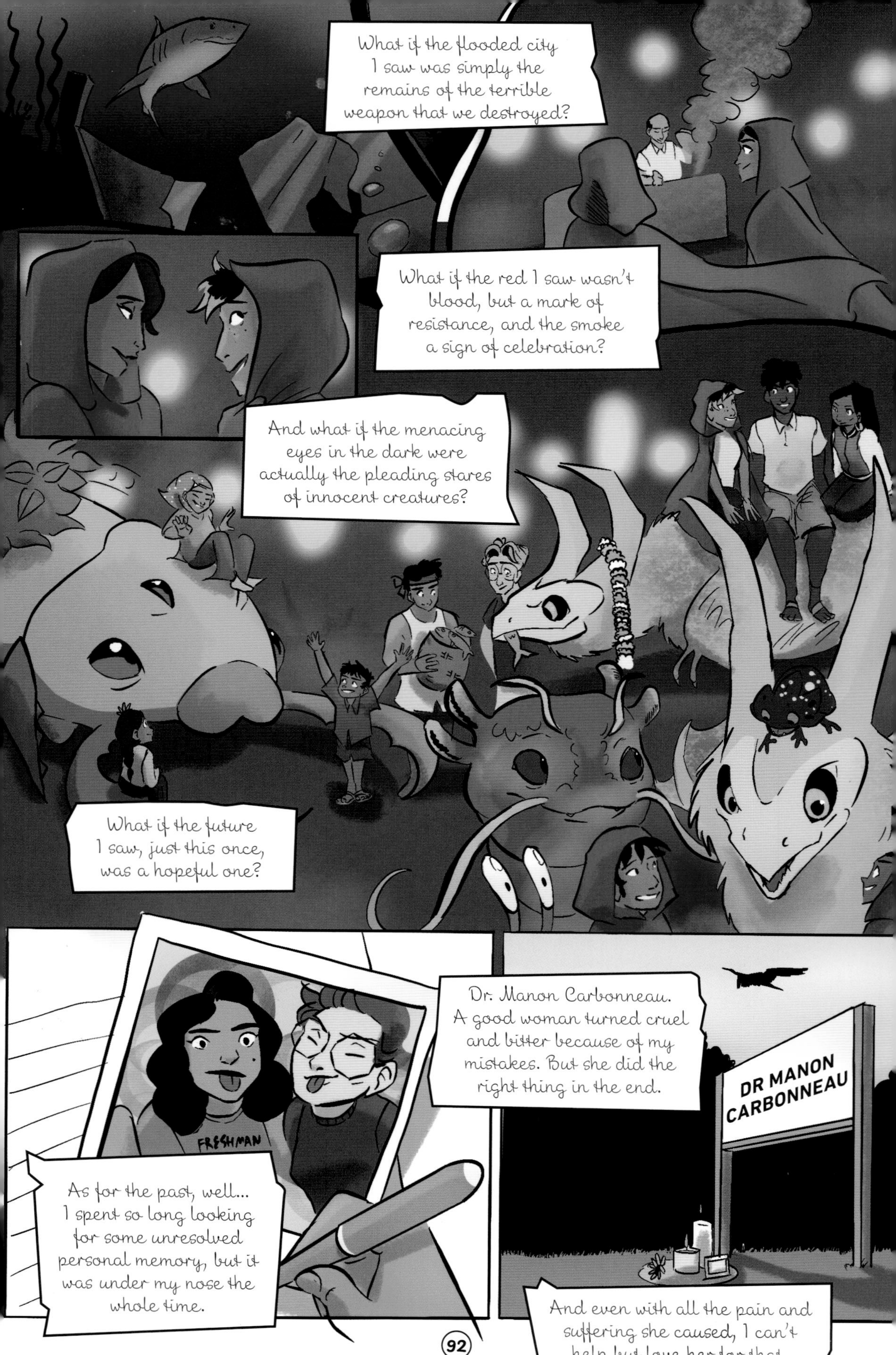

What if the flooded city I saw was simply the remains of the terrible weapon that we destroyed?
What if the red I saw wasn't blood, but a mark of resistance, and the smoke a sign of celebration?
And what if the menacing eyes in the dark were actually the pleading stares of innocent creatures?
What if the future I saw, just this once, was a hopeful one?
FRESHMAN
As for the past, well... I spent so long looking for some unresolved personal memory, but it was under my nose the whole time.
Dr. Manon Carbonneau. A good woman turned cruel and bitter because of my mistakes. But she did the right thing in the end.
DR MANON CARBONNEAU
And even with all the pain and suffering she caused, I can't help but love her for that.